LAMBS OF THE REICH

The Children of Nazi Germany

J. Thumann Molnar

PublishAmerica
Baltimore

First printing

This is a work of fiction. Names, characters, places, and incidents either are the product of the author's imagination or are used fictitiously. Any resemblance to actual persons, living or dead, events, or locales is entirely coincidental.

PublishAmerica has allowed this work to remain exactly as the author intended, verbatim, without editorial input.

ISBN: 1-60703-597-9
PUBLISHED BY PUBLISHAMERICA, LLLP
www.publishamerica.com
Baltimore

Printed in the United States of America

For

Karl Maximilian Thumann
1931–2000

***

Dedicated to my father who lived an amazing life. He was my inspiration. Despite hardship, danger and uncertainty Dad believed in his
dream, had the courage to follow it and the optimism to live it. His
daily example of faith, integrity, and hope gave me wings, and I will
ever miss him.

J. Thumann Molnar

To Emma Marie
Enjoy the book!
Janet Thumann Molnar
march 11/09

Prologue

1938

***

On that auspicious day the very air seemed charged with palpable energy as excitement transformed the population of the great city. Herr Wagner was one such citizen who embraced this festive mood, for the often sour-faced schoolmaster actually smiled this day. Neither could he deny the anticipation he felt. As the clock hands aligned at the precise stroke of twelve, he felt exactly like the fidgety children before him whose nervous little bodies strained to break free. Upon dismissing them, the exuberant tide burst from the school onto cobblestone streets escaping the bonds of textbooks, full of boisterous glee.

One child in particular imagined he was a wild bird taking flight. Scooping up a stick without breaking stride he played Hoffman's picket fence like a large xylophone as he ran past. The sun felt warm on his neck, which was unusual for October, and the clouds reminded him of the big puffs of whipped cream that crowned the fruit torten in Tante Olga's bakery windows. Golden leaves scattered on the breeze as he ran and even nature seemed to hold its breath as celebration overtook it. Yes, it was going to be a memorable day!

Papa had told him this special day would include a wonderful surprise when he got home. The child's birthday was still a few days away but his father was returning from business in Munich so he would receive his presents early. And to top this off, a parade! How lucky could a boy get?

Max waved at Rolf and Eric as they hurried home too, turning down the next block. Some of the children had uniforms to put on and a special part in the parade. For Max, it would be enough to watch.

He burst inside the door of his family's brownstone row house now alive with the aroma of fresh apfel torte and coffee. As usual, arms and legs flying, he sped past the table. One inch closer and the dessert would have been on the floor where the black bear of a dog would destroy it with delight.

The boy's mother, Anna, took a swipe at his backside but protested without conviction. Max was her baby, her gift at age forty-three, and she cherished him. Her smile crept from one rosy cheek to the other as she sent Max upstairs to change into clean clothes for the party.

She loved these happy family times and busied herself with food preparation as laughter and chatter surrounded her thoughts. Relatives kept adding to the presents piled up on the sideboard. Anna knew her boys were more than a little spoiled, being so much younger than their sister Liesl who was fourteen when Friedrich came, followed by Maximilian three years later. She sighed and shook her head. How could Max now be seven and Liesl grown and married already?! How time had flown!

Shouting and banging on the floor above interrupted Anna's reverie. She sighed and climbed the stairs to settle another argument. Friedrich's piercing voice was upset about something and she knew he would have his brother by the head, as he loved to wrestle. Max Schmeling his hero, recently lost the world boxing championship in June to the American black, Joe Louis. Friedrich boasted that when he grew up, he'd be a boxer and get even for Germany.

Anna found the boys as she feared, rolling around the room locked in combat and she set about to untangle them. How like Otto was her eldest son. Although both boys were lean and tall as she had been in youth, Friedrich favored Otto's pinkish complexion with straw colored hair and her own green eyes, while Max was tanned like she with dark blonde hair and Otto's blue eyes. The brothers also had different temperaments and days like these did nothing for her blood pressure that now rose as she struggled to calm the youngsters.

She tried not to show favoritism but it was difficult not to when Friedrich constantly picked on Max. At times when they only had each other she saw them play in an uneasy truce, hoping fervently they would be best friends. Yet more often than not and especially lately, Friedrich would find ways to punish his brother. Anna sighed, controlling her anger. She tried so hard not to let Friedrich get under her skin as she brushed dust balls off Max's sweater and lederhosen. She could swear her eldest son was not this unruly last year. Perhaps it was just a phase that boys of ten went through.

Anna scolded the boys and reprimanded Friedrich for soiling Max's clean clothes. After all, it was his birthday! Friedrich scowled and shot Anna a defiant look. The fight had been only because Max had "touched" Friedrich's new telescope. Otto brought it from Munich on the last trip, as it had been a gift from a client. Friedrich promptly claimed it for himself and Max had been content to let him.

The door slammed below as Otto arrived home amid laughter and much excitement and Anna hurried the boys down to the kitchen to join the melee. As the aunts and uncles joined them around the table Otto unpacked various treasures with the timing of a performer, each present exuding gasps and squeals from his audience. An exotic embroidered shawl was for Anna, a pair of field glasses for Friedrich, and various perfumes for Liesl and his sister. Max could hardly wait for his turn. Then at Otto's nod, Uncle Fritz went out the kitchen door and wheeled in the shiny new bicycle Max had dreamed of all year!

Max lovingly ran his hand over the chrome and breathed in the aroma of new rubber tires. Good wishes and congratulations faded into the background as his imagination took him on journeys yet to discover. He was brought back to earth however as his father spoke his name.

"I have one more present for you Maximilian, since you love little creatures. Enjoy!" said his father as he reached into a basket and pulled out a little box with holes in it and handed it to Max. Max gingerly opened the box.

"A hedgehog! Oh! Papa, thank you!" The little animal was barely five inches long. Max carefully began to reach in when Friedrich beat him to it. The hedgehog, being startled, rolled hastily into a ball wrapping itself around Friedrich's fingers, spikes digging into the soft flesh.

"Ouch!" yelled Friedrich, ripping his bruised hand out of the box. Ute, who always laughed when she was nervous, began to laugh hysterically, while Anna ran to get Friedrich's hand some soothing aloe and ice. Otto scolded Friedrich for his haste and Max ducked below the confusion to find the little animal that had fallen when the box toppled. He pulled off his soft sweater Mama had made and used it to gently scoop up the frightened little thing.

The episode died down with Anna and the aunts fussing over the unhappy Friedrich. Max cuddled the little hog that soon fell asleep and Otto muttered about the time flying, being a punctual little man. The household ran with strict clockwork when he was home and he prided himself on running a tight ship. Now he cleared his throat and tried to look stern for he would deny that he was really laughing himself and feigned worry over the wounded boy. He glanced around. Ah yes, he had one thing more to distribute.

Anna gasped when she saw the little flags. Even though she knew they were handed out along the street this morning she felt a sickly revulsion for the things actually laying there on her polished table. They were red with white circles and had crooked black "spiders" on them, as Max had put it so aptly. The family members divided the flags among themselves to wave in the parade, excited to show their support for their leader.

Anna hoped vainly that the birthday celebration would be enough and her family would be too relaxed with visiting and enjoying the party to make this side-trip out to the streets.

"More coffee or cake, anyone?" Anna inquired as she tried to divert their attentions to no avail.

"Look at the time, Anna! People are already lining up on the boulevard. We must get out there before the crowd is so large that we won't be able to see at all," Otto urged, "Who knows when the Führer will get to Düsseldorf again?"

"You go ahead, Otto. I must prepare the schnitzel for supper. I have no wish to see **him** anyway," Anna replied putting on her apron. Otto teased and cajoled but could not convince her. They always had this argument lately. Otto believed Germany had come out of the Depression because of Chancellor Hitler as many Germans did, and was heading for better things. After all, Adolf Hitler had just been named *Time's 'Man of the Year'* for 1938. Had not their fortunes improved when the Führer had put his policies into practice creating many new jobs?

Friedrich had gone upstairs to nurse his hand and his wounded pride. When he returned, he wore his new Hitler Youth uniform. It consisted of a brown shirt and black scarf held by a brown leather knot and worn over black shorts. A black belt with shoulder strap and light beige knee high socks above polished black shoes completed the ensemble. It gave him pride as he caught his reflection in the hall mirror and he straightened his back a little more rigidly. *'There, you handsome devil'*, he thought and winked at himself, running a hand through his wavy hair as he hurried to the door. He caught his mother's eye and saw her wince as she watched him go to meet his group.

Anna felt sick. She hadn't seen Friedrich in his uniform until now. Just this past week members of the Nazi Youth organization, *'Deutsches Jungvolk'*, had come to their door for the third time that month inquiring if her boys were at home. Twice she had lied about their whereabouts. But this time she was frightened as one of the large bullies threatened her. She still remembered his impudent grin, knowing that he had the authority to force her to obey. Whether they could actually take the boys away by force was something Anna did not want to find out. She knew it was mandatory for the boys to attend once they turned ten. And so the last time they came Friedrich who had passed his tenth birthday two months ago, was ready to join the Hitler Youth. What irked her was that her eldest son was actually excited to join! Thank God that Max was still too young to go!

The relatives and neighbors were preparing to leave next and called to Anna and Otto to join them as they hurried to the door clutching the flags. Otto wrapped his arms around his buxom wife and nuzzled her neck but to no avail.

Anna shuddered when she thought of the Führer, a foreboding always crowding her thoughts for she feared the future. She did not understand her own sisters and how they got caught up in the excitement.

Otto's assurances that all would be well fell ignored on her seemingly deaf ears. He soon gave up; it was useless to talk when she was like this. He joined the departing relatives for the motorcade was to arrive soon, scheduled for two o'clock. As the guests rushed out talking and laughing Otto forgot Maximilian.

Anna was still wrestling with her thoughts about this day when Betsy arrived twenty minutes later. She held a fresh bouquet in her arms. "Tante Betsy!" shouted Max excitedly, who came down from his room where he had gone to make a little bed for his new pet. He joined his aunt and mother at the table where Betsy unwrapped the flowers and Anna exclaimed over their beauty.

Betsy blushed. "I, I, thought the Führer might like, um, might appreciate this token of…our respect," she stammered not catching Anna's eye. Betsy was Otto's younger sister and though a woman of thirty-five, unabashedly had a crush on Adolph Hitler. She knew Anna disapproved of the German leader but didn't care, she thought he was wonderful. However her side trip to stop for the flowers had held her up and now she realized the party had left without her.

Anna could not bring herself to blemish this beautiful day with yet another long, un-winable argument so said nothing. Max was eager to get out into the sunshine and see the parade for even now marching bands were heard in the distance.

"Maximilian, would you like to go outside in the lane and try your new bicycle dear?" Anna asked, but knew what his answer would be.

"Oh Mutti, I want to see the parade and the bands and the marching soldiers first!" exclaimed the boy who thought the whole thing rather exciting. He looked around anxiously and noticed for the first time that everyone was gone without him.

"But the others have gone and Betsy is running late…" Anna's voice trailed off. She hoped that she had an excuse to keep Max home with her. The child pouted and looked for a moment like he might cry.

"Anna, Max can come with me," Betsy whispered. In weak resistance Anna nodded, resigned, as she could never refuse Max any wish. Betsy took her cue and hustled the boy out the door with a backward glance at Anna and a promise to take care of him.

***

Betsy's beautiful flowers took a beating as she ran the two blocks to the Konigsallee with Max in tow. The crowd was thick and restless along the boulevard when they arrived, jostling for a better position and twice someone had stepped on her only dressy shoes. She'd also been poked more than once by some zealous flag-waver. Her disappointment was mounting since she had to jump to see over shoulders, for like her brother Otto she was only five foot two inches tall. Max was wiry and could more easily wend his way through the throng.

Max was slipping easily beneath arms and around obstacles, trying to catch a glimpse of his friends as they marched in the parade with the older boys in their Nazi Youth group. He was impressed with their uniforms and could see their pride at the honor of being included in the festivities.

In the distance the motorcade was slowly rolling into the next block. A sleek Grosser Daimler-Benz open limousine with swastika flags mounted on each fender was moving ever closer. It transported the Führer himself. Betsy gulped. Her face felt flushed and hot yet she shivered and shook nervously. The crowd's mood seemed to electrify as the band music grew louder and Betsy knew she must make a snap decision. Could she get past this wall of a man who locked arms with his wife? Or possibly duck around that old couple without knocking them down? No. People would think her rude. The Führer was almost here.

What to do? Having a shy nature, Betsy knew she may faint dead away if the Führer happened to actually look at her. However, she had paid good Reich marks for this bouquet in the market and she wasn't going to waste it now.

She glanced about for Max and saw him just ahead of the old couple. 'Now or never', she thought. Betsy reached around the mountainous man and yanked a bit of Max's hair. He yelped and spun to look at her. She pushed the flowers into his hands.

"Max," she panted, "Maxie, please…give these to the Führer!!" The boy turned back to the procession staring in awe at the goose-stepping troops with fine uniforms marching in time, their polished boots clapping in unison. Wave upon wave of these cookie cutter soldiers grouped in regiments moved as one giant machine, stretching into the distance before and beyond the motorcade.

Two marchers carrying long vertical banners bearing giant swastika symbols passed in front of him. The banners were crowned with huge gleaming eagles that glared down from their haughty perches on the wild crowd. Following this came a truck whose sides bore more swastikas and the mounted loudspeakers blasting the music. Max realized he had heard this song before. "Deutschland, Deutschland, Uber Alles! …Germany, Germany over all!"

The limousine was now only thirty feet away. Max glanced back at his aunt then down at the flowers and around at the crowd. Where was Friedrich? He could do this. He was not afraid. He would be proud to give the flowers to their leader. Just then Betsy, with all the nerve she had left, ducked the big man and the elderly couple and pushed Max into the street. Max found himself staring into the face of the Führer.

To his amazement, Max could not move but only hold the flowers out stiffly in front of him. In slow motion his mind traced the memory he would have for the rest of his life. The Führer gave a signal and the motorcar stopped. He rose and locked eyes with Max. Max could no longer hear the music or the screaming crowd for the blood pounding in his ears deafened him. The Führer loomed above him, dressed in his military uniform and cap, the medals on his chest gleaming in the sun. He smiled.

Max stared back and fixated on a point in the middle of the man's little box mustache. Herr Hitler beckoned him closer and accepted the flowers while grasping Max's other hand in his right. Were those flash bulbs making spots in Max's eyes?! The Chancellor pumped his hand vigorously and then waved to the crowd who cheered in patriotic frenzy. Many hands reached out in rigid salute, others strained forward as if hoping to touch the imposing figure. Cries of "Heil Hitler! Heil Hitler! Heil Hitler!" echoed around him. The Führer sat down. The motorcade drove on.

Max's spontaneous encounter with Adolf Hitler was one of those moments in history that one does not realize is a turning point. That this man would affect his own destiny and the destiny of millions was something that Max couldn't comprehend, even if he could have foreseen it. Instead the child was caught up in the madness of being propelled into the presence of a demi-god. The boy saw only the adulation of the adoring masses, ignorant that one day this man would be revealed to them as the ultimate predator. Neither did Adolf Hitler know that this fair blue-eyed boy, a picture of Aryan perfection, in innocence betrayed his Jewish mother who waited at home and mourned for a Germany without hatred.

***

Part I

Chapter One

Anna

***

Anneliese Katerina Bauman was born in 1888, the same year that her parents left Vienna for Oelde, Westphalia, and across Europe the infamous "Jack the Ripper" was making headlines from London.

In Vienna the burgomaster, Karl von Lueger, had been aggressively outspoken in his campaign against the Jews. Although seen as a democratic, decent man and devout Catholic, he was opposed to Jewish capitalists benefiting economically at the expense of small tradesmen. He detested Jewish Liberalism and so united the Democratic, Reform and German National organizations under the name Anti-Semitic party.

Samuel Bauman, being both Jew and merchant knew this spelled trouble. He knew his history. For thousands of years one civilization or another persecuted the Jews. This simply was a fact. To protect his family he searched out a place where they could live in comparative tranquility. The village of Oelde suited Samuel and his wife Elizabeth perfectly. Life there was uneventful and quiet. Oelde's faithful were split fairly evenly between evangelical Protestants and Catholics, with very few Jews. And so like many ethnic Jews in the late 19th century, the Baumans embraced Catholicism. It made sense to Samuel to be part of a majority.

Annaliese or Anna, as she was called, was their second child and first daughter. They promptly had Anna and later the next seven siblings christened in the Oelde Catholic Church. They were a loving family as families go. Samuel was stern as men were often authoritarian in those times, yet her mother Elizabeth, though externally obedient, was a happy free spirit and the glue that held them all together. Eventually the family would number seven daughters and two sons. Their days would continue happily here in the little village and Anna and her family remembered them as joyful, golden years in their lives.

Samuel gained some respect in his adopted town as a fair man in his business dealings and to those in his employ. His wife Elizabeth was known for her community spirit, her well-behaved children, and her love of books. Anna inherited this love of reading from her.

Anna loved the classics and tales by the Brothers Grimm. From childhood into her teens she often preferred books to companions. Her sisters were sometimes playmates but Anna was closer to Max, her older brother. When not in school or minding her siblings for her mother, she was off roaming, dreaming of adventure.

Even though Elizabeth took her daughter in hand and tried to teach her needlework and other such domestic skills, she knew Anna would rather play in the woods with her brother and so allowed her this freedom. Elizabeth despaired of ever getting Anna into corsets and lace, but even this wild child eventually grew into the young woman they hoped she would be.

As Anna left childhood behind her romantic dreams replaced the tomboy with a new femininity. Like many young women embarking on the adventure of womanhood her heart now hoped for true love. She didn't have long to wait. One fine day in late spring she looked into a bookstore window and met a clerk named Hans Adler.

***

Hans' father had recently bought the little old shop and twenty-year-old Hans was to mind the store. The shop sat tucked in between the dentist office and the violin store, the little red door and six-paned windows overshadowed by meandering ivy above which a painted sign announced "Adler-Bucher". The books in the window beckoned her to far off places. Anna entered the shop where a shy, gawky young man dusted the books.

Young Hans remembered when he first laid eyes on the lovely blonde girl. He had been placing a series of shipbuilding books on the shelf. The shop bell tinkled as the door swung open. Hans turned to gaze into the prettiest green eyes he'd ever seen. He noticed little things like how she looked in the yellow dress she wore, with the sprig of edelweiss tucked above her ear. And her smell was somewhere between the aroma of lilies and fresh baked bread that he suspected she had just helped her mother make. He was totally enchanted.

"Excuse me, do you have any picture books about Egypt?" she asked.

Hans just stared at the lovely creature, both slender and buxom, with a confident air about her. He heard her ask something but was too tongue-tied to figure out just what.

"Think, Hans, think!" he told himself, but could not for the life of him remember what it was she wanted. All he could think about was how well her curves filled out her dress and with that, blushed as red as his shop door.

Anna thought perhaps he was a deaf mute. He surely was the handsomest mute she had ever seen. Not that she had met any, however. She smiled and watched as his neck flushed up to his ears and at once was charmed. She was just beginning to realize this past year that she caused men to react to her and it pleased her deeply. Gone were the years when Anna felt force-fed by well meaning family members because she was so thin. No, Anna had definitely become a woman.

"I, ah, could you, ah, please repeat that, Fraulein," he stammered, and knew he looked like a buffoon. With that he stepped forward to help her totally forgetting he was standing on a small stool. It was only a foot from the ground but made him misstep and he lurched forward, books in hand flying every which way.

Anna tried not to laugh and rushed to help him. As they piled up the books, straightening dust covers and bent pages, she observed him. The young man was tall and slim but muscular enough to be manly, she thought. He had auburn hair and round wire glasses that gave him a bookish look but certainly, Anna thought, the cutest dimples. His nervousness seemed to only endear her more.

Normally Hans would have died of embarrassment or gladly sunk through the floor forever, but this young woman made him strangely at ease, her bubbly laughter making him laugh at himself.

In the following months as Anna frequented the bookshop their weekly business turned to daily polite discussions. As the shyness developed into a friendship they had avid conversations about what they had read. Talk of travel, fantasy, adventure and the arts began to turn inward and centered more on their own dreams. As friendship grew slowly to love they planned for the future and a life together. However, into the second year of their bliss the couple found new obstacles brought detours to their hopes.

Anna knew her father was strict but did not anticipate the resistance she would have when she returned home one day with a new basket of books. She had been seeing Hans daily between her chores, her schooling now past for a year. Her mother had been presenting her discreetly to friends' sons at social gatherings or teas after church but could not understand why Anna seemed aloof to their polite advances. Samuel for his part was in no hurry to see his eldest daughter leave the nest, as she was help for her mother and siblings. He knew he could not hold her forever though, for he too saw that she attracted more than her share of men's stares when they were out in public.

Lately Samuel had curtailed her freedom for this reason and become unreasonable when Anna wanted to roam or took too long returning from an errand. Anna saw this as unjust since she was finally, surely an adult. Had not girls in the village married younger than she was now? She wanted Hans to approach her father but was frustrated that he seemed to hold back. His excuse was that he was only a poor bookseller while she was the daughter of a wealthy man. Hans had begged her to be patient. He worked extra hours in the evening for the butcher hoping to save money to afford the marriage.

This particular evening Anna had come in with a flush in her cheeks and light in her eyes. Samuel normally would commend his pretty daughter for taking in the fresh air but now suspicion clouded his reason. He called her into his study with a stern voice prompting stares from her sister Bertha at the piano, and the twins Ute and Olga who had been studying at the parlor table. Anna frowned.

"Young lady, what have you been doing so long?" Samuel asked a little gruffer than he meant to. The tone of his voice put Anna's back up when normally she would have been compliant.

" I went to the market for mother, and, and stopped at the booksellers, father," she began, feeling her cheeks flush. She knew it was almost dark and seemed even later than usual as autumn was almost at an end.

"Anna, you know you should have been home an hour ago. I do not wish to see you gallivanting around town, like, a, a loose woman…" he finished lamely.

"Father!" Anna's eyes flashed, for she could not believe her ears. "Is that what you think of me?!" Anna was almost in tears.

"Now, Anna. Of course not," Samuel tried to soothe the girl, "It's just that, well, you are a well brought up young women and respectable. You do not want men to think of you—"

"Think of me how, father?!" Anna interrupted, trembling. "I have never done anything to shame you or this family but I cannot live in a cocoon either!"

Samuel knew he was handling this badly and sent one of the younger children to fetch his wife. She'd know how to handle Anna. One thing Samuel had not bargained for were seven emotional daughters in his brood. Ach! Boys were easier. Why had he only had two sons? Yet such was his cross to bear. Oh, this modern age! Fathers surely didn't have this trouble when he was growing up.

Anna's mother arrived holding the youngest child on her hip. She smiled at Anna then sobered when she saw the unhappy girl and her husband frowning.

"What is this, my love?" she asked Samuel knowing that gentleness always softened his stern demeanor. She called to little Tina to take the baby and closed the door to the study.

"Elizabeth, speak to our Anna about what is proper for young women. She should not be out at this hour alone. She needs to stay closer to home or be chaperoned." Samuel began.

"Mother this is unfair! I am almost twenty-two years old! There are married women younger than I in town!" Anna pleaded with her mother.

"Now Anna, that is not the point!" her father retorted, " You are not married therefore you must heed my wishes!" Samuel was beginning to get hot under the collar, literally, for he wore a long beard that many patriarchs of the time sported.

Elizabeth could see her headstrong daughter was not going to back down this time for she hated to admit it, but both father and daughter were very much alike. She knew she had to intervene and save face for Samuel, yet soothe her daughter with the wounded pride.

"Please my loved ones, now let us just sit down and talk this through sensibly," Elizabeth took her daughter tenderly in her arms and brushed her hair softly, "There, there dearest," she soothed, "Father does not mean to hurt your feelings."

It would have been so easy to just bear the lecture to follow and leave the room but the passion in Anna's heart overruled her head. Blurting out her feelings she gave substance to what her parents had only imagined until now. That their Anna had found a young man and things would now be complicated.

What followed was a tirade from Samuel about what was expected of Anna, the unsuitability of the bookseller as a husband-to-be, and much weeping and carrying-on by Anna who felt surely her heart was broken and the sun would never shine again. It seemed Hans was right. Samuel would not consider this poor young man for his daughter. Unthinkable!

Elizabeth on the other hand, was wise enough to let tempers die down and knew that with enough time her husband would soften his stance if Anna could just not challenge her father in this thing. However, Anna saw this not as a testing of patience, but a fight worthy of a woman in love. Had she stepped back from the problem and waited Elizabeth may have been right, but it was not to be.

***

Anna grew defiant with time and as she clung to her hopes for a life with Hans her relationship with her father grew distant. A battle of wills had begun. It was finally agreed that if Hans came to work for Samuel and trained as the manager in Samuel's store, one day perhaps, he may be able to wed the "boss' daughter." To Anna it felt like a trap to keep her from marrying her beloved and as three more years flew by she felt desperate to take things into her own hands.

Hans had grown from an awkward young man into a handsome, well-built man and turned the heads of many of the town's young women. This irked Anna as she saw her youth fading away. She was already twenty-five and her father had still not permitted them to marry! Would Hans wait forever or feel that Anna just wasn't worth the effort?

One night Hans closed the store, for Samuel had gone home early and Max was to help him go over the account books. Elizabeth was away with the younger children visiting in Vienna. Anna's brother Max had proven to be a sympathetic cupid who often helped Hans and Anna spend time together and covered for their absences. He himself had been happily married for over two years by this time and felt sorry for his sister. His wife Heidi went along with the conspiracy and this evening was pretending to be Anna's hostess.

This particular evening as arranged, Anna arrived at the store as Hans locked up. It was another warm summer's night. Hans saw Anna's lithe form and shining blonde mane under the moonlight and soft lamps that shone on the age-old building.

"Ah, my Anna," Hans wrapped his arms around his girl breathing in her soft perfume. "It is wonderful to see you tonight."

"Hans, I am so unhappy. It seems like we will never marry," Anna almost sobbed as she felt a lump form in her throat, "I shall never be a bride if my father has his way."

"Now Anna, hush. Don't think such thoughts. I am soon able to purchase a little place for us and your father has hinted that he may give me more wages soon. I think he is happy with my management skills." Hans started to look hopeful.

As Anna gazed up at the handsome man she had such an urge to run away with him, anywhere but here. He looked lovingly at his bride to be as they moved into the shadows and kissed. Hans had to admit he found it harder and harder to keep chaste and honor Anna the way he wanted to. He dreamed constantly of when they would be one and wake together each morning. Anna seemed to read his thoughts and pressed closer to him. Hans had never suspected he would be celibate so long and this longing they felt did not help.

As surely as God made passion for lovers over the millenniums of time it enticed the two that night. On the soft moss under a grand tree and stars that burned in the vast heavens, in the fields Anna knew so well, Hans and Anna fulfilled their denied love. Anna felt that no couple had ever loved this much as she sighed contentedly in her beloved's arms.

A fitting tribute to this love should have been a home and babies, but happily-ever-after often exists only in books. A new barrier arose that summer of 1914, a conflict that swept everyone up in its path, soon to be known as 'The Great War'.

***

Chapter Two

Trial and Faith

***

Anna had always had a natural unwavering belief in the Almighty. She felt this connection as much while roaming in the wildflower fields as she did within the large domed cathedral where the church bells beckoned the faithful. She talked to God often as a child and never considered that He didn't hear her or answer in turn. Somewhere lately however, she had lost her way. She was madly in love yet deeply racked with guilt. Anna didn't know that God was still there for her even though she had replaced Him with her adoration of Hans.

After their first time it had been a month of secret trysts. Hans and Anna could not get enough of each other. Both felt the urgency borne of fear that this time was a brief gift that would be snatched from them forever. Yesterday their fears had taken form in the papers Hans had received, catapulting him into a fight he had no part in. Now she found herself in the cool womb of the cathedral kneeling in urgent supplication, the morning dew still wet on her boots. Turmoil engulfed her as she gazed up at the crucifix with Christ's likeness, and wept.

The old priest came over to the pretty young woman he'd known since her parents had first brought her to be christened in this very place. She was trembling. The candles on the altar flickered in the breeze of the drafty old church. He watched her. The sun's rays cut narrow blades into the gloom from the stained glass above, pouring a kaleidoscope of colors upon her head, which was covered modestly in a crocheted shawl. Her fingers gripped the back of the first pew where smooth grooves had formed from other worshippers' ardent petitions. Knuckles white, her lips moving fervently, God alone heard her plea.

The priest frowned. Did he even remember his own youth? Yes, as one looking on another's life. What could he say to her that would matter, that she would understand? At confession last week she had told him or rather indicated, a carnal sin. Was she pregnant? He hoped he was wrong. He reminisced about a time long ago when his own true love had once told him this news. Her father had sent her away from him forever. He, in shame and repentance had left the outside world for his God and never returned.

Ach, that was so long ago. He sat beside Anna and waited. "My child," he said softly.

Anna raised her head after a moment and looked at the kindly man. There was no judgment in his eyes. "Father," she spoke, " I have sinned. Now God has taken Hans away from me," she sniffled. "This is all my fault!" Anna wiped her eyes. " Did God send Hans into war to punish us?! How could He do this to us? How could He?!" Anna gripped the old priest's weathered hand. "We couldn't wait, couldn't wait any longer..." she sobbed, "Papa made us wait so long! Now Hans must go and fight."

Father Benedict felt helpless. He did not understand God's ways or His timing, but he did know that his God in heaven was faithful. The years had shown him this repeatedly as he had often witnessed amazing providence in his parishioners' lives and in his own. Looking back on the tapestry of these lives he had seen a wonderful pattern of answered prayers, miraculous events, and yes, sometimes even divine intervention. And finally healing that comes with acceptance of God's will. Yet sometimes, God also allowed grief and loss.

The old priest felt young people were impetuous, wanting all the answers now with no benefit of hindsight yet. He watched her trusting eyes, grasping at hope. No matter what he told this young woman, he could not turn back what was now in motion.

Father Benedict formed his thoughts. "My child, God does not punish us for loving another," he spoke quietly, "but His ways are not our ways. This war is not God's doing, it is the enemy who turns men's hearts in hatred on each other. God has graciously allowed us free will. What men do with that freedom defines them. Anna, if it is God's will, nothing can harm your Hans."

Anna spent a few moments digesting this. She then rose, wiped her tears and making the sign of the cross, asked the priest for a special favor. There was one thing left to do. Hans was leaving for military training tomorrow and she must not waste a precious minute. As she ran down the steps of the cathedral and out into the street she replayed the former week in her head. It all seemed surreal. It was then that the orders had come for all young men of Hans' age to report to the local conscription office for transport to the military training base. Had it only been a week? It seemed their happiness had flown a lifetime ago.

She did not understand how this all happened so fast. Father had been reading troubling things in the newspapers that she did not understand, frowning more and having quiet conferences with her brother Max and his business associates.

Last month they had read the news that Archduke Franz Ferdinand had been assassinated. Ferdinand's death orchestrated by the 'Black

Hand', a Serbian nationalist secret society, would set in motion a crazy pattern of events that now precipitated the world's first global war.

Austria-Hungary's outrage at the death of their heir gave them the opportunity to crush the Serbian nationalist movement and issue an ultimatum to Serbia that the assassins be brought to justice, effectively nullifying Serbia's sovereignty. The expectation was that Serbia would reject the severe terms of the ultimatum, thereby giving Austria-Hungary cause for launching a small war against Serbia.

Austria-Hungary knew Serbia had long had Slavic ties with Russia but did not really expect that Russia would care about the dispute other than by issuing a diplomatic protest. However the Austria-Hungarian government sought out her ally, Germany, to come to her aid if in fact the unthinkable happen and Russia declared war on Austria-Hungary. Germany readied itself.

As dominoes fall into one another, countries fell into the war aligning themselves on either side of the conflict. Austria-Hungary unsatisfied with Serbia's nominal response, declared war on Serbia July 28, 1914. Russia bound by treaty to Serbia, began mobilization of its vast army in her defense. Germany, allied to Austria-Hungary by treaty, viewed the Russian mobilization as an act of war against Austria-Hungary and with little warning declared war on Russia on August 1st. France bound by treaty to Russia found itself at war against Germany and by extension on Austria-Hungary. Britain allied to France by a loosely worded treaty, felt obligated to defend France, declaring war against Germany on August 4th. Britain was also obliged to defend neutral Belgium by terms of a 75 year-old treaty. Germany's invasion of Belgium on August 4th and the Belgian's appeal to Britain for assistance caused Britain to come to their defense. Like France, she was by extension also at war with Austria-Hungary.

Britain's colonies and dominions abroad also offered financial and military assistance. These were Australia, Canada, India, New Zealand and the Union of South Africa. Japan, honoring a military agreement with Britain, declared war on Germany in August 1914. Two days later Austria-Hungary responded by declaring war on Japan. Italy, although allied to both Germany and Austria-Hungary, was able to avoid entering the war arguing that their actions were 'offensive' and Italy was only bound by 'defensive' obligations. However in May 1915, Italy finally joined by siding with the Allies against her two former allies.

Sadly, this alliance system was largely to blame for the massive scale of the war, which would precipitate the downfall of the old European culture of kings and noblemen. Europe would be forever changed.

The conflict mushroomed in 1917 when United States President Wilson was forced to finally enter the war in April that year. Initially he had declared neutrality until Germany began practicing unrestricted submarine warfare, seriously threatening America's commercial shipping.

Hans and Anna were but two of millions whose lives changed over night. On their last evening they held each other and whispered promises of a future they hoped would come to fruition. Hans gave Anna a gold ring that had been his mother's, two vines intertwined with small hearts on either side of a pearl. Anna gave Hans an eagle pin that she attached to his jacket lapel, since his family name, Adler, meant 'eagle'. It seemed fitting somehow to give him this symbol of courage.

The priest was waiting as promised to unite them before the altar when they returned with Max and Heidi as witnesses to their wedding vows. They knelt before God and prayed for strength in the candles' glow. An hour later Hans could barely let Anna go when he boarded the train, his eyes locked with hers as he etched her face into his memory, their gaze holding on as the train pulled out of the station. It would have to be enough to keep them both through all that lay ahead. Anna did not move until long after the train disappeared over the horizon.

***

Anna's parents took news of her marriage as anti-climactic with so many other things of importance crowding their thoughts now. The war by simply existing had healed the rift between Anna and her father. He no longer cared about appearances or her husband's status and she no longer held a grudge over lost years. The priest had been correct in his assumption when Anna was found to be pregnant a fortnight after Hans' departure. This turned out to be an unexpected blessing. As Anna felt new life move within her, the family rejoiced for her bit of happiness. Hans was ecstatic when Anna wrote him the good news. Their sporadic letters affirmed their love and plans for their little family. Anna wrote pages full while waiting for news of Hans through months of silence and anxiety.

The Bauman family held their collective breath and prayed fervently for their sons as Max had also gone to fight soon after Hans left. Fortunately their other son, Bruno, was far too young to join. Hans' father Gunther was now a frequent visitor, welcome at their table. Many sons had left from the village and it drew the townspeople together in a common bond. People were moved to share what they had and mourn together as inevitably some were to lose husbands and sons as the conflict wore on.

Tiny Liesl Adler was born the day Anna received news from Hans. The letter in his hurried script had been passed hand to hand and returned with a wounded comrade in arms. At the time of writing he was fighting near

Verdun and his letter reflected his anguish at the futility of killing, for he hated no one. He feared he would not see his child and asked often after Anna's health. Was she eating well?

Soon after the war began Britain had initiated a Naval blockade of Germany preventing supply ships from reaching German ports. Proving extremely effective this cut off vital supplies from the German army and devastated Germany's economy on the homefront, leading to mass famine and starvation across the country. Anna's father eventually closed the store for lack of supplies. Few families in Oelde truly starved for this village had ample little gardens, but gone were the days of luxuries and extras.

Anna wrote back to Hans about his lovely little daughter. She had auburn hair like him and his shape of nose, her eyes, his ears. And she added her prayers for his safe and soon return. The baby was indeed a blessing for she gave Anna and the family comfort and much joy in their trial. The baby also was a favorite plaything for Max and Heidi's two children, and kept Anna busy for she worried much and ate little. Another month passed.

Daily she checked the mail for news of Hans and her brother Max. Finally, a letter. It comforted Anna that Hans had at last received news of his daughter's birth and approved Anna's choice of name. It had been his mother's. He sounded so homesick.

He said the troops were moving farther into the Western Front and he wasn't sure if letters would reach her now. What Hans' letters did not tell Anna was that there were many casualties. Trench warfare caused deadly head wounds. In this growing battle fresh technologies were pitted against opposing armies. New weaponry included planes, tanks, machine guns, long-range artillery and deadly gas. Hans had already lost almost half of his battalion and many hometown friends.

The young woman so briefly married counted the months, hoping vainly the war would end. She kept busy with Heidi and the other soldier's wives, sewing and visiting to keep the fear and loneliness away. She celebrated Liesl's first birthday and saw Hans in her child's smile.

It was Spring again. Anna rejoiced when the wildflowers popped up in the fields and took the baby out in the pram to see the green plants blossom. She was standing in the sunshine face raised to the sky, not far from the tree where she and Hans had lain that starry night. It seemed a million years ago. She felt rather than heard her mother approach. Anna turned, smiling, to see her mother's anxious face and then glanced down at the envelope with the black edging. In a heartbeat Anna's frantic denial at the contents of that envelope clashed with the realization of what she feared the most. Slowly the ground spiralled up as Anna fainted.

***

Unlike many others who were lost, Hans' body was returned to the village. The small funeral was held in the church where Hans and Anna had said their vows. Anna's father had purchased a corner of plots in the cemetery across the road for a family area. Hans was placed there near a grove of willow trees. Sorrowful relatives stood quietly, there was nothing anyone could say to comfort his young widow. Hans' baby was cuddled in her grandmother's arms happily sucking her fist, the child unaware of the father she would never meet. The pleasant breeze softly moved the leaves that hung above the grave. The broken-hearted woman who placed wildflowers there seemed now a shell of her former self. To hurt this much was more than she could bear and as she turned away from the fresh turned earth, Anna vowed to never, ever, love again.

***

Chapter Three

Otto

***

Otto Thielmann limped along the train platform in Hamm, the town of his birth. He had not been in this place in ten years. He looked around at the town and glanced at the cemetery near the tracks. The streets had not changed. Some of the buildings had stood vigil here for over two centuries and would remain when Otto was long forgotten. He had left at age seventeen, thinking adventure and the excitement of combat could wash away the feelings of bitterness. The father he was named for was gone, lying in the ground a stone's throw from this spot but he had no wish to forgive the man now, it was too late.

His mother was eager for him to return. Would she seem any different? Had time and the war changed her also? He grimaced in pain as he tried to lift his stiff leg onto the waiting buggy. The driver loaded his baggage and then offered to help Otto. Grudgingly Otto had to accept his aid, for he could not even do this one thing alone. His home was at the other end of the long boulevard of shops. What once was a simple jog for him would now be agony just to walk. As the horse clopped slowly up in front of the house Otto was flooded with memories of the last time he'd seen this place.

His mother opened the door to their thatched roof cottage, the tidy whitewashed walls with dark batten boards and heavy beams unchanged, the home she had first entered as a bride. She looked expectantly at the man in the doorway. He had her son's eyes but gone was the youthful boy she remembered. Instead, a sad-looking man with a tired countenance begged her to know him by his slow smile and outstretched arms, his cane propped against the door frame.

"Otto..." she began, and as he stepped painfully forward, she saw his legs. Turned slightly inward as though pinned together at the knees, it was now evident why he had spent many months in hospital. The shrapnel which had cut him down had almost made him an amputee. Therese was a resilient woman and not a stranger to battle wounds herself. She embraced her son as surely as she had dreamed this many times.

Otto and Therese spent the long afternoon talking. His luggage stood by the door as daylight turned to shadows. Otto told his mother about the lonely, long days and nights in the trenches. How he prayed to return home and the regret he felt at leaving so hastily. His guilt over abandoning her and Betsy, unprotected from his father's wrath. How he was spared when a grenade exploded too near, killing his comrades yet leaving him with the daily reminder of pain. And as they talked they slowly rebuilt the lost years of their lives. Healing began then as he let the past fall behind.

"I have forgiven your father, Otto," she said simply, while holding his hand as an assurance he was really there. "If I can forgive the beatings I endured surely now you must forget the memories of them. You were only a boy and couldn't protect us."

Otto knew she was right. She had always said, probably as a way to cope with life then, that one should not dwell on the bad, but only the good things in life for life was short. Otto smiled at the woman he thought was a saint. St. Therese, the optimist.

Otto told her that after the war and several operations on his legs he had stayed in Düsseldorf and collected a meager veteran's pension. He lived frugally and watched for opportunities. Otto's best feature fortunately, was his mind. He had always been clever in school and vowed that he would at least have wealth some day even if physical strength was denied him. He must have something to attract a wife. Since he was able to sit comfortably for several hours a day he obtained work in a bank and began to save what he earned. That was 1921.

That year the Allies presented a bill to Germany for war reparations due to damages caused in the war that Germany had started and its effect plunged Germany into disastrous inflation. This bill came to thirty-three billion dollars. The currency exchange which had been four German marks to the U.S. dollar, fell to 4,000,000,000 per dollar by 1923, and Germans lost everything.

Early on Otto had purchased gold ingots whenever he could. He had figured out what was happening before many common folk who were now burning marks for fuel like worthless paper since it cost more to buy the fuel than burn the marks. Otto had lived on little, held onto his little pile of gold and waited. After four years he had been at the right place at the right time and bought a small but lucrative commercial property from a bankrupt business at a fraction of what it was worth. Otto knew the hard times could not last forever and had plans for the building. He had leased it to tenants for a meager rent to carry itself.

Otto had thought now was as good a time as any to reunite with his family and bury the past. He was the son and heir and it was up to him to look after his mother and sister. And so he had returned feeling less a man than before, but he would overcome. He had his mother's character to thank for his tenacity. Her strength in dealing with adversity dwelt in Otto as well. It had always served them well in dealing with Otto's father.

Betsy would be home soon. His mother had prepared the main floor bedroom for him which had once belonged to her and the elder Otto. Since he couldn't manage stairs well his mother insisted this was to be his new room. She set about preparing the table. The delicious aroma of kartoffelsuppe and milchwurste wafted through the house and his growling stomach reminded Otto that he hadn't eaten since early morning. He poured water from the ewer into the washstand bowl and splashed his tired face. He had one more person to face and her acceptance meant everything.

He heard the house door open and someone enter. The voice had to belong to his sister. He had not seen her since she was ten. Otto came out of the room hesitantly, wiping his neck and hands with the towel. Betsy turned from unwrapping a cake and stared at the brother she vaguely remembered. Otto in turn stared back. This petite young woman of twenty smiled shyly and then surprising him, ran to throw her arms about his neck.

Otto's eyes stung. It was not like him to cry but it felt so good to be welcomed. He hadn't been sure of this reception before. Memories of his little sister crying the night he left used to give him nightmares. Even at ten she had been aware of the situation and begged him not to go. She had been a bright child and not immune to the ravings of their drunken father and frightened mother. He had pried off her clinging arms amid promises to return and then left and not looked back. The shame he had carried for years had built a hard knot in his chest. Forgiveness truly is a wonderful thing. As Otto felt the knot melt he knew now that he was truly home at last, as the shadow of the youth was comforted in the man that wept.

***

Otto awoke the next morning with a new lease on life. Things would be better now. He had a plan. Phantoms were buried and change was in the wind. He just knew it. First a job, then who knows? Even though dull, nagging pain was his companion it was amazing how joy made the trial lighter.

He limped about the yard, clearing and chopping wood for the stove, piling the kindling up orderly. He mended what he could around the house and helped Betsy make a wonderful supper. Years of living alone and his culinary inventiveness made him a surprisingly good cook. The two spent the day chatting about their plans and dreams and becoming once more a brother and sister, albeit on a new adult level that pleased them both.

After supper the little family sat around the table long after the twilight was gone, so glad were they to be together. He had been foolish to stay away so long. Tomorrow, Otto told himself, it will be time to make the rounds and renew acquaintances.

Otto had learned not to take offense when people stared at his awkward gait or turned away in ambarrassed silence. One developed a thick skin if they wanted to survive in the world. What did bother him however, was pity from beautiful girls. As though it were obvious that they would never consider him anything but a cripple. He believed there was someone for him, however. Otto Thielmann would show them all. He approached love as he did any other need, with a purpose and a plan.

Two weeks after his return home he had secured a job. He was to be a clerk in the town office. Though the pay was not large he had his pension, his home, and his family back. That was enough for now. Yet to have a wife and children would make his life complete, so Otto would make it happen soon with any luck at all.

***

The day Otto met Anneliese Adler he knew it was meant to be. She did not know it, nor did she take any special notice of him, but he just knew. And he would ensure his hopes came true.

Otto had been tasked to make a business trip to the nearby village of Oelde for the Hamm municipal office. He was bearing contracts to have signed by the mayor or burgomaster of Oelde for the purchase of coal which the Hamm mines produced. As Otto entered the Oelde Rathaus building he followed the polished hallway past the pictures of town patriarchs and various official looking certificates, to the main office. There he saw several office workers trying hard to look busy. Otto had been observing many women as he worked daily in Hamm and knew what he was looking for. He was keeping his eyes open for opportunities in Oelde.

There were attractive women here but one was obviously expecting a baby soon, another wore a wedding ring. Otto could see no prospects here. After the documents were signed Otto left the office. As he came out into the sunlight from the darker recesses of the building he happened to see a blonde woman sitting alone at a table at an outdoor café across the boulevard. Her head was turned away from the warm sunshine as she read. Otto glanced at his pocket watch. Ah, a little before noon. He crossed the road and hoped he might strike up a conversation at least. Who knows, she may be single, he thought to himself. In any case he was hungry.

Although he pretended not to notice, he observed how women treated his disability. Otto would never consider marrying a woman who pitied him or mocked his inadequacy, however subtle. He also had no patience for those who felt uncomfortable or awkward in his presence. He just felt he would know the right kind of woman by her poise should he ever meet her.

Otto had a sense of humor and could also laugh at himself. But he would never have believed that such an awkward, undignified chance meeting could change his destiny. As he approached the tables he suddenly slipped on some bit of food. He promptly went down in a heap, thinking as he did so that he surely made an impression only not the one he hoped to make. It was fortunate that he landed on his soft leather satchel and his pride was the only thing wounded.

At this moment there was no one around as the café regulars had not arrived for lunch yet. Anna abandoned her book and rushed to aid the gentleman. She put her hand forward to help but did not grasp his arm. She waited patiently until he got himself situated properly to stand and then he accepted her aid gratefully. Otto watched her. The woman was polite and sincerely concerned but not flustered as some women would be. She had a beautiful smile but in it he detected no sense of amusement at his misfortune, or condescension on her part. Anna had passed his secret test before they were even introduced. She invited the man to sit a moment fearing he had hurt himself.

"I am afraid that is more common than you think," Anna said, as Otto sat at her table brushing off his trousers. "The pigeons raid the leftovers on the café tables and often drop bits of food. I have slipped here myself before." As Anna spoke she had a lingering sense of deja vu. Long ago she remembered meeting another man who fell with an armload of books. She had come to his rescue too. She smiled wistfully at the memory.

"I appreciate your help, Frau-?" Otto began, hoping she would correct him. She did not. Yet he did not see a wedding ring and hoped somehow she was available.

"Frau Adler," she finished for him, and Otto felt deflated. Just his luck. Anna noticed his subtle reaction and did not know what compelled her to reveal more information, but added, "My husband was taken in the war." Otto felt sorry for her but secretly began to hope.

The owner of the little eatery came running then with apologies, offering free coffee and pastries. Otto accepted gratefully as it gave him an excuse to sit with the enchanting blonde lady. He was thankful she did not make excuses to leave and was willing to let him buy her a coffee also. The truth was, Anna needed an excuse to spend a few more moments in the sunshine. She was still a woman who loved the outdoors and most of her duties for the Krause family kept her inside.

Otto found her easy to talk to and she did not act like other women he met who affected airs, she was as he found her, real and down to earth. A bit sad perhaps but who didn't have some problems in these times? They chatted until Anna insisted she must return to work. She said she was the head housekeeper in a large household and had only stopped to enjoy the sunshine after shopping at the market. Otto made his farewells but knew he had to see her again.

A few days later business matters found Otto in Oelde again and he made sure he was there just before lunch. This time she was not at the café however and Otto chastised himself for not asking her where she lived before. He did not want to pursue her too quickly and have her frightened off, but this woman was to be his wife and the matter had to be handled correctly. He dejectedly decided there was nothing to do but return to Hamm when fate stepped in and showed Otto he must be the luckiest man alive.

As he approached the train station, Otto almost ran into Anna as she shepherded a pre-teen girl before her from the doctor's office. "Oh! Excuse me!" Anna said, as they almost collided. Then she saw who it was. "Herr Thielmann! I am so sorry, but I was just trying to get this sick girl home. This is my daughter, Liesl. Liesl, this is Herr Thielmann." Liesl, who had the flu was miserable indeed.

Otto could not miss this opportunity surely sent from heaven. "Please, call me Otto," he begged. "And let me get you a ride home. She seems too ill to be out." Without waiting for a protest he was able to get the attention of a cab, the horse drawn buggy still in use in the town. Anna and Liesl had been dropped off by the one of the kitchen help and had planned to walk the short distance back, but saw wisdom in his offer as Liesl did look rather faint.

Otto accompanied them making sure they arrived safely, for he really had to see for himself where Frau Adler lived. Even though Anna had told him she worked for a wealthy industrialist, he was suitably impressed as the buggy rounded the drive before a very large mansion. Indeed, Otto thought it must be one of the largest homes he had ever seen. As he helped Anna out of the carriage he inquired if he could be of more service. Anna declined, thanked him and turned to go, but Otto would not give up that easily.

"Frau Adler," he cleared his throat nervously, "There is a symphony concert at the Opera House in Hamm next week," he was now grasping for a reason to make her see him again. "I would be so honored if you would accompany me." There, it was out. Until this moment he had not even thought of the concert though he had seen the posters. Otto had always prided himself on his ability for quick thinking in a pinch. He'd often credited this ability for saving him throughout battles during the war.

Anna hesitated. She assessed the man. Though not a total stranger and though he seemed to be kind, she really knew nothing about him. He sat very upright in the carriage, hands crossed atop his cane. He was somewhere between twenty-five and thirty she judged, but seemed more mature. His hair was the color of pale wheat and neatly combed. He wore what must have been his best suit. His demeanor was dignified but she could tell he was nervous, almost pleading, like that of a schoolboy. Anna could not bring herself to let him down. She nodded.

"I have seen the poster advertising it, Herr-" she corrected herself, "Otto." Anna smiled then, "I am fortunately not on duty that day, so, I would be glad to come." Anna beckoned to one of the maids who had come out to the driveway then, and the girl helped Liesl into the house with a word from Anna who said she would be right in.

"I, I am very happy, Frau Adler," Otto beamed.

"Anna," she corrected him. Otto pre-arranged to come for her in the early afternoon that Saturday so that they had time to make the trip back in time for the concert. As the buggy turned back down the drive Otto leaned back into the leather seat and smiled, self-satisfied. He felt his life take a new turn again. His plans were now in motion and he would prove to be the best suitor ever, and she would not deny him. He whistled as he set out for home.

***

Anna wondered if she had made a mistake as she climbed the sweeping main staircase of the mansion. She knew it was a harmless concert but was not naïve enough to think that a man would not continue to pursue her once she showed the initial interest. It was just that she was happy enough here and fortunate to be in a position of authority. She had a lovely home for Liesl to live in, enough food, and a certain range of comforts. However if she was honest with herself, she was also lonely.

The first years after Hans had died were sheer torture. She had shed a million tears which were still not enough to kill the pain in her heart. Then after the war, she had a few young men who had expressed interest and come around, but truth be told, she was not interested in any of them and certainly not fun to be around. They had eventually stopped calling. Her parents' encouragement had fallen on deaf ears and even her brother Max who had come home to them, could not persuade her otherwise.

She had secured a job as house maid for the Krause family when she felt it was time to move out on her own and she had worked her way up into the prime housekeeping position within four years. Her attention to detail, hard work and fairness were not overlooked by the mistress of the house. Lately however she had felt her youth escaping and her vow to never love again became a self-imposed sentence she no longer wished to live under. She had dreams of more children, a happy home and her own hearth. But who would want a middle aged woman now? Though Anna was only thirty-six and looked younger, she felt eons older. She guessed that her sudden acceptance of Otto's offer was in reality nothing more than one last chance to feel wanted again.

As Anna turned in to Liesl's room in the servant's quarters she did not expect her daughter to be awake and waiting for her. The girl certainly was ill but had a frown on her face.

"Mama! How could you?" Liesl pouted, and shivered as she pulled the covers up closer to her neck. Anna felt the girl's flushed cheeks and forehead and poured water for her from the bedside table pitcher.

"How could I what?" Anna pretended naivete, but thought she knew what Liesl was going to say.

"Mama, he's crippled! And you said you would go to a concert with him!" the girl accused. Anna felt Liesl was being snobbish, a trait she did not appreciate in her daughter who actually was growing quite spoiled from living amidst such luxury. Anna could not be harsh with her sick child however.

"Liesl, he is not crippled," said Anna matter-of-factly. "Or else he would be in a wheeled chair. He just has trouble walking because of a war injury. And since when have you thought that someone with a disability not worthy of a little happiness too?" Anna admonished as she tucked the girl's bedding in.

"He is too short!" Liesl pointed out, as if that were that and Herr Thielmann not to be considered as a serious romantic option.

"Liesl, let us not get ahead of ourselves. It is only a date, not a lifetime we are talking here." Anna hoped she sounded light hearted and dismissive. She too noticed that she was almost a head taller than Otto, and was sure that she was older. And he did seem to walk with great difficulty. Anna wondered if she could marry a man who would surely need some special care as he aged. She came out of her musings though and felt she was being silly. This was only one date. Offers for an interesting evening didn't come along all the time now and Anna was getting older. Although still attractive, Anna knew she was not the svelte girl she had once been. She worried that she would not have many more opportunities in life. Anna determined that she would not allow her daughter to ruin this chance to enjoy something once more.

And so the day of the concert, Anna had arranged for Liesl to spend the night at Max and Heidi's home. When Otto arrived Anna was waiting, breathless and expectant. Otto's luck held. It seemed he had met Anna at just the perfect time in her life. Too soon and he wouldn't have had a chance. The woman that she was now yearned for more than life had dealt her. And it was this fertile ground on which Otto found he could spoil and dazzle Anna, treating her like a queen. Having a sister and mother he adored, no one could ever say that Otto Thielmann didn't know how to treat a lady.

And so this date became the first of many and slowly, with a tenderness borne of respect, Otto truly won the heart of Anna Adler. She did not compare this man with the memories of Hans for it was not the passionate, all encompassing true love of youth that she felt for Otto, but a warm and loving caring for a gentle man. Otto teased her often and the companionship of laughter and happy times were theirs as he assured her of his undying love, after all, he had 'fallen' for her that first day, hadn't he? Liesl even grew to respect the man she soon called 'Papa', and Therese and Betsy came to love the sweet woman that Anna was.

At first Samuel and Elizabeth had worried that Otto could not properly care for Anna with his disability but as Samuel came to know him, he saw in Otto a hard worker with a brilliant mind. He soon realized that Otto was a good match for Anna and was happy that his daughter would at last have a home of her own. Anna and Otto were married with their families looking on. It was late 1924 and hard times were but a memory. Surely now life would be better.

***

Chapter Four

Into the Night

***

In 1920 the National Socialist German Worker's Party or Nazi party as it came to be known, was nothing more than a largely ignored fringe group with a following of a few thousand. Within three years however this growing movement had begun to stir the political pot. A rising star, Adolf Hitler, had become their new leader by virtue of his gift for oratory. His one claim to fame was Germany's Iron Cross medal which he earned in the Great War and that was awarded to him interestingly enough, because of a commendation by his Jewish superior. Adolf's talent for speech making began to draw crowds like moths to a flame. Bolstered by his growing popularity and thirst for power he prematurely attempted in November of 1923 to overthrow the German republic by force in the foolishly conceived Beer Hall Putsch.

As increasing inflation sparked unrest and chaos, Hitler's Nazi Party saw an opportunity. It was time to strike. Hitler had rushed into a meeting of businessmen in a beer hall in Munich with Hermann Goring and some armed men claiming that the Bavarian and Reich governments were dissolved and this Nazi revolution was the beginning of the new government. He attempted to kidnap the three highest officials of the Bavarian government. Though he extorted support from them under gun point and with the help of General Ludendorff, his bluff was discovered when he left the hall to attend to a problem elsewhere in the city. Order was restored as the army rounded up the Nazi thugs and stamped out the rebellion. It had been a foolish gamble for Hitler to attempt the putsch without the support of the German Army. The result of this hastily conceived plot bought Hitler nine months in prison.

Not to squander time he decided to write his lengthy and rambling diatribe, *Mein Kampf* meaning literally, my struggle. In his writings, Hitler began with his childhood following the path that ultimately led him to a political career. It was influenced greatly by his youthful days of poverty in Vienna following the deaths of his parents and opened his eyes to despair and social inequities.

His daily observances of the common man's plight led him to an inspiration: two methods which could turn around a society. Firstly, by creating improved social conditions by establishing strong social responsibility among the public; secondly by combining citizens' keen awareness of social responsibility with ruthless determination to prune away all problems incapable of being improved. As he saw it, the two biggest perils to Germans were Marxism and Judaism. He also adopted the solution of selective breeding and the idea of weeding out the 'parasites'. He felt to preserve the superior German racial stock unmixed in purity, was tantamount to maintaining Germany's pride, leading to patriotism and fulfilling their purpose the Creator meant for them. In *Mein Kampf*, Hitler also outlined his eventual plan to ultimately conquer Europe's nations for the expansion of Germany's territories for the German people.

After his prison release he again reinstated himself as leader of the Nazi Party. Since the disastrous Pusch, Hitler realized his initial folly.

When the opportunity came again he would use Germany's own democratic rules to win by election while his government waited in the wings to step in and take over. During the next few quiet years Hitler bided his time waiting for Germany's then solvent economy to falter and need a saviour.

***

When a new currency called the Rentenmark was introduced to replace the worthless Papiermark, it effectively stopped hyperinflation and the German economy recovered. Otto and Anna were married during this time when the future looked bright. Germans enjoyed peace and a little prosperity for a time unaware that a brooding poison was waiting patiently beneath the surface to erupt when the time was right.

Otto relocated his family to Düsseldorf shortly after their marriage since he felt this was a sound economic move and they made plans to increase their little family. Anna was nearing the end of her child bearing years, her biological clock ticking quickly, so their priority was set on having her pregnant. However two miscarriages later Anna despaired of ever providing Otto with the children they both so desperately wanted.

As human nature often is when hope falters, people turn back to the faith they've abandoned when angry with their Creator. This was where Anna found herself one day as she knelt anew at the altar of God. Her constant prayers were for children she knew would bring Otto pride and make their lives complete. Anna repented of the years she blamed God for the tragedy that took Hans from her. And just as the childless Hannah of the Bible had once petitioned God for a son; Anna also wept on her knees as the afternoon sun fell, until finally she felt a release in her spirit and knew that God had answered. In 1929 Anna finally carried a child to term and gave birth to their first son, Friedrich, early that year. They were filled with joy. Even Liesl was excited to have a little brother at last and became almost a second mother to the child, carrying him around like a doll and spoiling him so that his every need was catered to. While Anna made a home, her husband was busy with another plan.

Otto decided to increase his holdings. The commercial building he had purchased for a song in hard times had multiplied in worth and was sold to purchase two others. One of these two was a 3-storey building housing six side-by-side apartments on Hohe Strasse. It was old but surprisingly sturdy, of brick construction. The top floors were afforded a view of the nearby Rhine river to the west and each home had small gardens in the rear. Having grown up with a carpenter father Otto used the one thing he received from him, the skills to improve his holdings. Otto filled all but one of these homes easily with other tenants saving the largest for his own family. This brought him a tidy income for a time.

Their happy ordered life might have gone on like this indefinitely had an event not rocked the world of 1929. On Tuesday, October 29th, the Wall Street stock market collapsed in New York. From across the ocean the repercussions reverberated around the globe; the Great Depression had begun. Financial markets were affected worldwide. The German economy built out of foreign capital mostly by loans from America, was very dependent on foreign trade. These loans were suddenly called in and the world market for German exports dwindled. German workers became unemployed as production levels fell. Banks failed throughout Germany. Hard earned savings accounts disappeared. Inflation resulted bringing hardship to families needing to buy costly necessities with devalued money. Poverty and despair became the norm for former middle class families overnight.

The Thielmann family weathered the hard times as well as any other and since the tending of a garden was necessary just to have vegetables on the table, they grew what they could and traded for the rest. As long as they had food and peace, Otto hoped they could outlast the storm. Priorities had narrowed to basic survival. And survive they did.

Otto navigated hardships by making his own luck, a philosophy he adopted from being independent at an early age, unable to rely on his father. Since Otto had put all his earnings into the properties he owned he really had no savings in the bank to lose. He had learned after the war not to trust paper currency or anyone else with one's savings including financial institutions. By being a sympathetic landlord and not demanding full rent he had the loyalty of his tenants and was able to hang on to his holdings, though barely.

By mid-1930 the German democratic government had begun to fall apart under such pressures. The political parties of the Reichstag squabbled amongst themselves unable to agree or unite and solve the nation's plight. This finally forced an election to be scheduled for September as the nation looked for anyone with solutions to save them. Hitler had known his time would come. Now that it had arrived, Adolf Hitler was prepared.

The Nazi party was ready and launched a fantastic election campaign that captured the attention and hopes of millions of impoverished and destitute Germans. The well-planned Nazi juggernaut overwhelmed the masses with its polished and carefully orchestrated political theatre. Rallies included staging, lighting, and swastika symbols that set the mood for the charismatic leader and gifted orator. Hitler played his audiences like a tightly strung instrument, whipping them into a pseudo-religious passion by playing on their emotions of envy and hatred of injustices done to the German people. His speeches built up to a frenzied climax while his almost hysterical audience became willing to act on whatever he demanded of them. Some even called him the "New Messiah".

Here at last was a man who seemed to have the answers that Germany was looking for. His promises included something for everyone from the common man to the industrialist, to all classes and the army, restoring order from chaos. He also promised to tear up the Treaty of Versailles, which limited modernization and the army to a limit of 100,000 men. He would end reparation payments to the Allies that Germany still made. So it was on September 14th, when the masses had voted, that the Nazi Party rose from the smallest German political party to the second largest. Hitler moved one huge step closer to his goal of total power. Before he would realize his dream however, power was to change hands several times prompting three more elections.

When Chancellor Hermann Muller resigned in 1930, Heinrich Bruning became the next chancellor and one of the last men in Germany to oppose Hitler. He truly had the best interests of the people at heart. He was responsible for getting President Paul Hindenburg re-elected to keep out Hitler and preserve the republic. He also put a ban on the Sturm Abteilung, or 'Storm Section', Hitler's own private army. These SA bullies accompanied Hitler on his rallies and encouraged supporters to carry out acts of violence against Jews and left-wing political opponents. Bruning also toiled on the international scene to help the German economy by seeking an end to war reparations. But his economic policies in Germany itself failed to stop the economic deterioration with now nearly six million people unemployed.

During this time of national chaos, Anna found she was expecting again in spring of 1931. The prayer she had made for more children was being answered, even now. Welcome news, though the family like millions of others scraped by while the future of Germany was up for grabs in a desperate type of political chess game.

October marked the start of political intrigue that would destroy the fledgling republic and bring Hitler to within just 15 months of his goal. It also was the month that tiny, premature Maximilian was born to the Thielmanns.

In fear of another miscarriage Otto had sent Anna to Oelde in September. He hoped in the care of her family, the peace and quiet of the country would be better for her. It was while there and almost eight weeks early, that Anna gave birth one evening. Otto arrived almost too late from an appointment in the city. Rushing to his wife's bedside he saw the stricken faces of several of Anna's sisters and initially feared for her.

Shadowed by a priest who had just arrived, Otto spied the wrapped bundle that appeared to be a small puppy judging by its size. Picking up the child, he unwrapped it. At first he doubted that the tiny, red boy with pencil-thin limbs would live, he fit so neatly into Otto's palm. The baby had a weak, pitiful cry, and Otto's heart feared for him. However until now, he didn't know the extent of his wife's stubbornness or her apparent direct line to heaven, for she firmly took the child to her breast and shooed the astonished priest from the room. It seemed her well-meaning sister-in-law had summoned the cleric to administer the last rites.

The relatives waited skeptically but were astounded when days passed and the tiny infant actually grew stronger. For although only three pounds, tiny Max would not only survive but thrive with all the fierce love of a mother who refused to ever lose another thing she cherished.

Several weeks later, the family returned home with a much chubbier baby and their joy was complete. Though hard times abounded Anna and Otto felt blessed. Adversity only seemed to make their family stronger, making them closer.

As the tides of history pull them along some humans blindly trust the fates, others turn to God in times of need. Anna chose the latter for she had finally found fulfillment in trusting God as she saw His goodness in all things. It was this faith that would sustain her for the rest of her life. And it would sustain them all as their beloved country was pulled deeper into an abyss that no one truly saw coming, even as they fell.

Chapter Five

The Witching Hour

***

In May 1932 Chancellor Bruning was asked to resign by President Hindenburg, who replaced him with Franz Von Papen of the Catholic Centre Party. Papen decided to gain the support of the Nazi Party by lifting the ban on the Sturm Abteilung and other radical decisions. During this time there was open warfare on the streets between the communists and the Nazis, wherein eighty-six people were killed. Papen's reactionary policies upset Kurt von Schleicher. He persuaded several government ministers to turn against Papen who then resigned from office. Schleicher now became chancellor of Germany. Since Schleicher attempted to control the activities of the Nazi Party, Papen and Adolf Hitler collaborated to topple Schleicher from power.

Struggles escalated as storm troopers freely attacked socialists and communists. Incidents such as these worried many Germans and in the November 1932 elections, support for the Nazi Party fell. However, the German Communist Party gained favor winning more seats. Hitler reacted by creating a sense of panic, stating that Germany was on the verge of a Bolshevik Revolution that only the Nazis could stop. Franz Von Papen who was now vice-chancellor, along with a group of prominent industrialists who feared such a revolution, sent a petition to

President Hindenburg requesting that he appoint Hitler as chancellor. Papen persuaded him that if he appointed Hitler the new chancellor, Papen would be able to prevent the Nazi leader from introducing his more extremist policies. Finally they were able to wear down the resistance of an old and tired Hindenburg who gave his consent.

On January 30, 1933, at age forty-three, a teary-eyed Adolf Hitler left the presidential office as a victor and Chancellor of Germany, stepping out into the cheering crowds of his supporters. He had won.

A telegram was sent to President Hindenburg from former General Erich Ludendorff who had been Hitler's ally in the disastrous Beer Hall Putsch. It read, *"By appointing Hitler Chancellor of the Reich you have handed over our sacred German Fatherland to one of the greatest demagogues of all time. I prophesy to you this evil man will plunge our Reich into the abyss and will inflict immeasurable woe on our nation. Future generations will curse you in your grave for this action."*

***

Weeks later Hitler became absolute dictator in Germany as he instructed Nazi thugs and murderers to seize power from legitimate public offices using the Enabling Act, passed by the Reichstag to give him full powers. To belie rising public concern over this regime of gangsters, he initially played to the world press. Pretending to serve democracy with staged displays of subservience to an ailing President Hindenburg, Hitler ensured that photographers duly recorded it all.

The mysterious burning of the Reichstag on February 27th became the first symbol of freedom and democracy to go, a democracy that Hitler had never meant to adhere to. Murders of communists and dissenters followed swiftly, birthing a tyranny and legacy that were to become benchmarks of Hitler's rule.

The Bauman and Thielmann family members had different opinions about this new leader ranging from initial indifference to shock, when the life they took for granted began to change rapidly. Otto read the papers daily to see what would happen. Anna was raising small children and pretended to be preoccupied with her babies so she wouldn't have to think about the world beyond her doors. Friedrich was soon turning five and Max was still a nursing toddler. Anna wondered what would happen to these and other innocents in Hitler's new Germany.

A new ban on Jewish owned shops was implemented on April 1, 1933. It was the first of some four hundred laws and decrees that would eventually be imposed on Jews during Hitler's twelve-year reign. Dismissals followed. Jews could not hold civil service positions and were prohibited from serving as lawyers or doctors in state-run institutions. Then they were forbidden from being journalists or owning newspapers, and even finally banned from the arts and entertainment industry.

Germany became a police state over night. Given free power of arrest, jails quickly overflowed with people as fifty thousand Nazi storm troopers replaced the former police officers. This facilitated the need for large outdoor prison camps which then birthed the concentration camp system.

Those who opposed Hitler were not forgotten. Many who mistakenly under-estimated Adolf Hitler did not escape his revenge, such as Kurt Von Schleicher. His mistake proved fatal. During the Night of the Long Knives the Schutzstaffel or SS as they were known, acted on orders to murder him in his Berlin residence on June 30, 1934.

The Night of the Long Knives became a turning point in the history of Hitler's Germany. Adolf Hitler was now supreme ruler of Germany with the self-granted right to be judge and jury. He alone had the power to decide whether people lived or died.

This purge was kept secret until Hitler himself revealed it on July 13th. During his speech he called the purge: 'Night of the Long Knives' (a phrase from a common Nazi song). Hitler stated that over seventy-five people had been assassinated in the purge. He had not let the courts deal with the conspirators because he alone was responsible for Germany, he said, and therefore was its supreme judge.

The final barrier to his plan of solitary rule was erased at last, with the death in August of that year of President Paul Hindenburg, leaving Hitler against Hindenburg's wishes to proclaim himself the holder of both offices of chancellor and president.

Now Ludendorff's eerie prophecy would come swiftly and devastatingly. It testified that one common man, the son of a civil servant, could so ignite havoc that it would echo around the world. Adolf Hitler rose from obscurity to infamy merely armed with driving ambition, a passionate conviction and a plan that bore the fruit of hatred, touching not only every German citizen but also whole nations.

Later those who survived would indeed curse his name, for this evil like a tumor wove its tentacles directly or indirectly into the lives of those caught, pressing on the nerves and the heart of each home, institution, nation and belief. Those not strong enough to resist were caught up in the vision, blindly following. Germany's march into the seemingly endless and all-encompassing night had only just begun.

Chapter Six

A Holiday

***

Early in the Hitler years, happy times still abounded in the Thielmann household for again the economy began to improve. The little boys were a constant joy and Anna had her cup of happiness full. Liesl was a great help to Anna as her brothers were into everything and always under foot. Anna determined not to let politics or her fears affect their lives. Otto soothed her fears and was ever the optimist as he saw a new, strong Germany, and hoped for more.

Otto was now in sales and traveled often and each reunion at home was cause for rejoicing. On one upcoming trip Otto would be returning to Hamm and Oelde, and convinced Anna and the boys to come along to visit family while he made the rounds of clients. The bonus would be attending the country fair in the area. The rare opportunity offered was all Anna needed to pack.

This August morning in 1936 found the family at the station early and aboard the train just as the sun backlit the sleeping houses. Soon they were clicking along as the inner city buildings and warehouses gave way to smaller homes and farms. The mists in the fields began to dissipate as the rising sun sparkled lazily on a meandering creek alongside the tracks.

The boys could hardly contain their excitement and pointed out the cows and sheep and early farmers at work in the fields. When the train noisily braked at the Hamm station Friedrich and Max wanted to be first off on their great adventure. If one did not notice the military presence hulking quietly about or the bold swastika banners hanging from each station's rafters, it still often felt like the Germany of Anna's youth.

Otto had his papers in order as he commuted often and didn't foresee a problem for his family. His hunch was correct as the few soldiers that stood about in clusters talked amongst themselves and seemed concerned only with their morning coffees. No one bothered the family as they hunted for a cab to take them to Otto's mother's home.

The children chased butterflies and hunted for tadpoles in the grass that grew along the boardwalk as their parents organized the assorted luggage. A cab soon arrived and took them the short distance to Oma Thielmann's cottage. Betsy opened the door and hugged Otto and Anna fiercely, bringing them into the kitchen wafting with the aroma of pancakes, sausages and coffee. Therese stooped and enveloped the two boys in her arms.

"You've grown so much my little men!" their Oma exclaimed happily, "Come and see what I have for you!" Upon which, Max and Friedrich ran into the yard to find new kittens. There were two tabby, one almost black and a tortoise shell colored one which Max picked up. The mother tabby cat seemed content to allow it since they were a few weeks old now and had opened their eyes, but watched from the cool shadow of the porch.

As the boys played and ran about the large yard they picked pea pods and carrots from their grandmother's garden and found sticks to have a sword play with. The noonday shimmered with the promise of a hot afternoon and this brought out the fragrance of the patch of dill that their grandmother grew.

The adults enjoyed the leisurely brunch but Otto needed to leave for his rounds with customers, promising to return and accompany them to the fair in the evening. The week continued in this lazy pattern with the women venturing out to shop and visit friends on the long days. Anna relaxed and grew tanned, refreshed by the country air and almost forgot the tension she had felt in Düsseldorf.

The fair was wonderful, with many types of pastries, cakes and sausages for sale, and quilts and other handmade items that attracted Anna. Home made toys, table games, and music delighted Friedrich and Maximilian who ran between the tables and vendors with glee. For Otto, the highlight was an aircraft newly launched in May of the previous year. He had been intrigued with aircraft since his youth. The Hindenburg airship was often seen in the distance as it traversed Germany's skies, but the ship so named for Germany's past president was to make a special low flight over the fair grounds.

Otto bustled his brood ahead of him as the scheduled arrival grew near. They were lucky enough to find a few seats on some temporary bleachers near the bandstand. Indeed, the crowds were in awe as the ship grew from a distant saucer to a massive monster that covered the sun. It was close enough that passengers on the ship could be seen smiling and waving.

Little Max stared and clung to his mother, overwhelmed with the enormity of the craft as it flew low over the fair grounds. It reminded him of the huge bed sheets on washday that his mother hung out to dry in the sun, large and white and terrifying if they fell on you.

Friedrich clutched his father's arm and pointed at the shining sides as it reflected the sun from its taught, streamlined skin. Huge lettering proclaimed its name as the Hindenburg floated majestically over them.

Otto had recently read about the ship in the Düsseldorf paper. Visually striking, at 804 feet long and 135 feet in diameter, it was only seventy-eight feet shorter than the doomed oceanliner Titanic. It was equipped with cabins for fifty passengers and a crew of forty. Although the Hindenburg was originally intended to be filled with helium, a U.S. military embargo on helium led the creators to modify the ship's design to use flammable hydrogen as lift gas with the added benefit of raising the ship's lift capacity about eight percent more. The designers weren't overly worried about using hydrogen since it was used successfully without incident before. Four Daimler-Benz diesel engines gave it a maximum speed of eighty-four miles per hour.

Now flying in a large arc it sped up and sailed off into the blue, as crowds below clapped and waved. The thing was a tribute to German engineering. The bands played a military march and Otto's heart swelled with pride. How he wished he could be up there! The Hindenburg had another engagement tomorrow for it would trail the Olympic flag over the stadium in Berlin, as the Eleventh Olympiad would begin. Tragically, the Hindenburg would fly cross Atlantic for only another year before a flaming disaster would claim it in America.

Otto watched the mighty airship disappear into the horizon. Tomorrow it would impress the visitors that were now pouring into the country for the Olympics. He pondered over the face that Germany would present to the world.

Hitler had spent forty-two million Reich marks building a huge Olympic sports complex hoping to impress the nations with Germany's wealth and prosperity. His focus was on showcasing Aryan superiority to the world. Initially he refused to allow Jewish participation in the games, causing much outrage and calls for an international boycott of them. The

United States initiated a vote and participation in the Olympics was finally approved, though by a narrow vote in favor.

Otto was shocked by the recent changes on his last trip to Berlin. Tourists arriving were treated to the spotless city where any misfits or undesirables were previously removed to a special detention camp away from Berlin. All buildings were adorned with Olympic flags and Nazi swastikas alike. Mysteriously, the 'Jews Not Welcome' signs that had been everywhere were suddenly missing from hotels, restaurants and public places for the duration of the Olympics. Nazi storm troopers were also ordered to desist from any mistreatment of Jews. Even the anti-Semitic newspaper, *Der Stürmer* was removed from newsstands.

What Otto couldn't see was the subtle policing. Newly arriving international Christian and Jewish leaders who wished to investigate stories of Jewish persecution for themselves, or visitors wanting to interview Jews about daily life in Nazi Germany were directed to contact the Gestapo first, basically to be watched until they departed.

Otto mused over these changes and had mixed feelings about the government. Being an optimist, he fought the fears that choked his thoughts. He wanted to believe in a better Germany, that the economy would continue to improve, and a new, strong nation would emerge that had much to offer the world. Had not most of the top thinkers, inventors and scientists come from Germany? He believed in giving the Nazi government a chance to prove itself and certainly some good things had already been accomplished. However, it bothered him to see rising open Semitism, that now suddenly seemed to have disappeared over night.

A tug on his sleeve interrupted his thoughts and returned him to the present. For now he would not worry, but enjoy this family holiday. He looked forward to his visit with his father-in-law and Anna's brothers.

Their discussions always presented a new perspective. He glanced down at the tow-headed Friedrich who had licorice on his grinning face, and smiled himself. This family was worth everything and he would protect them no matter what the future held.

Chapter Seven

Shadows

***

When it was time for the second leg of the trip the family was to make the short journey to Oelde, and Therese and Betsy could hardly let them go. The passing of years seemed to make each visit more precious and time more fleeting. Max developed a persistent sniffle and Therese worried that he had caught cold while playing in the shallow stream at the rear of her property. She offered to keep him in bed while the family traveled on to Oelde but Anna would have none of it, and Max wanted to see his cousins as well. They waved as the train pulled away promising to visit soon again.

Seeing Oelde again was to relive many memories and Anna's parents embraced their daughter, who always tended to cry when she was happy. Anna hugged her brother Max. She had always kept a special bond with him, as they were the eldest siblings. Heidi greeted her warmly too and it had been a few years since they were together. Her other siblings were all married and had children of their own and now a few grandchildren too, so Friedrich and Max had many cousins to meet. Samuel and Elizabeth were now into their early seventies. Anna was glad they seemed in good health but mourned the passing of time that brought wrinkles to her beautiful mother's face. It was good to just sit and talk into the night and she treasured their time together.

Elizabeth exclaimed over the growth of Friedrich and remarked that Maximilian was no longer a baby. News was exchanged but no one wanted to taint the conversation with the rumors they had all heard, or even mentioned the political scene in Germany. That evening Anna's spirits were revived and she thanked Otto as they cuddled in the great feather bed in the guest room. It was a wonderful vacation. Neither realized that joy would be short lived for Max had gotten progressively worse these last days of the holiday.

The early morning of the third day brought gasping and choking sounds from the little room where the boys slept and Otto awoke from a tugging on his sleeve. A disheveled and sleepy Friedrich announced that Max was choking. Anna and Otto sprang out of bed as one and though the movement shot pain through Otto's legs, he was almost as fast as Anna at the door.

Maximilian's eyes held the panicked look of someone who couldn't breathe and this was confirmed by the bluish tinge around his mouth. Anna was terrified as Otto lifted up the child and cradled him in his arms. Soon the household was up and a car was sent for to transport the boy to the hospital.

The hours passed as a nightmare and as the doctor scraped the thick grayish coating from the little boy's throat, the nurse began to prepare the oxygen tank and mask for Max. Anna prayed and scolded herself for allowing the child to catch a bad cold, but was totally unprepared for worse news. The waiting was agonizing until the doctor sat down across from them in the waiting room and cleared his throat.

"Um, yes, it appears the child, Maximilian? …Has contracted the Diphtheria virus. I am sorry to say it is very contagious. You must leave him in the hospital. We will do whatever we can for him. Please bring your other son in to be checked as well." The doctor appeared as though he tried to say it kindly but hope was missing from his features. Otto and Anna did not need to be told that death claimed a percentage of those contracting this disease.

"There are new vaccines being developed that we could try…" the doctor's voice faded out as Anna covered her face with her hands and wept into Otto's shoulder. This was her fault! Or could Max have caught the virus from someone at the Fair? Either way, she had fought to keep him from harm ever since he was born so tiny and had fit into Otto's palm. She surely could not lose him now!

Friedrich, who was healthy as a horse, somehow escaped the disease despite playing daily with Maximilian. It was decided that he would spend his days with cousins while Anna almost lived at the hospital. Otto had to work but returned early each day, his mind clearly not on his sales.

Liesl, who had kept house in Düsseldorf, contacted them daily on little Max's progress. Even Therese, Betsy, and Heidi also spelled off Anna so she would leave Max's side and at least eat something. Days turned to weeks, as it became a touch and go battle for the child's life. Anna spent many hours on her knees to her Lord. She pleaded for her baby, promising that he belonged to God and she would instill faith in him, if only God would spare his life. That night was the worst so far and hope was almost gone. Amazingly, he made it through again.

Liesl arrived one afternoon distraught that she may not see her little brother alive, for weeks had gone by with little change. She was shocked to see the waif in the large hospital bed. He looked a bit like Max, but was the size of a three-year-old. Yet he was weeks away from his fifth birthday. She stood behind the curtain that hung by his bed struggling for composure so that her crying would not frighten him. Then Liesl knelt by his bed, covering the little hand that lay beneath the sheet with her own hand. Maximilian opened his large blue eyes and smiled when he recognized his big sister.

"Hello little brother," she began, smiling bravely, "I missed you! You must get well and get out of this bed now for I have a gift for you." Maximilian grinned weakly but his eyes still sparked with all the inquisitiveness of a child. Liesl produced a picture book filled with all sorts of dogs. She held the book up so that Max could see the colorful pictures and turned to a page with roly-poly black puppies.

"See here Max, this is a picture of your new puppy. I have him at home waiting for you. If you would just try and get well, you can come home and play with him. He doesn't even have a name yet, so you can name him. Alright?" Liesl was smiling but tears were gently moving down her cheek behind the mask she was required to wear. The boy smiled and slowly the little hand crept up from beneath the blanket and reached to wipe one away near her hair.

Liesl didn't care if the nurses chastised her or not. Glancing quickly around she gently hugged the little boy to her, whispering that she loved him dearly. "Mama and Papa are so worried about you and Friedrich has no one to play with. Please get better dear."

Amazingly, Maximilian began to recover within days of Liesl's visit. Whether this was due to her visit or just the long awaited answer to prayer, it was welcomed either way. It was decided that since Max's birthday was so near anyway he should have a party with all the relatives before leaving Oelde.

Their decision to leave Friedrich with relatives all this time now caused a problem. Summer was at an end and Friedrich missed his friends at home. Due to Anna's constant vigil at the hospital and Otto busy with work, Friedrich grew angry and petulant. Anna knew it was her fault that little time was given to the seven year old, and tried to comfort him. She was upset when he turned away from her one day when she attempted to hug him. It would also have broken her heart had she heard him mutter that Max should die.

Preparations and excitement abounded but even though Anna included Friedrich in everything, his resentment and jealousy got the better of him. Though others celebrated that Max was on the mend, Friedrich changed that summer. A contest of wills had begun. Now Friedrich competed with Max for every bit of attention, toy or favor that was up for grabs. Otto spent more time with Friedrich, taking him along on short day trips. Anna spoiled him a little, trying to make amends to Friedrich, but to little avail. His parents both hoped Friedrich would grow out of it soon.

Chapter Eight

Kurt and Liesl

***

Liesl became a young woman during the years in Düsseldorf. She was lonely for her cousins in Oelde, and too many years as an only child made her hate solitude. She had developed an outgoing personality and became quite independent. The vivacious girl was also quite pretty with her mother's green eyes, Hans' auburn hair and slim build. She also attracted young men at the dances and school functions, and one of these was an intense young man by the name of Kurt Schwartzkopf.

Initially, Liesl thought he was too interested in politics. His years of attendance in the *Hitler-Jugend*, as was required of all males from age fourteen and up, had made a loyal follower of Kurt. He really took every thing to heart and seemed the perfect poster boy for the ideal Aryan, believing in the dream that was The Third Reich with its unfailing loyalty to the Führer.

As her mother had loved to debate with her father years ago, Liesl relished discussions with Kurt, lately about the Reich. She and Kurt disagreed regarding the Nazi principles taught about the place of women and men. Liesl had attended a *Jungmaedel* group for a time as well, but balked at the creed that implied her utmost purpose was only to provide a home and hearth and healthy Aryan babies to raise up loyal to the Führer.

Kurt in turn pointed out all the good that their leader had done since coming to power. In Hitler's election campaign he promised to abolish unemployment. Fortunately for Hitler, the German economy had already begun recovering by then. Some of his policies however, actually did reduce the number of people unemployed in Germany.

Certain policies involved removing some freedoms from employers, such as banning the introduction of labor saving machinery and requiring employers to get government permission before reducing their employees. The government also gave work contracts to companies that relied on manual labor rather than machines. One example was the government's massive motorway program. The result of this scheme was Germany developing the most efficient road system in Europe.

Adolf Hitler removed taxation on new cars. Being a car lover, Hitler wanted every family in Germany to own one. He was even involved in aiding in the design of the Volkswagen, or 'People's Car'.

He also encouraged mass production of radios, probably because he saw them as necessary to supply the constant stream of Nazi propaganda to the German masses.

Hitler tackled youth unemployment by the forming the Voluntary Labor Service and the Voluntary Youth Service. They were used to plant forests, repair riverbanks and help reclaim wasteland. This actually was a positive action giving youth a purpose and involvement, bolstering their self-importance as Hitler praised youth as being ultimately important to the future of Germany.

Liesl had to agree that Kurt was correct in some of his points. What she found unacceptable was that unemployment for men was also reduced by almost forcing women to leave the labor market. Female doctors and civil servants were dismissed while other married women were paid a lump sum of a thousand marks to stay at home. And so the discussions went.

When politics were not being discussed Liesl found Kurt a fun and interesting companion. Their dates often found them rowing down the canal, or sitting at an outdoor café with friends, or bicycling to the meadow for a picnic. As her friendship grew with Kurt, Liesl worried over the growing mutual attraction between them. He was just a little too Nazi for her mother's liking and Liesl knew that Kurt was probably headed for a military career. How this would affect his future could have repercussions if she married him. Being even part Jewish was not a popular thing these days and the whole topic made Liesl's head pound. Why couldn't they just be left alone!

Liesl had approached Kurt on the "Jewish topic" early in their friendship to "feel him out." His stance at the time had been almost indifferent and he had encouraged Liesl not worry.

Sometimes one's heart betrays one's head and the result often is that you can't help who you fall in love with, as Liesl's grandmother, Oma Thielmann used to say when speaking of her own marriage. Liesl was certainly in this predicament now.

In spite of their differing views Liesl and Kurt were surprisingly compatible. A deep thinker, Kurt's careful and serious nature was balanced by Liesl's gentle laid-back attitude and easy smile. As opposites often attract, they were good for each other. Kurt was also an only child of elderly parents, and though confident and an over-achiever, he always seemed a little lonely to Liesl. Kurt admitted he needed Liesl, and found he enjoyed her larger family and their acceptance. So, in the autumn of 1937 Liesl married the dashing Kurt, now a young military officer, and they rented a little flat not far from Otto and Anna and her little brothers.

Otto respected his new son-in-law and Anna welcomed him, though with some reservation. He just was too enthralled with the new regime and its leader for her liking. However Kurt tried hard to please and wanted to fit in with his new in-laws. The newlyweds spent many happy hours with Liesl's family around the table, and Anna's cooking soon won his palate.

However, fate steps in when unexpected. Though Kurt was not cruel or without conscience as most who had hardened themselves to become Hitler's ideal, his hopeful zeal was noticed as his superiors saw in him a faithful tool for the Reich. He carried out orders religiously to the delight of his commander, and began to rise in rank and power. Soon a candidate for the Schutzstaffel, by early 1938 he was an SS officer. He felt honored to be part of a new, proud Fatherland that had been so humbled after the Great War. Kurt knew the world would now have to sit up and take notice of his beloved Deutschland.

Where the Jewish problem was concerned Kurt had once felt they probably deserved to be mistrusted, for he could never understand a Jew's knack for business and profit. He never agreed with open persecution however and in times where few could be trusted, he fortunately kept this opinion to himself. In one of those ironic twists of fate Anna's son-in-law was soon promoted to Regular Leader, two levels below Supreme Leader, effectively becoming a muscle in one arm of the cancerous regime that now choked the heart of the Fatherland.

Chapter Nine

Changes in the Wind

***

Human nature being what it is or motivated by self-preservation, the old adage, "If you can't beat them, join them," seemed to the the standard of the day. Many applications for membership to the Nazi Party came flooding in during the early Hitler years. Industrialists, bureaucrats, even intellectual and literary figures were standing up to be counted with the new leader. Original party supporters soon cut off new memberships from these latecomers, mocking them.

There was another flood in the opposite direction as well as over two thousand writers, scientists, and various artistic people abandoned Germany to enrich other lands, especially America. Albert Einstein was one who never returned. Those who remained were a strange mixture of optimists and the fearful. Some of both were represented in the Bauman and Thielmann families.

Jewish persecution was on the rise and relentless in Nazi propaganda. Samuel Bauman wondered if it would ever end. He thought he had dealt with the problem of persecution when he had taken his family to a country village to live. He had raised his children as Catholics instead of Orthodox Jews and hoped that they could live peaceful lives away from the prejudice he felt as a boy. He only hoped God understood that he hadn't abandoned his faith all those years ago, only changed the form of worship.

A generation later when Otto met Anna he cared not that she was Jewish. She didn't 'look' Jewish with her dark blonde hair and Aryan appearance, so it had never been an issue. This new regime however made it a point of interest and now it could not be ignored.

One day Kurt came home with a strange request that frightened Liesl. She hurried to him as he closed the door, and deep in thought, sat heavily in his chair. Removing his military cap he rubbed his face with his hands brushing his hair through with his fingers. Liesl saw the worry lines in his forehead and tried to ease them with her caress.

"What troubles you, love?" she tried to inquire lightly. Liesl was no fool. The increasing tenseness she felt each time she read a newspaper or overheard whispered gossip caused her stress. She knew if she felt it Kurt's worries must be magnified.

Kurt paused, not sure how he could reassure her. Could he even trust his own staff when traitors were everywhere, or be sure that his plan would work? The Geheime Staats Polizei, or 'Gestapo' as it was known, muzzled Hitler's political enemies and even snooped on the members of the Nazi hierarchy within at all levels. In 1936 the Reichstag had passed the Gestapo Law that forbade the affairs of the Gestapo to be reviewed by the courts making them effectively above the law.

Gestapo agents operated amidst a web of informants that could be anyone. German citizens lived in fear that anyone they knew, even the postman or neighbor could be suspect. Those who disagreed with the regime dreaded that a chance careless word or anti-Nazi sentiment could result in a summons to the Gestapo Headquarters in Berlin where interrogation by sadistic torture was the order of the day. Victims whisked off in the dead of night were later sent to concentration camps, if they survived. In reality not only Jews, but also indeed the entire population was held ransom in Hitler's Germany.

"Liesl, we must have a new strategy," Kurt began, his voice low, as if afraid the walls could hear him. "I want you to arrange a meeting with your parents. We will take everyone's identification papers from your mother's family including you and your brothers. I must take them to a…an acquaintance, and he will make some slight changes."

Liesl realized what Kurt proposed was placing him at great risk. "You mean to have our heritage stamped out, is that it?" she asked him, a little more harshly that she meant it to sound.

Kurt knew Liesl was touchy on the subject but pulled her onto his lap. "Now dear, you know what surely must be coming as I feared. We talked about this before. If I don't have the papers changed now we may not have another chance. Things are coming that I can't talk about. It is better that no one knows that there is any Semitism in your family at all. Your grandfather was wise to raise and baptize them Catholic. It will make things easier for me now."

Liesl held her breath. She knew Kurt was putting his job and possibly his life on the line for this. She sighed, kissed him and whispered into his ear, "I will arrange it."

Kurt had a few favors to call in with a certain government clerk and it didn't hurt that he had dirt on the man that effectively ensured his silence. However, the forged documents had to be prepared discreetly and quickly. He couldn't bear to think that his precious wife and her family members were in danger of being caught in the Nazi anti-Jewish "web" that was tightening daily.

This year Kurt had witnessed a cunning plan unfold. Firearms registration had been mandated in March shortly after Kurt's SS appointment. He knew the next inevitable step would be the enacted law forbidding Jews to own or carry weapons, requiring them to turn over their guns to government authorities on pain of incarceration penalty if found otherwise. Kurt had foreseen it coming and knew he earned a position of trust with his in-laws a few months before when he had helped them bury their hunting long guns on Samuel's land. Samuel, Otto and Max had all wisely refused to register or surrender their right to arms.

Now Kurt knew he must be careful as he was about to erase all Jewish history from the identification of those he cared about. Kurt did not believe in God, but if God did exist, he hoped that He would protect those who believed in Him. For now Kurt's 'god' was the new Reich and he believed in its ability to turn his beloved Germany into a powerful and mighty country to be proud of. Yet he was not naïve enough to ignore the rising trend towards tyranny and abuse of authority the Nazis freely wielded.

Kurt sighed as he hung up his uniform jacket and lightly touched the lapels where his own authority lay for all to see. He had considered briefly his small part in this corner of history but realized if he was careful and lived by his wits, the opportunities for good out-weighed the bad. He could not in good conscience refuse to use his position to benefit those who needed him, including his family. And so he swore to himself as long as he had any clout at all, he would do his best to treat all men fairly and do his utmost to thwart those who would promote the malignant evil that was poisoning the new Reich.

Part II

Chapter Ten

The New Order

***

Young Maximilian Thielmann began to form a plan. The seeds of anxiety that birthed the plan were planted in him even before Max met the man in the motorcar. A child can sense his mother's fear and while not understanding why she fears, absorbs this.

Friedrich and Max were growing up in the belly of the Third Reich. Their mother tried to cushion this reality especially for Max, since Friedrich embraced the excitement of belonging to a new, proud Germany. Being Max's closest comforter and ally she strove to fiercely protect him from the madness that was changing their world.

His father feigned normalcy, providing comfort and assurances even while his own optimism waned. Though Kurt had effectively ensured that their papers were in order and Anna could not easily be accused of being Jewish, Otto knew she did not feel safe. Daily people of her race were picked on and even denied citizenship in the land of their birth.

In Nazi Germany being Jewish was considered a racial designation and Jews could not become non-Jews in the eyes of the government by simply not practicing their faith, marrying an Aryan, or converting to Christianity. If one grandparent either male or female were Jewish, even someone who actually adhered to another religion could be subject to the race laws. Laws that were recently made public regarding the banning of inter-marriage between Jews and Germans of pure blood. Jewish shops were now marked clearly segregating them further.

When Max went to bed he could hear his parents speak in hushed tones having soft arguments in the kitchen below. Reaching down beside his bed, he sunk his fingers into curly fur, assured by the warmth of his big dog, Heinz. Turning to the wall Max retreated to his imagination and for him it was panacea. It took him other places when reality was becoming too strange. A dreamer was born in Max because he chose to see the world as wonderfully as the magical places his storybooks depicted. He was secure in his family home and that was enough.

Yet below his window changes had occurred daily. Where once laughing mothers pushing baby prams had strolled the city sidewalks, now soldiers walked two by two as gloating bullies.

This cradle of hatred made Max and Friedrich pawns like all German children, ripe to be molded by its leader. Success with this generation depended upon usurping their parents control to instill the Nazi ideals. Hitler knew he must control the very thoughts of the German people. Three years before in his attempt to purge 'un-German ideas', huge bonfires had been ordered to annihilate thousands of books and the words of some of the world's great thinkers.

In reaching for the nations' children, the Hitler Youth Organization overtook the training of children in elementary and secondary schools. Basic math and science skills suffered as priority was placed on military-type subservience to the Fatherland, drilling them to serve as unquestioning soldiers instead. This was done so they would obey and thus be ready to fight to the death for 'the cause'. Young minds were pliable and easy to instill with the race superiority ideals of the Nazi propaganda machine. Hitler once stated that he wanted, "a brutal, domineering, fearless, cruel youth…that is how I will create the New Order."

In 1938 Max was in his second year of school. He had fallen behind in his battle with Diphtheria the year before and only his love of stories helped him persist in learning to read now. Though Anna helped Max practice each evening, he still struggled to catch up to his classmates.

Then something, or rather someone wonderful happened. Young Kaethe Kaufman had noticed the sick boy who returned to school and it bothered her to hear the other boys' laughter when Max couldn't spell words that the class already knew. She had seen him on her block after she had moved in last year and had longed to join the children when they played outside. So that spring day Max looked up to see the girl standing beside him.

"May I sit here?" she inquired. Max nodded. Being a motherly type, the little girl perched beside him on the curb and set down her lunch pail. She spread her book open across both their knees and matter-of-factly began to read. It seemed the most natural thing in the world to Max as the two children read together and a friendship was born.

Soon they were playing together daily as Kaethe was accepted as one of Max's group. The two became fast friends since Friedrich was now off with his older pals. Coolness had developed between the brothers since Max's illness.

Months passed and the summer came. It was filled with the sweet joys of childhood as Max and Kaethe waded in the creek nearby, catching frogs and minnows, while Heinz barked and splashed them. Little picnics and bicycle races down to the pastry shop where Tante Olga would give them a tart were great fun, and often the children would raid the apples that hung over the fence behind the store. When summer turned to autumn again they sat near each other at school, whispering only when the quite deaf schoolmaster was turned toward the chalkboard.

Something bothered Max that had occurred often of late. Several children were being taunted on the schoolyard, and he was not ignorant of the racial slurs that were being directed at Jewish children like Kaethe. The schoolmaster seemed unable or unwilling to stop it. Once Max suffered a bloodied nose for helping little Josef Rosen escape some bullies. Another day, Max wisely enlisted some nuns passing by who grabbed the youths by the ears and administered a tongue-lashing.

At home, Max asked his mother about the trend. She sat him down and held him a moment. "Max, people can be cruel. If parents don't teach their children manners and compassion, how are they to learn? You were not raised like them. You are dear, and full of kindness. Be brave son, and stand up for the persecuted. I am so proud of you." Anna knew that to be Jewish in this time and place was a fearful thing. Some day soon, she would have to tell Max and Friedrich about their heritage from her. Otto had thought it wise to omit that information, since Anna and her family were baptized Catholics anyway. She sighed, contemplating if this was the time, but was interrupted as Otto came in the door. The truth would have to wait for another day.

***

It was this October that Max had his seventh birthday and it bothered him a little that his best friend had not been seen that day or come to the parade. Upon returning home Tante Betsy made sure that any who had missed it would know about Maximilian's encounter with the Führer, and Max became a celebrity of sorts on his street. This had odd implications.

For some reason Kaethe was not allowed to come out to play with him and he hardly saw her for a week. Even in school she did not speak to him. While neighbors and other children envied his good fortune, Kaethe seemed distant.

Friedrich was terribly jealous of Max and wouldn't speak to him either until being the brother of the local celebrity suddenly brought himself some attention. This soothed his ego and so he changed his mind now being willing to boast about Max meeting the Führer as if they were great friends. This, strangely, brought the boys together again.

Soon however the novelty blew over and Max's celebrity waned. Kaethe eventually was allowed to play with him again. Max didn't know that she had spent the week crying and begging until in resignation her mother and father decided the boy was not to blame for attracting the attention of the hated man.

It was early November now and Otto was reading the newspaper, frowning at an article on some latest mistreatment of Jews when the children ran in the door. Otto always made sure he didn't discuss upsetting things with Anna in front of the boys. He noticed that Max was spending a lot of time with a certain little girl, a pretty little thing with rosy cheeks and bright, friendly eyes. Though glad that Maximilian had found a good friend Otto knew she was the daughter of the Jewish family down the street. He hoped that they would be left alone since they were kind, decent people. Anna also visited them with a torte one day and became friends with Kaethe's mother.

"Don't you approve of her, Otto?" Anna asked, observing Otto's frown as she pummeled a dollop of dough.

"Well, of course! It isn't that, Anna. It is just that Max is quite fond of her, isn't he?" Otto said slowly.

"Is that so bad, Otto? They like to read together and Max has really improved!" Anna smiled. She was always in a good mood when making bread. It was a comforting ritual and she loved to bake for her family.

"I know." Otto was happy that Anna could not read his thoughts right now. Though he pretended nothing was wrong he hated to admit that maybe Anna was correct. Daily observing societal changes and the tightening web of restricted freedoms, Otto assumed more hardship was intended for Jewish families. He did not like what he was reading.

Upstairs, the children were looking through Friedrich's telescope. Kaethe ran her fingers along the smooth, cool metal. She peered through the lens and turned away when she saw the strolling soldiers on the street below. Her parents had also been noticing changes and restricted her play to within the rear yards of the flats, forbidding her to play on the front streets now. Kaethe turned her attention to the little hedgehog and gently stroked him. Max could see she was bothered by something.

"Max", she began, "What did the man in the motorcar say to you?"

"Nothing. He just smiled at me," said Max, noticing Kaethe had become quiet, her brown eyes almost sad. It was slowly dawning on Max that something was terribly wrong and realized the man with the moustache had something to do with it all.

"Why did you give him flowers?"

"Tante Betsy bought them for him. She, she likes him." Max shrugged. He felt uncomfortable. He did not like where this conversation was heading.

"Mama tells me that he is a bad man. She has been crying and asking Papa to move us to Uncle Yacob's farm in the United States." Maximilian was mildly alarmed but nodded mutely. "Mama says I must stay invisible and play where the soldiers can't see me," she continued, " Will you be invisible with me, Max?" With that, she took Max's hand and pulled him down to the floor.

The two children sat for a moment then crawled under Friedrich's bed and lay down on their stomachs, chins in hands, and both peeking out at the sunny room. With quilts pulled down over the edge of the bed they called this their fortress, and it seemed that nothing could touch them there. With Heinz beside them like a huge fluffy sentinel they were for the moment safe indeed.

Max reached for some picture books and pulled them close. They were books about airplanes, Max's favorite thing. "See these airplanes, Kaethe?" he began as he tried to soothe the little girl, "They can fly you to the United States. I have decided to fly there too. Then we'll never have to worry about the soldiers. Alright?" he brushed her hair away from her cheeks as he tried to comfort his friend.

"When will we go, Max? Papa says we are trying to get a travel card, and then we will go away. I want you to go too."

Max frowned. He did not want Kaethe to move away and pretending they would go together was much nicer. Their plans were interrupted as his mother called upstairs for Kaethe to come down; her mother was there to get her.

Max hugged Kaethe and assured her it would be all right. He waved from his window as Frau Kaufman hurried Kaethe along the rear lane behind the yard. The child turned to look back at Max and smiled for him though sadly, and he felt a shiver as if some foreboding omen passed between them. He did not know how right he was.

Chapter Eleven

The Night of Broken Glass

***

Three days later came the awful day. Max was home with the flu and had been sleeping. In his half-sleep he heard bells and cymbals and drums which waking realization slowly turned into the sounds of breaking glass and slamming doors. Then the awful sounds that so scared the child that he wet his bed. Women screaming, loud male voices shouting, then, shots rang out. Heinz began to bark wildly jumping at the sounds coming from the window. Sensing Max's distress, he ran back and forth growing louder by the minute until Anna ran in and calmed him down.

The terrible sounds did not stop however but would intensify in the hours to come. Anna held Max protectively as if against the assault and confusion happening below. She was glad she was home and hadn't gone to the market as she had planned. Now she worried about her other son and prayed.

A half hour later Anna jumped when their own back door slammed and a wild eyed and pale Friedrich ran up the stairs. Some of his friends from the Hitler Youth had asked to participate, pointing out known Jewish residences for the soldiers but Friedrich begged off since he was feeling sick. It was the truth. The trembling boy ran to his bed and stopped his ears with his fists, shaking. Anna rushed to comfort him also.

What madness was this?! Surely all hell was loose in the streets!

It seemed an eternity until a worried Otto made it home at suppertime and held Anna while she sobbed into his shoulder. Feeling as helpless as she, Otto knew if he dared attempt to help his neighbors or stop the madness he might never return. And thus, he felt a coward.

As the evil day bled into the night the horror went on. Otto and Anna could not believe the surreal scene before them when they chanced a glance from darkened windows. Down the street as far as the eye could see, Jews were systematically being dragged from their homes, their belongings thrown through closed windows down onto the street now littered with glass and broken dreams. A backdrop of crimson and yellow flames made dramatic strokes against the canvas of the indigo sky and they realized disbelieving, that it framed a synagogue burning.

These marked ones had once been a vital part of this society. They were local shopkeepers or shoemakers, lawyers and doctors. No matter, these non-citizens as they had recently become were now devalued, beaten, shot, or marched toward waiting trucks as Nazi thugs destroyed their homes and loved ones. These who suffered beyond the haven of the Thielmann family's own untouched home were not evil criminals. No, they were simply Jewish by fault of birth. Surrounding neighbors who escaped were those who by virtue of their "pure" Aryan blood watched simply from behind their lace curtains and did not venture out.

What would become known to future generations as the Holocaust had truly begun. And this infamous night would be known mockingly as 'Kristallnacht', the night of broken glass.

***

The next morning the pogrom of this night was blamed on a Polish-Jewish man who had murdered a Nazi official in retaliation for the harsh treatment of his family. No one was fooled. Judgment was coming anyway and the excuse of this night just gave Hitler's henchmen their chance to take action sooner.

The Kaufmans were gone, their home an empty shell. Otto and Anna called on them as soon as the SS thugs had retreated from their nasty business. Hurrying through the chaos and destruction one could almost believe a hurricane or some natural disaster had hit the city. Otto shook his head. He would never have believed this could happen here. He had such high hopes for the new government and it had seemed for a time to be the answer to Germany's troubles.

The door stood open to the once quaint and cozy home. Though the lock was broken from being forced open and the home appeared to be ransacked it also appeared too that the family could have fled before the onslaught. The drawers were pulled out and clothing was missing from them and the wardrobe closet. Silver menorah candlesticks and mementos that had adorned the sideboard were absent as well. Family pictures were missing from the walls and the home had a look of abandonment. Could a family torn from their home in such brutal urgency have packed even these items? Almost relieved, Anna began to have hope that they fled before the onslaught unscathed.

When they returned home Otto assured Max that this was most likely the case and affected a cheery countenance to convince his son of their escape. Max envied Kaethe if this were in fact true. One day he would go also. It made more sense all the time and when his time came, he would leave this cruel place. He would go to America to see Kaethe. He also believed fervently that she had gotten away with her family.

Friedrich and Max were further grieved when they returned to school. Classmates who had somehow escaped the purge of Kristallnacht were not overlooked. As if the recent scourge were not enough, all Jewish children were now forbidden to attend German schools. The atmosphere was somber and quiet, as scattered desks sat empty that were once occupied by these shunned ones.

Nazism encouraged bullying and Jewish children had increasingly become targets. Others like Max who guarded friendships with Jewish pals were secretly glad their friends were saved from the tide of ongoing abuse that was rising as German children were encouraged to mock and hate them.

Now sadness turned to relief for Max since Kaethe and her family had surely escaped. But Max felt his loss. A loss that was magnified in countless homes, in countless places as loved ones were severed from their families. The hopeful waited in vain for some news, to find them again. Most were gone, never to return. He fell into a restless sleep to that troubling thought.

Later Anna checked on her sleeping sons that night, tucking their blankets securely around them. Gazing at them peacefully breathing, to her they seemed safe and secure for now. Softly touching Friedrich's curly locks, and Max's cheek, she wondered how much longer she and Otto could keep them safe in these troubled times.

Cursing the evil that preyed on the vulnerable, Anna slowly lowered herself to the floor. Kneeling down by her sons' beds, she was silhouetted in the moonlit room as tears began to flow down her cheeks. The stresses of recent events seemed too much for her. Now pouring out her fears to her God, she silently wept for all the children. Some were the sacrificial lambs that through fault of birthright would increasingly face the fires of persecution, while others like her sons were forced to participate in charades of grandeur orchestrated by a dangerous madman. That they should daily witness such horrors broke Anna's heart. And so she prayed for protection for all the innocent lambs of the Reich.

Chapter Twelve

Promises

***

On the tail of that terrible November an uneventful and quiet Christmas came. The boys still enjoyed gathering the boughs and making candles for the Advent wreath in anticipation of Christmas Eve as they had other years, though their joy was tempered. As children do they dreamed of things they hoped Father Christmas would bring them. Anna did her usual baking of pfefferneusse and stollen bread in preparation of the holiday. Liesl came over to help with the decorations and placing candles and candied marzipan on the tree that Otto brought from the forest. The family laughed and played together, the boys holding on tightly to routine.

One evening a week before Christmas the brothers were called to the kitchen. Anna had convinced Otto to tell them about their half-Jewish heritage. She felt it was important somehow to identify with the persecuted. It would also strengthen their character when hard choices had to be made. Otto began, telling them about the importance of family ties, but the need for secrecy. Anna also briefly explained the history of the Jewish people and why her father had hid that fact.

Max just sat quietly, wide-eyed, his thoughts whirling with the implications of that revelation. Friedrich would have sworn under his breath, if he weren't afraid of quick retribution from Otto. The nine-year-old was very upset and Anna tried to comfort him, but to no avail. It didn't seem that any explanation would suffice to a boy who daily witnessed harsh treatments of Jews. How could they tell him such news! The boys didn't have to be told twice that the information was confidential. It could mean the destruction of their family.

As Christmas neared, Friedrich settled down. He was still young enough to be affected by the infectious joy that surrounded the season. Otto came home Christmas Eve early, to the strains of the Blue Danube waltz playing on the old gramophone. Coupled with the aroma of fresh sweetbread baking, his wife smiling with flour in her hair, what could he do but sweep her in his arms and waltz her around the kitchen? These were needed sweet diversions to the depression that had overshadowed them lately.

That evening the Thielmann family went to church for midnight mass, joining other families for the walk to the cathedral as the Christmas bells peeled clearly in the winter air beckoning believers to worship. Since the horrors of Kristallnacht Hitler had set his sights elsewhere for the moment and the old feelings of awe and reverence returned as Christmas touched tender hearts once again.

Max raised his face to the softly falling snow and stuck out his tongue to catch the huge flakes as they fell and caught in his lashes. As music wafted from the massive pipe organ inside the family mounted the cathedral steps to the strains of 'Silent Night'. It was Anna's favorite and she clutched Otto's hand as the words "Stille Nacht, Heilige Nacht..." floated on the chill air. They joined hands with the boys. Family was even more precious now and they counted their blessings that they were still together. In the altar's soft candle glow they prayed for their friends who were now gone, possibly forever. Faith was an important lifeline more than ever as they searched for answers from above.

For Christmas Kurt was allowed two days off for festivities so he and Liesl came for a brief visit. He was a very busy man now and visits were becoming rare. While the adults gathered to talk quietly and privately amongst themselves the children were relegated to the upper bedroom.

Having a son-in-law in the Schutzstaffel had already proved to be a trump card for Otto & Anna. The marriage they at first feared to be a disaster would indeed be a saving grace. Because of Kurt, Anna's parents and one brothers' family had wisely emigrated to the States under assumed names Kurt had acquired for them months ago, to unknowingly escape Kristallnacht. All this was possible because Kurt was an officer, an ironic blessing that made them almost untouchable.

When Kurt entered the boys' room awhile later two pairs of questioning eyes met him. Pride and fear wrestled in Friedrich's heart as he beheld his sister's husband in his uniform, the light glinting off the medals and collar pins with the double stylized SS. Kurt opted to wear it for the very reason that it sometimes kept away prying eyes. He knew that there was an informant on this street and until he knew who it was, it was better to be feared than become a victim.

Max associated that uniform to the evil deeds he had witnessed and this belied his fondness for the man. The dog Heinz barred his teeth and lowly growled under his breath until Max pulled on his collar. The boys waited silently. Could Kurt still be a friend, or foe?

It was true that Kurt had an authoritative presence that commanded respect. In fact his confidence intimidated other officers as well as his subordinates, making those who might cross him very careful. His eyes gave nothing away and you couldn't read him unless he let you in. He could be ruthless with those he despised, or smooth as silk, a dignified gentleman. How he chose to use this kept spies within the Nazi hierarchy off balance. He wore this power like a mantel and it would later save him in his line of work.

Kurt sat carefully on the foot of Friedrich's bed. "Hello little brothers! How are you both doing today?" he began wanting to maintain their trust, yet understanding their confusion. He knew that Max had just lost his best friend, possibly to an enemy dressed as he was. Kurt had early on developed a friendly comradeship with the boys upon his marriage to Liesl but knew it was now on shaky ground. He needed to affirm that nothing had changed between them.

"Friedrich, Max…I want you to know that you are both dear to me. I would never let anything happen to you, " he paused as he held their attention, "please believe me. I wear this because I believe in a new, better Germany. However there are those who are filled with hatred and want a different Germany." Kurt almost faltered for a moment as he wondered, how do you tell children about evil and ambition?

"Ours is a great country and there is nothing wrong with pride in that. Some of the world's best inventors and scientists are German…" He felt he was messing this up as he searched for words and the boys stared at him. Talking to adults was a piece of cake compared to the wide-eyed innocence before him now. "…and we must stand up when we are called upon to do our duty. I must serve as an officer for my country but I do not have to agree with the methods of those who violate my conscience."

Friedrich nodded, still suspicious, and Max cocked his head, confused. Kurt scratched his ear and tried again. "I am able to perform more good for those who suffer if I use my position to help them, than if I were to resign and run from the responsibility. Do you understand?"

Despite some of the words Max thought he understood. Kurt was really a victim of sorts like they all were, unhappy with the changes around them but unable to stop it. Yet here was a grown-up trying to ask their forgiveness for his part in it all. Max went over to Kurt and touched the braided lapel on his left shoulder.

"It is all right Kurt," the boy began, " You are a nice man. You don't want to hurt people…you didn't send Kaethe away…did you?" Max asked slowly, as if afraid to hear the answer.

Kurt hugged the boy then and reached for Friedrich as well. "No! No, never!" A lump forming in his throat, Kurt paused before he spoke. He felt he had slipped up. There had been no time to warn them about Kristallnacht coming. He should have helped them at least save their friends. He had hoped the attack was to be confined as a demonstration of power in just the Jewish ghettos, not the massive strike against Jews all over Germany that it was. Ninety people died that night as identical scenarios played out in every city and town. Additionally, thousands were loaded onto trucks and sent to concentration camps. To add further insult the Jews were blamed for the carnage and made to pay dearly for the clean up costs resulting from that day.

Kurt now wanted to make a difference. He was currently assigned in an administrative capacity which gave him opportunities to 'lose' or alter important documents, identities, supplies and orders, and try his best to confuse and confound the Nazi agenda with red tape that slowed them down.

Also good at reading people, Kurt knew how to choose his staff. He developed allies in useful areas with ties to Intelligence. He was clever at covering his tracks. With only a few narrow misses Kurt would navigate the next years true to his word, covertly causing chaos while appearing to be the hardnosed, efficient leader he wanted them to see.

Kurt cleared his throat and looked directly into their faces. " I swear to you boys, I will try to foil attempts to hurt the Jewish people if it is in my power and try hard to be a force for good and not evil."

The boys clearly understood. It was what they were planning to do themselves. In appearance they would be loyal little Aryan soldiers learning the Nazi Creed at school and attending the Deutsches Jungvolk, goose-stepping to the command of their Nazi teachers; all the while vowing to be a thorn in the Reich's toe if they could.

Friedrich and Maximilian's relationship had turned a corner after Kristallnacht. Together they planned to do what they could to throw a wrench into the Nazi machine, and so began a partnership of sorts. Pranks had to be planned carefully and soldiers were often the targets. Thus began their own private war against the Nazis. Though Friedrich steadfastly refused to believe that his mother's family were Jewish and thus would deny it his whole life; he hated the Nazis for what they did to Jews and those that opposed the Reich.

***

Chapter Thirteen

Pranks

***

Both being pranksters at heart, Friedrich and Max's plans often got them into trouble. Sometimes they were caught and sent off to bed with warm bottoms from their father's belt when a complaint was made or a warning issued due to some adventure that went wrong.

Such was the Halloween night when they had poured water over Herr Diesel's door because he refused to give out candy. It had been an unusually cold night and in the morning his door was frozen shut. They still remembered the swift punishment they received when they were anonymously reported by some snitches. The boys had worn paper masks they had made from the popular Beistle Luhrs Halloween characters. With their faces covered who could have known who they were?

When spring came another opportunity presented itself as unexpectedly as the warmer weather. About a mile from home and an easy ride on their bicycles was a munitions factory on the edge of the Rhine. Max and Friedrich, being boys, decided to check it out with their friend eleven-year-old Rolf. It was decided beforehand that when they went on "undercover missions" Heinz would have to stay home. The dog put his paws on the gate as Max rode off and gazed after him balefully.

The factory was surrounded by a high fence topped with barbed wire to keep out inquisitive climbers, like those that were watching it now. Parking their bikes in the trees the boys crawled on their bellies in the grass up behind a gentle knoll. There their position was hidden from any watcher who might gaze out from the factory yard yet it gave them a perfect view of the top of the fence and chimneys. The huge generator that powered the plant was to their left inside the fence.

Rolf wanted to throw some firecrackers to make the factory workers think they were being shot at but practical Friedrich felt this was like teasing a sleeping dog. It would only make them get caught without causing any real damage. Rolf was always up for any mischief and had joined the "Foil the Nazis" club of thinking. Better yet, he could be trusted not to squeal if they were caught. Not one of the boys considered the real possibility of being shot themselves.

Friedrich had been practicing and was pretty good with rocks. His idea was just to take out one of those glass insulators and hoped to cause an electrical short or even a blackout if they were lucky. This would cause a bit of chaos and they could ride home exultant that they had slowed the Nazi's bullet making production down. They were certain the cause of the problem wouldn't be discovered until they were long gone on their bicycles, thus making it a safe enough plan. They must never be caught, they all agreed on that point!

So it was decided. Friedrich scooped up a couple of rocks the size of small eggs and warmed up his arm. He would aim first for the power pole as practice. If he hit that at forty feet he would try for the power station itself. Being on the backside of a hill had its problems as well as benefits. While one could not be seen from the factory one must also aim high so the rock could arc over the hill, and this made it harder to aim straight.

He let the first rock fly. It arched high and true and seemed to be a great shot. Then, as the rock began its swift descent a soldier's head appeared suddenly above the hill. It had not occurred to the trio that a guard might be on his rounds outside the factory. In one of those improbable moments that one may think, what if, 'if' happened. The boys held their breath in unison watching as the soldier arrived at the same point as the rock. To make matters worse the man glanced up at the moment of impact. The rock would have bounced off his helmet had he not looked up and possibly just knocked him over. As it was, the missile hit just above his left eyebrow and knocked him flat. He lay there as if dead, his rifle nearby.

The boys' eyes were round as saucers. For seconds no one moved. Then with speed borne of terror the boys jumped on their bikes and raced for home. As if chased by demons they pedaled faster while imaginations ran wild, perhaps expecting a convoy of soldiers to overtake them any moment. They didn't stop or hardly breathe until braking inside their rear yard. The boys stared at each other, panting. Then as the remembrance of the event replayed in their heads, the trio collapsed in heaps of laughter until they were almost in tears. What a day! What a score! They defeated a Nazi soldier! What fun! Making a pact of secrecy, Rolf headed home.

In spite of their mirth the brothers watched the streets for patrols and expected a knock at the door any moment throughout supper. Anna inquired as to the snickering during the meal but the boys did not want to feel Otto's belt when he returned home, so told their mother it had been a wonderful day exploring on their bicycles.

That night the boys lay in their beds and discussed the day. Max was having second thoughts, his sensitive nature and compassion getting the better of him. "Maybe the soldier is badly hurt. Or worse, maybe dead!" Max worried aloud to his brother in the darkened room.

Friedrich scoffed at this. He would not accept guilt or responsibility for an accident. He hadn't known the soldier was even there, much less targeted him on purpose. "I'm sure he's fine Max! Don't even worry. Besides, like Mama always says, things happen for a reason. Maybe he was a bad man and supposed to get a rock on the head. How about that?" Friedrich teased.

The seven-year-old Max wasn't so sure, so said a prayer for the guard before he went to sleep. He wasn't sure God would forgive them if they had killed him.

The next day Otto sat in his favorite chair after the meal and read a small newspaper article to Anna. "Hmm, it says here that a soldier on patrol outside the Rheinmetall plant was found unconscious yesterday. They assume he was attacked by a rock thrown from over the fence. Local authorities believe it may have been an attempt by underground resistance to attack the plant but are curious as to why they stopped there." It also says, "If a rock is the best they can do the Reich has little to fear," Otto read. "Hmph, sounds more like youth than resistance fighters to me."

Friedrich choked on his milk at the last comment spurring Anna to heartily pound him on the back and scold him for drinking so hastily. Max just smiled into his plate.

Chapter Fourteen

A War Is Launched

***

Having lived through cycles of good times and bad Otto wondered if worse was on the horizon. He and Anna had both felt the effects of food shortages in the last world war. It seemed the writing was on the wall, Hitler may just propel them into another fray, who could know? In the spring of 1939 Otto purchased a plot of land on the edge of Düsseldorf. It was too common to have back lane gardens raided when people were desperate. So most Saturdays now the family went out to the lot where Otto busied the boys with helping Anna till the ground or pick weeds, while he drove large metal stakes into the property line and erected a fence.

As summer rolled around the wisdom of the plan was proving itself. A new chicken coop surrounded by trees stood at one end unseen from the road, and the property was surrounded with a high fence topped by barbed wire. Healthy rows of vegetables grew there now. The journey from home was a short bicycle ride for the boys who collected the eggs and fed the hens.

August arrived and Adolf Hitler survived an assassination attempt. Otto read this news in the morning paper to Anna as she served him coffee and a fresh apfel streusel. Anna shook her head. There would be no relief for the world just yet. She would just have to pray harder that God in His mercy would remove the awful man from power. She knew thoughts of murder weren't Christian-like but she thought God just might agree with her.

Thirteen years before in his book, *"Mein Kampf"*, Adolf Hitler had outlined his planned domination of Europe. If the book had not been largely ignored at the time the powers of the world may have recognized the enemy sooner and saved themselves a second world war, and the loss of millions of lives.

Hitler now cited the harsh limitations set against Germany in the Versailles Treaty as an excuse to acquire land where German-speaking people lived. When Great Britain and France allowed Germany to take control of Austria and Czechoslovakia without a shot, it was felt that appeasing Hitler with this concession would avoid any bloodshed. However they had gravely underestimated him if they thought the matter was over. They didn't realize that Hitler wanted much, much more.

At the end of August Himmler hatched a plan that would give Germany an excuse to invade Poland, their next victim. The Nazis dressed an unknown prisoner from one of their concentration camps in a Polish uniform. Placing him at the border between Poland and Germany they staged an attack, shooting him, and spread the lie that they averted a Polish attack against a German radio station.

Early the next morning on September first German troops invaded Poland in an all-out attack known as a Blitzkrieg or lightening war. The sudden air attack destroyed the Polish air force virtually while on the ground. The bombing of roads and bridges and killing of not only marching soldiers but also civilians caused chaos and hindered any further mobilization of Polish forces.

This time he had gone too far, prompting Great Britain and France to send Hitler an ultimatum. He was to withdraw German troops from Poland or there would be war. Hitler refused, thus forcing the Second World War on September 3, 1939. Australia, New Zealand, India and South Africa would join forces with Britain and France that day. On September 10th, Canada also joined them as they went to battle with the Third Reich.

***

Chapter Fifteen

Daily Trials

***

As 1939 faded into 1940 the war continued to heat up. Denmark and Norway were entered by German troops in April, Belgium and Holland were invaded in May. It seemed that there was no stopping Hitler's ambitions.

In the Thielmann house life went on as usual, daily functions bringing some sanity to an uncertain future. Otto still traveled, now selling hardware to manufacturing plants. When he was home he and Anna made plans and Otto spent much time in the yard studying drawings of bomb shelters. Anyone who knew Otto knew he was well prepared, always a step ahead of the game. And so weekends found him digging a shelter with the boys running errands and helping out.

One constant irritation was that Friedrich had to attend the Deutsches Jungvolk meetings, which his mother and father were helpless to stop. Soon Max would be old enough to join too, meaning Hitler's clutches would take another son. It was bad enough when Friedrich learned the Jungvolk Oath, swearing allegiance to Hitler, the 'savior of our country".

One Saturday, Anna heard Friedrich reciting something as she put clean towels away in a closet outside his bedroom. The door was ajar so she peeked through the crack. He was looking into the mirror, a frown on his face as he tried to remember the words on the paper before him. Anna couldn't help leaning closer to hear those words. She hoped it was schoolwork but was shaken as she listened. It was the Hitler Youth Prayers modeled after the Lord's Prayer; to Anna's horror and consternation, absolute blasphemy!

"Adolf Hitler, you are our great Führer. Thy name makes the enemy tremble.

Thy Third Reich comes, thy will alone is law upon the earth. Let us hear daily thy voice and order us by thy leadership, for we will obey to the end and even with our lives. We praise thee! Heil Hitler! "Führer, my Führer, give me by God.

Protect and preserve my life for long. You saved Germany in time of need. I thank you for my daily bread. Be with me for a long time, do not leave me, Führer, my Führer, my faith, my light, hail to my Führer!"

Otto would not let Anna give Friedrich a scolding, reminding her that if he did not learn the words, he would be disciplined. They simply had no choice about this brainwashing. They could only teach them the truth at home and hope their example would sway them from being affected too deeply. As with eight million other boys in Europe, Friedrich's attendance was mandatory. Friedrich explained the purpose of it when asked by his parents what they were taught. To learn military athletics or 'Wehrsport', that included marching, trench digging, map reading, use of dugouts, and how to get under barbed wire. Friedrich didn't want to upset his mother so omitted telling about the other important techniques, such as bayonet drill, grenade throwing, gas defense, and pistol shooting. Otto could only assure Anna that attendance in the organization would at least sometimes keep the boys out of trouble.

***

One cannot lock up the house and wait out a war. Life goes on and Anna determined that life should be as normal as possible. Yes, the rations had less variety than at the beginning and certain things were only a memory, never mind long gone luxuries. Little things like stockings were unimportant in summer yet Anna smiled to see younger women still attempting to follow fashion by drawing lines up the back of their legs. This worked fine, until it rained.

Anna brought fresh bread out to her boys one warm Saturday afternoon with her preserves and lemonade. Otto wiped a handkerchief across his brow and drank thirstily. It was hard to believe this lovely day that a bomb shelter of all things, would ever be needed. As yet the Allies were nowhere near the city but that did not mean it would never happen.

Max reached for a slab of thick, hot sweetbread, and slathered a good bit of butter on it only to take a bite and spit it out. "Mama, what is this stuff? he cried, disgusted.

Anna looked apologetic. " I'm sorry Maximilian but butter is not so easy to be found these days. And when you can get it, it's very expensive. That is margarine. If you don't like the flavor just use the preserves."

Otto frowned at his son. "Max, you must be appreciative to eat at all. It is not your Mother's fault that there is no butter. She does what she can for you." Max looked contrite but he hated this terrible tasting stuff!

Common in wartime markets now, the margarine was developed by a half-Jewish scientist named Arthur Imhausen who ran a factory in the Rhur area. Having first synthesized soap from coal, he next developed a way of making margarine from coal. He had succeeded to Hitler's delight, as Hitler was a vegetarian who only ate margarine. Normally, being even part Jewish would have doomed Herr Imhausen to a concentration camp, but he received money and aid from the Nazis to produce a type of margarine that was so durable it didn't spoil. Hitler was thrilled and in 1937 told Imhausen that he and his family would be treated as honorary Aryans. Eventually the scientist received two of Germany's highest military medals for his fat-synthesis work. Thus, he survived the Third Reich. Fortunately for him, Hitler had his own double standard.

Since the outbreak of war in September rationing cards were issued for the populations' usage. Certain luxuries were not to be found anymore and Max and Friedrich missed the cream torten they used to buy from the bakery. Chocolate was becoming scarce as well. So Anna baked sweetbreads for the boys when she was able to get sugar.

Trades around the neighborhood began to become common and soon Anna was known as the "egg lady". One day she found a stranger at her door. He apologetically asked if he could bother her for some eggs. She only had six until the boys could go the next day to collect and two were for baking, two were promised to Frau Hagerman.

He offered oil in trade and seeming honest enough and a little hungry, she decided he needed the remaining eggs more than she did. It seemed a good trade at the time for he profusely thanked her, tipping his shabby hat and bowing as he went. She needed oil to bake anyhow, so cheerily set about to do just that when he left.

Anna hoped her neighbors would not give out her home address without her permission anymore. She made a mental note to tell her neighbor, Frau Mangold not to broadcast about her egg supply all over Düsseldorf! Or, she mused, it could have been that nosy Frau Unruh down the block who seemed to personify her surname, 'troublemaker'.

As Anna busied herself making cinnamon cakes she thought about the scene at the meat shop only the day before. First Frau Unruh had complained to Herr Adelman the butcher about the price of the milchwurst, then discussed with Frau Potthoff her views and approval of ethnic segregation a little too loudly. She had seemed to stare down Frau Adelman as if to challenge her objection, and then openly stared into the home at the back of the store. Anna had a mind to clobber her with the sausages she had just purchased. Ah well, there just was no accounting for bad taste. Maybe the woman was just plain miserable.

When the cakes came out of the oven, Anna was aghast. Yes, they smelled like cinnamon and apples yet there was another odor she couldn't put her finger on. Anna sniffed them suspiciously. They had an oily sheen to them that she couldn't account for which puzzled her as she had followed her recipe as usual. Yet her thrifty upbringing would not allow her to throw them out. Ah well, she thought, they could cool while she went to the market. She would decide later what to do with them.

This particular Saturday, Friedrich was serving as altar boy for the evening service with Father Klaus. The family had been gone an hour when Friedrich rushed home ready to raid the kitchen, hungry and in a hurry. He had been out with his friends since breakfast and those cakes smelled so delicious! As Friedrich hurried past the sideboard he lifted two of the little cakes onto a plate with a spatula and poured some cider to go with it, heading up to his room.

Friedrich gulped the food without really tasting it, washing it down with the delicious cider. He emitted a hefty burp while brushing his wavy hair. He wanted to look his best. Stepping into his good lederhosen and wiping his mouth with the back of his hand, he flew down the stairs two by two. As his parents and Max arrived home Friedrich was hopping on his bicycle. He waved. They would see him at mass in under an hour and he didn't want to be late.

Anna and Otto were proud of Friedrich's maturity of late and his willingness to please. The priest who Friedrich was taking catechism classes from had reported pleasure at his progress. And so the family made sure they were not late this night. As if they could be with punctual Otto in the lead.

As Otto, Anna and Max filed into their pew they waited for the processional to come in. They knew that Friedrich was to follow Father Klaus and carry the large golden cross down the center aisle.

Friedrich had wondered as the priest put on his vestments and prepared to lead the boys into the mass, why he had gulped his food so hastily. Twice in the last minute he had burped loudly and shamefaced, blushed a deep red. The other two boys giggled. His stomach was now doing somersaults and making noises like a kettle coming to boil. Would he be sick? He half-heartedly pulled on the white tunic over his clothes. His mother had ironed it and it smelled clean and fresh. He didn't want to disappoint her either. Unsure whether to bow out, his stubbornness won over when the priest kindly rested his hand on Friedrich's shoulder and nodded that he should follow.

As they entered the vestibule Friedrich glanced toward the congregation through the heavy wooden doors and decided he must not fail his post. After all, his family was here and papa especially came home early to be here! And so ready or not, Friedrich led the other boys down the aisle.

Normally the beautiful music would thrill his soul and Friedrich tried to concentrate on that, but this time it was to no avail. Each step now was agony as Friedrich's stomach complained louder than ever. As the sweating boy passed the family pew to his horror his bowels suddenly failed him. The mysterious oil mixed with thin stool shot down his legs before he could even react. Never in his life had he been so mortified!

Two things now happened quickly, though to Friedrich they seemed to unfold slowly, as if an eternity passed. Otto saw the problem and being next to the aisle, relieved Friedrich of the cross while guiding Max into position with a firm hand. Surprised, Max took the heavy cross and shouldered it, stepping into his new duty as if he had rehearsed it. Next Otto guided the bewildered and terrified Friedrich as they retraced his steps up the aisle, while those who had missed it wondered at the stench that seemed to rise from the carpet suddenly.

Anna would have laughed at the absurdity of the scene had she not felt so awful for her son. And so when Max had set the cross into its stand and departed to the side, Anna beckoned and the family left quickly and quietly.

At home nothing was said to the shamed Friedrich who raced upstairs throwing himself onto his bed with hot tears spilling into his pillow. Otto gently helped his son clean up, providing towels while Anna filled a hot bath. Their silent support and unconditional love helped the boy through the event though Friedrich refused to help with the sacraments any more that year.

Needless to say the oily cakes went into the stove and made wonderful fuel. It was some time before Friedrich himself could see the humor in the situation but knew that no boy ever had a more faithful family.

***

Chapter Sixteen

A Trap Is Set

***

Max sat on his bed drawing birds one late spring afternoon as the sun shone lazily through the lace curtains and the breeze gently moved the branches on the tree outside. In full bloom, the fragrance of apple blossoms wafted in the window. The tree's shadow made patterns that moved across his paper as he sketched. He had become quite the artist of late as his pencil recorded the still gentle world of nature around him. The awe of childhood had not yet been taken from him. He carefully colored the feathers of the bluejay he was sketching and satisfied, jumped off the bed to pin the picture to his wall.

His room felt safe. A haven. Max was not a coward but he was shy and careful by nature. He thought about Kaethe. She had disappeared as if by magic. What would she tell him now if she could? Had the family stolen away by night crawling through ditches, suitcases and satchels in tow? Had they been caught? No, he wouldn't let himself entertain that thought. Had they met a boat or perhaps a plane to fly them to safety across the ocean?

Max knew that Uncle Bruno had taken his own cousins six months before that and lived safely in the United States. He hoped for and pictured Kaethe there as well. Someday, someday he would join them.

Being bored, Max decided to see if his mother had anything good in the cooler. Or maybe she baked the day before. As he descended the stairs and entered the kitchen Friedrich burst in the door. He was excited and his cheeks were rosy. "Max! You must come now. We're going to set a trap for the Faust bunch. They are going to get it!"

A gang of boys headed by the Faust brothers, were local bullies who lived across the tracks and loved to pick on younger kids. Fritz Faust was also a group helper in the local Nazi youth Chapter and prided himself on being chosen for this important task. He apparently embodied the ruthless youth that Herr Hitler so prized. The gang had challenged Friedrich and his friends to games and contests that often broke into fights. It was an ongoing problem and Otto had forbidden Friedrich to any further association with them.

Max knew that Anna had gone to the neighbors' house for an hour. He was always ready for a good trick but also knew that often he felt his father's belt when their innocent 'fun' was reported. "I don't think so Friedrich, father said we couldn't have anything to do with them anymore."

"We aren't going to even see them," Friedrich protested, "Rolf saw them drive away with their father and the others won't be around with the Fausts gone."

"What do you want to do?" Max frowned. He was excited to hear the plan but apprehensive as well. Friedrich's ideas often meant trouble with Otto.

"Rolf and Klaus are coming too. We'll dig a hole in the meadow path near the tracks. They come through there often to our side. No one will see us, since a thicket and trees hide that part of the path. We'll have to work fast and cover it. Then, when they run through there later they will fall in! We'll put lots of water in the bottom and make it mucky. Won't they be surprised!" Friedrich's eyes glistened with the anticipation of seeing Fritz Faust and his hoodlums covered in mud.

"I don't know…" Max said slowly, " If you think it will work?" He began to get excited too, though doubtful of not getting caught. The Fausts deserved it. They were such rotten characters and were always causing someone at school to cry.

It didn't take long to convince Max and soon the brothers were handing out shovels from Otto's garden shed. They also packed a tarp, a water jug and some rope on their bikes and were off.

It was nearly suppertime when the sun dipped to the west and the hole was ready, the fresh dirt dispersed among the grass and the bottom wet enough to make a quagmire. It had taken twenty or more trips to the stream with the jug to accomplish this. The older boys stretched the tarp over the hole. It finally measured almost three feet deep and three feet in diameter. The younger boys tied the tarp loosely to pegs in the grass. Max and Klaus, Rolf's younger brother, spread handfuls of dry dust, rocks and twigs across it to hide the pit. They stood back and surveyed their work with satisfaction.

"If you didn't know it was there you wouldn't even guess it," Rolf boasted with glee eyeing their successful trap. Hoping to stay and watch for the Fausts to return and run down the path had been the plan. However supper wouldn't wait and regretfully the boys trudged to their bikes, shovels in hand and headed for home.

Max and Friedrich squirmed all through supper and Anna noticed their restlessness. They must have had fun today, she mused. They came in dirty and their clothes went promptly into the wash basket. She thought often how different it was raising boys now, compared to her experience with Liesl. Supposing that boys were just made that way, always hard on the furniture and their clothes and always into mischief. She loved them dearly anyway.

As Anna sighed and turned back to take more soup from the stove, Friedrich shot Max a meaningful glance and nodded toward the door, a silent signal to go and check on their plot as soon as supper was over.

The meal dragged on it seemed because Otto for once was late for supper and then decided to quiz the boys on their schoolwork, whether they had done their chores and homework, and what they had done this particular Saturday. Max ran up to his room and produced the bird sketch for Otto who dutifully admired the very lovely birds. His little Max was indeed quite an artist and Otto wished to encourage any talent in his boys.

After an agonizing amount of time, the supper dishes hastily washed, wiped and floor swept, the boys were allowed to go out for a while. Otto felt since the days were getting longer and they were longing to go outside, the fresh air might be useful for a good sleep.

Jumping on their bicycles the two could hardly wait to see if they had caught the wicked Fausts. Even better Max imagined, would be if they caught a Nazi soldier! He knew this was a long shot since the soldiers rarely went into the little meadow with more important matters like harassing people in the city. Max followed Friedrich as they stopped at Rolf's house and he scooped up a pebble to fling at the boy's bedroom window. In a moment Rolf looked out, looked back at something and then made a sign that he would join them. Poor Klaus had to stay in as he had to practice piano.

It was difficult not to race into the meadow but Friedrich cautioned that if they actually caught the Fausts, it had better appear that they just 'happened' upon the scene than had planned and executed the trap themselves. The trio of bicycles rounded the last block before the meadow in anticipation. It was almost totally dark now. However if they thought they would find their enemies in the muddy hole silently cursing, they were in for a surprise.

Before they even headed down the path they could see something was up. A military vehicle stood halfway down the path just before the trees. Several people stood around watching as headlamps from the truck illuminated the spot where they knew their trap was. Friedrich stopped his bike abruptly almost causing Max to run into him and Rolf jumped off his bicycle as well. Amid barked orders by one soldier and a nasty spiel of cursing from a loud woman, two other soldiers seemed to be pulling something from the hole. The boys held their breath, dumbfounded.

First a bicycle with a bent wheel appeared, then a broken basket of groceries. Assorted fruit was scattered around the mouth of the hole, a cake upside down a few feet away. Finally, a disheveled woman emerged hoisted up by her armpits, her knees and coat covered in mud. Max was sure he had never heard such language in his life. "Dumbkopf! Dummer esel! " she spouted red-faced, which were the milder of her many expletives. She vented her wrath at the soldiers who were only trying to help, but she had to rage at someone. Max's eyes widened upon recognition of the bedraggled creature that huffed and puffed in the truck's headlamps. It was Frau Unruh from their street! Max remembered her because she often scolded the children for picking apples from her tree as they hung over the fence. She also had a yappy little pug and a petulant daughter of sixteen who liked to flirt with the soldiers who strolled by their front steps.

Max tugged Friedrich's sleeve as the boys suddenly seemed of the same mind. They turned their bikes around and as nonchalantly as they could muster, mounted and rode back the way they came. They surprised Anna when they came in and went straight to their room.

"Can you believe that?!" exclaimed Friedrich when the door was safely closed. Max shook his head. He didn't know whether to giggle or just be relieved that no real harm was done to the woman. No one who could yell that loudly could possibly be hurt.

Friedrich snickered. It was after all, pretty funny. However it was not what they planned and at some point the Fausts still had to be dealt with.

"Do you think she is really alright?" Max said, second-guessing his first assessment of the situation.

"Of course!" answered his brother assuredly, "You could hear her half way across the city, I'm sure. If she was really injured she would still be there, no soldiers would have heard her yelling."

"What do you think will happen now?" Max was suddenly afraid of being tracked and imagined their father answering the door and innocently being arrested.

"Don't worry," Friedrich bragged, " The tarp and rope we left there are common in any hardware store. And I am sure no one saw us this afternoon." Although for all his bravado, Friedrich was secretly afraid that he was mistaken.

Next morning Anna returned from the market where she ran into Frau Mangold who passed on the tidbit of gossip that the whole neighborhood was buzzing with. The new topic was the unfortunate Frau Unruh and her misadventure of the evening before. Apparently Frau Unruh escaped with minor bruises, but lost her bike and cake and a bit of pride. Ironically, due to the attention and expressions of sympathy, she actually basked in the limelight that the mishap brought her making the event almost worth the trouble.

Otto visited the boys' room at bedtime. He was not a showy man given to overt displays of affection, and had rarely hugged or kissed his boys since they were little. Thus a bedtime visit usually meant punishment for some misdemeanor. Both boys exchanged glances holding their breath for the inevitable scolding and strap.

Otto cleared his throat and paused, which made Max squirm and Friedrich break out in a sweat. "My tarp is missing from the shed," he said. They waited. "Also, the shovels are dirty."

Max gulped. Why didn't Friedrich say something? Both boys just knew what was coming now, until Otto surprised them.

"I want you boys to clean the shovels in the morning and sweep up the mud, do you hear?" Otto tried to appear stern. They knew he meant business. Both boys nodded mutely. "Friedrich, I will get a new tarp when I go for garden supplies next week. You boys will help with the new garden." It was a statement, not a request. Though they would have helped anyway it was their father's way of saying he knew. Purchasing a tarp right away would only confirm suspicions about who was responsible for the hole in the meadow. "Good night." With that, Otto turned and left the room. The boys stared at each other, mouths agape. What, no strap?

When Otto climbed into bed beside Anna, he chuckled. "I am so glad that the miserable woman didn't really get hurt. I would have hated to punish the boys for doing everyone a service. I'm sure they didn't mean to catch her specifically, but I think they won't try that again."

Anna sighed and snuggled close to Otto. "No, but they will think up something new. Whoever that hole was meant for, I think they couldn't have caught a more deserving person." She yawned, "I'm only sorry I wasn't there to see the launch." With that, Anna chuckled and turned over. "Anna!" Otto scolded mockingly. Every once in a while he was shocked by the spunk in his normally gentle Anna.

Days passed by as the boys waited, expecting retribution eventually. However it never came. Although the gossip-turned-informant on Hohe Strasse had herself become the victim, she for once could not inform on those who caught her. Their identity remained a mystery, as luck would have it.

Chapter Seventeen

Evacuation

***

During the summer and autumn of 1940 Hitler brought more attacks on London and British airfields and in retaliation bombs were rained on Berlin and Hamburg. He had also launched unrestricted submarine warfare. In September Germany's Jews were ordered to wear yellow stars for easier identification. In November the Soviet leader Molotov and Hitler met regarding the topic of "the new world" for a premature discussion of who would dominate Europe's countries, like two small boys dividing up marbles. Otto shook his head as he read the news daily watching as the world fell apart. Alliances and pacts were made or postponed as Hitler met with Mussolini and later Franco to try and achieve his ends.

The unpleasant business of war would one day soon affect them all. Yet so far, other than living under certain restrictions and amid shortages, their family had been reasonably safe. Soon however, they knew they would have to make a decision. Germany's child evacuation program had begun last year. Named the Kinder Land Verschickung (KLV), it served to remove children from the cities. Transporting children to rural areas for a "holiday" spared them from increasing inability to feed them and danger from bombing by the Allies. Schools and the Hitler Jugend (HJ) jointly ran the organization until the HJ took over the lead role this year.

Until 1940 there had not been many planes near Düsseldorf but Otto knew it was only a matter of time. Important factories were built along the Rhine and a clever opponent would surely seize the opportunity to strike where it hurt Germany the most. Berlin had been the first city to evacuate its children last year and other cities were preparing to follow suit as the war heated up.

Otto assured Anna that he had built a strong bunker in the back and they would use it to protect themselves when the air raid sirens began. He omitted that a direct hit would render it useless. And so the family practiced and drilled and plans were drawn up in event of separation from each other. They made up codes and means to contact one another, should the unthinkable happen.

While radio and German newspapers praised the victories and advancements of Hitler's armies, they waited for the next shoe to drop. It was bad enough to have a war on one's hands but now it was coming to their own soil and closer than ever. The Allies were advancing.

The Christmas season was almost upon them when bombs hit Düsseldorf and a few days later, Mannheim. Max was playing in the new fallen snow just before suppertime. He almost jumped when the air raid sirens first began their incessant whining. He glanced up and around, running into the street to see if he could spot planes. Yes, there they were to the northwest! Just small dots in the sky, growing larger, but Max was so excited he couldn't move. Fear mixed with the thrill of seeing up close the actual bombers he could identify in his airplane books. Not hearing when his mother called him, he very nearly flew off his feet as she grabbed his arm and yanked him into the yard. Friedrich was helping Otto lift the bomb shelter's heavy metal door that Otto had procured from a scrap dealer, as Anna and Max rounded the garden. Max shouted for Heinz who had started barking loudly when the sirens began.

Firmly shut in, the family now huddled in the shelter as Otto lit the lantern making sure the blankets were passed around. It was very cold in the bunker. Friedrich had snatched the newly baked bread from the stove where it was cooling as he had run past on his way from the house. No sense wasting the warm bread that made his mouth water. He tried to make a joke about the inconvenience of being bombed at suppertime. It fell on silence as they waited.

The first sounds were of distant droning planes, which then became louder as the planes flew overhead. The whine of falling bombs preceded explosions that shook the shelter so that the bread stuck in Max's throat like dry lumps, the concussions causing dust to fall on their heads. Bottles of water and supplies rattled and clinked together on makeshift shelves Otto had built. Surely their home would be safe, they hoped, and Anna prayed to that end. Eternal minutes passed as the bombing continued. Finally, there was silence.

Emerging from their friendly tomb in the ground the family surveyed the yard. Other than pieces of scrap wood, bricks and mess lying about from the building across the street being hit, their home was almost untouched. Inside the house Anna picked up broken dishes that had bounced their way off of open shelves. The kitchen windows had broken but remained in place. Otto began taping them up.

Having survived their first encounter with terror from the skies the boys' silence soon turned into post-stress excitement and they talked excitedly throughout supper. But that night it was hard to sleep and they lay in their beds watching the skies apprehensively through dark windows until sleep took them in exhaustion.

The next day brought sorrow mixed with relief that only two people were killed on Hohe Strasse. In the ruins that now stood across the street they had stark reminder that war had come to them also. Most of the neighbors attended the funeral of elderly Herr Spratt who had been sickly and bedridden and his daughter Elsa, who had nursed him. It was supposed they had nowhere else to go when the bombs hit. Across Düsseldorf the deadly numbers were higher. It had begun.

As the boys explored the neighborhood to see what other damage had occurred, they came across St. Stephen's churchyard. Most of the church's stained glass windows had been blown out and the steeple had toppled. The cemetery beside the church had suffered a direct hit leaving a huge crater where weathered stone crosses once stood. Of course the result was that everything that once was there now littered the road. As only children can see it, the macabre gives way to reality. Soon a game of kick the can was underway, the skulls of the formerly departed providing the balls.

***

Christmas was somber and even though the family did not starve, they and others missed the treats and plenty that were taken for granted in peaceful Christmases past. Families were just glad that the bombing had ceased for now.

Max obtained an important task in the spring of 1941. Father Klaus asked the eager boy to be a bell ringer for Sunday mass. Max was elated! He had watched other boys get to ring the large bells that hung high in the cathedral tower rafters. At last Father had deemed him of sufficient weight to pull the huge ropes that rung the bells. What a thrill! Max had almost let go the first time he jumped on the ropes and got the ride of his life high above the floor! Jump and pull, tug and fly! Rolf's brother little Klaus was the other ringer, and the boys quite enjoyed themselves.

Max loved going to church. He believed in God, his mother having firmly planted the seeds of faith in him. Not only because she believed but to train her children in principles and values that belied the feared Nazi brainwashing that produced eager zealots from impressionable youth.

During mass his eyes roamed up the massive marble pillars that held the vast dome above, and he gazed at the painted angels there. His eyes drank in the exquisite carvings of the Holy family statues in the vestibule. Stained glass windows high on either side of the sanctuary depicted scenes from Christ's life. In awe, Max learned reverence for God and appreciation for beauty and order. Sometimes the strains of the pipe organ that covered the entire west wall balcony brought him to tears. Music brought him to a place where he felt sure God must dwell. But Otto thought the boy was daydreaming and not listening and sometimes Max felt Otto's stern frown that brought him back to earth. Why did the priest have to intone in Latin? How could a boy understand that?

Outside St. Mary's Cathedral, which to date stood miraculously untouched, reality could not be denied. Increasingly war turned ugly. Where once stately, ornately fashioned buildings and centurion stone homes once stood, now ruined skeletal ribs of these former homes poked awkwardly into the sky amid the rubble like ugly pockmarks on a once beautiful face.

Can innocence be restored to children of war? Max's soul could not reconcile the beauty of spiritual things with the evidence of the cruelty of men. As months passed, his eyes and mind were assaulted into witnessing the stark realities of death that now rained down. Never having experienced death before, suddenly he must avert his eyes, for the stench of it now surrounded them. Like broken dolls, human limbs lay in the rubble and on the road after the bombings. More often lately this tragedy was repeated.

Bombing continued sporadically over the next year and the shelter Otto built proved safe enough for raids were concentrated further north and west. For a time they had a reprieve they hoped would last. However Otto was correct in his fear that cities along the Rhine were soon to be targets. He knew too that the decision about the children had to be made soon. Lists were posted instructing the days the trucks were to be leaving for camps and rural villages where children were to be billeted. Names of families listed by street were posted, instructing them to have their children packed and ready to go.

Anna argued with Otto at night as they lay in bed and discussed the future. It was Anna's favorite time to discourse on important things when she had Otto's full attention. She said she was not ready to part with her sons just yet and would think up excuses to tell the KLV if they came for them. After all, there had been no air raids for nearly a month now. She preferred to fool herself pretending that they were over. Otto sighed and gave in. He wanted the boys to be safe but at least the two were united in their belief that the boys shouldn't leave them until they had no choice. It broke both their hearts that they should miss even a day of their sons' lives.

Too soon the decision was almost made for them. On the afternoon of July 31, 1942, Friedrich had decided to take a bike ride with Rolf. Otto warned him not to venture too far in event of an air raid. Friedrich nodded as he ran out the door. He wasn't worried, like most youth with the attitude that they are somehow invincible and untouchable. They had been lucky so far hadn't they? Having turned thirteen recently he was just beginning to enjoy the company of girls. He and Rolf had met Helga and Sabina at the theatre house last week. They hoped the girls would be back in the area and headed for the theatre in high spirits. Fifteen city blocks seemed like nothing when on their bicycles and anticipation gave them wings!

The outing started promisingly for Sabina and Helga were also hoping to meet the boys and had gone to the theatre daily in search of them. Although shy and awkward the bloom of new experiences made their time together exciting, the flirting harmless. The boys tried to impress the girls by walking atop the rock and mortar cemetery fence, and then attempted to knock birds off the power lines with stones until the girls squeamishly begged them to stop.

Later while leaving the theatre house, the young people's laughter filled the early evening air. The promising day had ended and Friedrich was surprised how quickly the evening shadows were darkening into the night. Regretfully the boys realized they had to go. Promising the girls they'd be back the next day, the boys mounted their bicycles and headed for home.

Friedrich realized they had stayed too long and feared Otto's punishment. Though it had been over a year since he had administered the strap, Otto always warned that Friedrich was yet not too old to feel its sting if he disobeyed.

Pedalling swiftly, they were still ten blocks from home when the air raid sirens suddenly burst to life. Streets that were dark to begin with now saw remaining lights being extinguished rapidly to make harder targets. An eerie finger of fear raced up Friedrich's back and Rolf shot him a look of terror as the two youth pressed more urgently on their pedals, propelling them down the darkened streets.

Droning deadly messengers now dived low over the city, delivering the kiss of death. One cannot know until they experience the whine of bombs falling, the breathless terror of waiting for the hit. As bombs found their target, nearby explosions shot flames and blackened missiles of stone and debris into the sky and jaw numbing waves swept over the riders. Friedrich felt tears sting his cheeks as flash-heat and the stench of sulphur burned his nostrils and another home or business became a tomb of rubble. Time stood still as his pedals seemed to turn infinitely slowly like the dreams one has of trying to run under water. The safety of shelter still seemed a million miles from them.

Tears now ran freely down Friedrich's cheeks as the certainty of death reached for him. Then at last, there was home in the next block! He glanced toward Rolf as he pointed to their refuge. Rolf who had been there a moment before was gone. He had been right beside him. Why couldn't he keep up?! Friedrich tried to look over his shoulder but had to pull quickly to a stop, turning as he did so. His mind could not comprehend what he saw.

Thirty yards back his friend lay motionless, his bicycle nearby. A deadly black pool was spreading beneath him. No, no, it couldn't be! Friedrich's thoughts blurred, all noises around him now became dull thuds in his mind. Otto appeared from nowhere and pushed the shocked boy toward home. Limping hurriedly as best he could to the slain youth, Otto tried to pick him up but found he could not. The young man's head was blown apart, the contents spread out around him, a puzzled countenance his death mask. Otto turned and ran back toward safety.

When the bombing stopped almost a whole city block to the south was gone. Shrapnel from one of those targets had found Rolf and took him, only a few feet from Friedrich. Friedrich lost his best friend and his naiveté in one night.

Neighbors rallied around Rolf's parents and their remaining children, Klaus and little Sophie. The grief bound them together as they sat numbly throughout the small funeral. A closed casket like a lonely sentinel mocked the promise of a future gone forever. Innocence dead, the bloom of youth and freedom forgotten, all these Friedrich buried with his friend. That July night was the first massive Allied bombing on Düsseldorf and over a thousand civilians died that night. As the tale of that terrible night spread along the block, neighbors called Friedrich a miracle, to have survived.

Friedrich's mind reeled as it replayed the horrific memory over and over. He could feel only guilt for surviving when his friend did not. Could that have been chance? Now when he needed his family the most, a grave decision had to be made. Unfortunately there was for Otto, no choice.

***

Otto was quiet, his heart heavy. There would be no more excuses; he had almost lost a son. Even though the boys wept and pled with him, Otto's mind was made up. He must stand firm. Liesl came over to see them the evening before leaving, which was spent assuring each other of their love. Otto gave his sons what instruction he could because they were becoming men too quickly. He knew this might be his last chance.

That night Max stroked his little hedgehog and set it back into its little den lovingly. Mama had said he couldn't bring his pets where he was going. She promised to take care of them for him. And so he fell asleep with hot tears as he cuddled the huge form of Heinz the dog. Friedrich was quiet, his face turned to the wall, yet sleep wouldn't come.

Next day the trucks came for the children. Anna who had spent the night crying was up early with the boys' bags ready for travel. A large truck stood in the square where a KLV aide loaded up the last of the children before Max and Friedrich reluctantly climbed aboard. The aide closed the gate on the back of the huge military truck and Anna thought she would be sick. Her eyes red from crying, Otto hugged her, assuring her all was for the best. Max waved and Friedrich tried to look brave and yet felt miserable. The family did not know when or heaven forbid, if, they would see each other again.

Max was still only ten but was actually one of the oldest children in the truck, after Friedrich. He held the hand of little Fritzy Schruber who was crying loudly, assuring the boy of five that all would be well. Max determined he would act like a man and help the others. He would make his father proud. Trying to frame their faces in his mind as the truck pulled away, his father, mother and sister waved, and Heinz looked woeful, as if he too knew Max wouldn't come back for a long time.

As the truck headed southeast onto the highway it rumbled noisily, bouncing over debris and downed lines, detouring around piles of bricks and rubble. Düsseldorf faded into the skyline and the brothers wondered what the future held. They both hoped that at least they would stay together.

Chapter Eighteen

Obbach

***

The journey was long and for the brothers, quiet. Friedrich was morose and introspective, Max, lonely and confused. After two previous stops and devouring the contents of the lunch pails their mother had packed, the boys' dusty journey ended in the village of Obbach northwest of Schweinfurt. Friedrich read the road sign as the truck turned down the village street. Their destination had been a surprise to even them.

They were disappointed hours before since they had long since passed the turn to Oelde, realizing that they weren't being sent to their grandparent's town as hoped. Apprehension turned to relief now as first one brother and then the other was called from the roll that the KLV worker held. When about six children of varied ages had disembarked the truck left for its next destination, those few who still remained onboard looking sad and already missing their comrades.

Carrying their suitcases, the children were lined up and matched up with families who waited for them expectantly. It would be difficult for a while, this living with strangers. Some of the host families looked as uncomfortable or unsure as the children. First Friedrich was paired up with an elderly farmer and his wife, the Melmans. They were looking for a strong older youth to help with the cow milking and chores around the little farm. But as Friedrich looked back for Max to join him, another couple came forward to claim him. The Brauer family had two teenage daughters and no boys, so they looked forward to having a boy join their family.

Max's bottom lip trembled just for a moment. No, he wouldn't cry. It was all he could do to will himself to move, this didn't feel right and he felt awkward. However he remembered Otto's words and would do his duty. After all, he reminded himself; these kind people were offering to keep him safe. He must remember to be grateful. With a backward glance at Friedrich who was heading in the opposite direction, Max stiffly nodded to the Brauers who smiled at him, knowing he must be afraid.

By the time they had walked up the street to the Brauers' home Max had convinced himself that life wouldn't be so bad; he could endure this. Herr Brauer assured him the village was small and he would have ample opportunity to see his brother.

Upon entering the rear of the residence he began to feel better. It was a comfy home with a hearth, cozy kitchen and baking smells that reminded his stomach that it was time to eat. Clocks of every size and shape hung in the hall, marking the passage of time with their comforting tick-tock. The front of the house was a storefront with long, mahogany cases of glass revealing watches of all types. Beautiful cuckoo clocks and miniature grandfather clocks with polished brass pendulums hung on both sidewalls.

Frau Brauer chatted continually telling him how welcome he was and that he wasn't to worry, life here was peaceful and all would be well. She showed him up two flights of stairs to his little room where Max would have a world of his own there. It was the attic room in the top peak of the house with a little window at one end. A single frame bed with a great fluffy and colorful quilt stood on one side with a cupboard, chair and washbasin. A chamber pot peeked out discreetly from the bottom of the bed. Max set his little suitcase on the bed. Frau Brauer set about placing the contents into the drawers, and Max opened the cloth bag he had carried. Emptying boots from the bag, he found his first comfort at the bottom.

There he had packed his airplane encyclopedia and his artist materials with paper, and Friedrich, God bless him, had contributed the much fought over telescope. Max set about to position the telescope after Frau Brauer left, telling him supper would be in ten minutes. Max looked out through the lens and imagined he saw Düsseldorf outlined on the horizon ahead, but it was too far away. Max supposed the lens was dirty but upon further inspection realized the haze was caused by smoke and flak from distant anti-aircraft guns.

He would not forget, he would pray for his family each day as his mother had instructed him and he knew they would do the same. He lay down on the quilt and sunk gratefully into the eiderdown with a sigh. If only he could rest for a moment…

It was dark when he awoke. The Brauer family had left him sleep realizing the trauma of the day must have been too much for him. A lantern turned low provided a soft glow. Unsure of where he was Max sat up, disoriented. As realization washed over him he almost cried, but noticed the glass of milk and large ginger cookies on the little cupboard. He ate them gratefully, filled the chamber pot, and crawled under the eiderdown quilt. "God keep you safe Mama and Papa," he murmured.

The next morning Max was surprised that the washbasin had fresh water and a soft breeze blew in the gauze curtains beside the bed. His clothes were laid out for him. Washing and dressing quickly, he carried the chamber pot down the two flights of stairs and stood on the threshold of the kitchen as four pairs of eyes appraised him.

"H-Hello," he stammered, "I thought you must want me to empty this." The girls giggled. Herr Brauer put down his fork and knife and came to claim the chamber pot without a word. Frau Brauer beckoned to Max and pointed to the wall sink so he could clean his hands. He then sat down in the only spot left.

"Maximilian, this is Frieda and this is Gretchen," introduced the mother as she smiled at her girls. Both frauleins were blessed with flaxen hair and freckles. Frieda was almost a woman and Max noticed her large bosom and blushed. As biscuits and porridge were passed around Max was surprised that the food tasted so good. He couldn't remember when he last tasted fresh cream or butter. Frau Brauer was frying eggs on the stove, and Max's mouth watered.

Max was small for his age since his bout with diphtheria and had grown thinner as food shortages increased in the city. Sometimes despite Anna's best efforts to keep her family fed, they had been hungry lately. The table before him now seemed like an ample feast.

"You may call us Margrete and Pieter," said Frau Brauer, gesturing to her husband who felt the formal titles too stuffy since Max may be with them a while. Being summer, there was no hurry to enroll Max in a school and he was free to roam the village once he had learned what chores were expected of him. He was relieved to find some free time to explore and look for Friedrich.

After breakfast Maximilian, who had now reverted back to his full name because Margrete liked full names, was to learn his chores. Though the girls took care of dishes, Max was to empty the garbage which entailed crushing the eggshells into the leftover crusts, porridge and coffee, and feeding it to the little pigs they owned. He was instructed that nothing was to be wasted.

The property was actually just an acre but had a little chicken coop, pig sty and small barn at the back that doubled as a smoke house. Between these and the porch at the back hung Margrete's wash line and an ample garden, which reminded Max of Oma Thielmann's yard. It also smelled somewhat of dill and had neat rows of vegetables such as potatoes, beets, onions, radishes, and corn, that all looked delicious to Max. Max especially eyed the ripened peas and fluffy carrot tops hoping he was allowed to raid them once in a while. A small patch of raspberry canes and strawberry plants grew in one corner and a huge rhubarb plant grew in the other back corner. The fence on the left actually held grape vines where a few grape clusters peaked out here and there.

Maximilian was called over by Pieter who showed him how to hone the knives on the sharpening stone. With small circular motions he demonstrated how to get the blades sharp enough to split a hair. Next Max collected eggs and fed the hens, which had been a familiar chore at home. He was also to help gather wood for the stove and pile it next to the house.

After lunch he was allowed to explore and found to his delight a small general store with a gasoline pump at the near edge of the village. Had Max any money, he would have spent it on the candy, which was displayed in large glass jars on the mahogany counter. The kind man who ran the store could see the want in the child's eyes and knowing he was newly arrived, treated the boy to a black licorice to Max's delight.

Upon leaving the store Max continued to explore. He found the village laid out similar to a large wheel, the town centre being the hub with large yards and streets that branched off from the main street, which was made of cobblestones like at home. In fact most of the homes were also built of stone and heavy beams, or whitewashed. He found a blacksmith, tiny bakery and small school. A post office looked forlorn with its windows covered and a lock on the door. Not that Max expected to get any letters. The post had been suspended with war matters and survival taking up everyone's time. Two churches in the town serviced the faithful, both Catholic and Lutheran. With little more than fifty buildings, most of those residences, the village took less than an hour to explore.

The small farm that Friedrich now resided at was at the far end of the village, the home tucked in behind a small slope amid rolling hills. Max set out to find his brother. The house looked deserted when Max knocked at the door and no one answered so Max decided to walk around it. He almost ran into a massive shepherd dog that could have knocked down the slight boy if he had jumped on him. The dog took a protective stance and growled low in his throat.

Maximilian was a bit frightened but remembered how other children feared his own big dog Heinz at home. "Here boy, it's okay boy…there, there," Max murmured, holding out his hand for the large canine to sniff. At that the dog came near, sniffed and circled Max and then began to wag his tail slowly. By the time Max came around the house, he and the large dog had made friends. The yard was empty except for chickens that roamed freely so Maximilian continued to the barn about a hundred yards away.

It smelled of hay, manure and large animals. The rhythmic sound of milk spraying into a pail could be heard in a stall further down. "Hello!" Max ventured, not wanting to trespass, but dying to pet the huge horse that flicked a fly away with his ear. The horse surveyed Max with his large soft brown eyes and whinnied.

"Ho! Who is that?" inquired the farmer who as yet, Max couldn't see. Max ventured closer and rounded the stall to see Friedrich next to a large, boney brown cow with teats in hand, frowning and concentrating on the business of milking, not wanting to spill a drop.

"I-I'm Friedrich's brother, Max," announced Max, not sure if the farmer remembered him.

"Humph," mumbled Herr Melman, eyeing him suspiciously then remembering the registration the day before, held out a huge leathery hand to shake Max's own. Max had not seen such a big man in his life. However Friedrich did not turn or even acknowledge Max and kept up his milking. This puzzled Max who attempted to tease him.

"Hey brother! You are becoming a real farmer! Where did you learn that?" Max grinned and bent down to inspect the technique.

"Where do you think dumbkopf?" snapped Friedrich, "I'm a quick learner."

Max was unsure how to respond to this and made light of it. "Well, you sure did learn fast since you've only been here one day," said Max, genuinely impressed. Max watched his brother finish, wipe the teats off as he was shown and carefully remove the bucket so the cow wouldn't kick it and waste the milk. Max then followed the farmer and Friedrich out of the barn into the sunshine as they carried it to the separator. He was awed to see the metal contraption separate the cream from the milk and was allowed to sample some with a small dipper as Herr Melman explained that it would be made into butter that afternoon.

Max asked Friedrich if he wanted to explore but Friedrich only shook his head and told Max to run along. He would see him another day as he had much to do here. Rebuffed, Max was puzzled and a little hurt by Friedrich's reaction. As he walked back to his new home he couldn't understand how the only blood relative he had in this place didn't want to see him.

Being young and adaptable, Max didn't realize that Friedrich was having difficulty dealing with the trauma of his friend's death and separation from his family. Added to the moodiness of puberty, this made Friedrich an unhappy youth. Everything here was strange and so different from the busy city. Friedrich was depressed.

Max was bored and a little sad. If Friedrich wouldn't play with him what was there to do? The other children from the city that had been left in this forgotten corner of Germany were all too young. He noticed too on arrival the day before, that older men, some fathers and the very young comprised the males of the town. Those between seventeen and forty had left to fight.

Maximilian had been here one full day. He sighed. It was going to be a long war.

Chapter Nineteen

A Friend

***

He supposed that he must explore on his own, until he felt rather than saw a pair of eyes watching him. He turned to see a boy of about his own age with very black hair, dark eyes, and a quizzical expression leaning on a feed wagon. Maximilian walked over and introduced himself. The boy just stared.

"You are one of the billets, right?" he asked Max. Max nodded. "Where are you staying?" the boy demanded, and Max felt he was being rude since he had not yet told Max his own name.

"I'll tell you if you tell me your name first," ventured Max. The boy considered this and then smiled for the first time. "Name is Dieter, Neuman," he finished.

"Max Thielmann," said Max. "I live with the Brauers now." That bit of information seemed to make Dieter warm up to him since he was a bit envious. Dieter had a crush on Frieda, or at least her shapely body. He quite envied Max's close proximity to the blonde goddess. Soon the boys were exchanging information about their likes and dislikes, differences between the city and rural towns, and Dieter was especially interested in what the bombing had been like.

Max told him about the shelter his father had built and the terrifying sounds which shook the very city as the bombs exploded. He couldn't bring himself yet to talk about Rolf, it was too recent, and too surreal. Max brought Dieter up to his room asking Margrete permission as they entered the house and she nodded with pleasure. It was good to see the boy making a friend and there were few his age here anyway.

Dieter peered one-eyed through the telescope at the distant outline of the horizon adjusting the focus. Then he sat on the bed and spied the airplane book that Max had brought. Excitedly the boys pored over the book pointing out German and Allied planes and their markings. Dieter claimed to have seen this one and that one fly overhead and Max found in Dieter a kindred spirit when it came to planes.

Dieter also filled Max in on some gossip since everyone here knew everyone else. Seventeen-year-old Frieda was actually engaged unofficially to Melmans' son Reiner, who was serving as a pilot somewhere in Hitler's Luftwaffe. Another son, Karl, was in seminary in France. Dieter's brother Paul was sweet on Gretchen, and so it went. When Dieter went home for supper Max felt he had made a friend and felt a lot better than the day before about his relocation. He only hoped Friedrich would adjust as well.

As August passed Max and Dieter played in the gullies and streams around Obbach, got to ride Melmans' horse and found enjoyment in boyhood. The other younger children appreciated having Max around too, for he had a great imagination and was adept at thinking up games. He also didn't mind playing with them sometimes and so quickly became popular in the village.

The hard part was evening, often at first he cried himself to sleep when he thought of his parents and Liesl and Kurt. He wondered if they missed him as much as he missed them. Strangely, he also missed Friedrich. It seemed sometimes that he was far away instead of just the other end of the village. Friedrich was always too busy to see him and certainly didn't want to play anymore.

September first, the village children went to school. Fraulein Kessler the schoolmistress was a spinster of perhaps fifty with graying temples and curls that escaped the netted bun at the nape of her neck. Thin and prim, she sat ramrod straight. But far from being a disciplinarian, she was patient, displaying an avid interest in her pupils. Her warm brown eyes missed nothing and the corners of her mouth perpetually turned upwards which gave her an amused look. Maximilian loved her immediately. She was a welcome change from his previous schoolmaster, strict Herr Wagner.

Thus, Max began to do well in school for he actually enjoyed it. The first week the children who ranged from first grade to eighth grade in one room, were treated to an outing. Under the guise of Science the children were to catch frogs and tadpoles for a biology lesson. He had never experienced school like this! Each day he hurried home to report the exciting events of the school day to Margrete who by now seemed like a surrogate mother to Max, who missed Anna terribly.

Max wasn't bored with lots to do, his chores, school and the Hitler Jugend program to attend. But he hated learning and repeating all the oaths, prayers and pledges that glorified his nation's leader. It wasn't that Max was unpatriotic, but it was hard to pretend a lie. He knew that the leader was ultimately responsible for the horrors that now plagued his country daily. His mother had told him so. Even though the small chapter existed here and met as was mandatory, it did seem to Max that most people's attitudes here were opposed or at least indifferent to the Nazis, a welcome relief from the constant presence in the cities. He at last was settling into his new life. However joy is fleeting in wartime, as he found in the early hours of September eleventh.

After midnight Max dreamt that bombs were dropping around him. Waking in a cold sweat he jumped from the bed onto the cold floor to gaze disbelieving through the attic window. On the far horizon somewhere to the northwest was Düsseldorf, his home. The distant sky glowed with dancing firelight of violent devastation. In truth, planes dropped their deadly cargo on the sleepy city. As Max watched and began to cry, Gretchen and Frieda quietly entered the room comforting the boy who imagined horrid things. It was the second time a massive Allied air strike hit the city. And when it was over, thousands of civilians were no more.

Max became physically sick with worry. Margrete allowed him to stay home from school the next day, comforting and assuring him. She hoped she was right. Max developed a habit of checking through his telescope often, hoping to see something to give him hope, to assure him that everything was fine. For the event would repeat itself over and over each time the planes attacked. And Max would wonder for three long years whether his family had survived each fiery onslaught.

Chapter Twenty

Bad News

***

It seemed that the Thielmann brothers had been transported in the nick of time. The Allies were now becoming relentless in their bombing, especially in targeting cities and factories along the Rhine. Almost daily now, dogfights took place in the skies to the west. Whenever they could from relative safety Max and Dieter would watch in morbid fascination. When other children would scatter and run home these two would troop out to a favorite spot they had picked to be their fort. They would scan the skies over the Bavarian countryside with Dieter's father's field glasses, naming the planes that performed daring aerial maneuvers.

Unknown to the inhabitants of towns and villages southeast of the Rhine area, an Allied miscommunication would treat them to a light show that autumn of 1942. Gearing up for an offensive utilizing almost eight hundred aircraft, Lancasters, Halifaxes, Wellingtons, Stirlings, and Mosquitos were to be deployed over mid-western Germany. The Pathfinder marking plan proceeded as planned until an Oboe Mosquito mistakenly dropped its load of target indicators miles away from the actual target area. This caused part of the Main Force to waste bombs on open country.

While the bulk of the operation caused extensive damage in the center of Düsseldorf, the countryside southeast of the city was also bombed that cold night. Citizens of the towns for miles around watched in awe as bombs fell in the open, yet not one targeting their own homes. This could be seen far away in Obbach as well. The children saw only the planes in their choreographed aerial dance, the bombs falling safely far away. In their haven far from harm, for the time being they were spared the devastation of those bombs.

***

Christmas passed as no other had for the brothers, being the first one away from their loved ones. Friedrich and Maximilian spent the afternoon together but reminiscing was painful. Each wondered if they even still had a family, but didn't want to say that aloud and trouble the other.

Max had received little presents from the Brauers and thanked them gratefully, but it just wasn't the same. Retreating to his room with his presents and new warm coat that the talented Margrete had sewn for him, he thought of other Christmases. Lying on his bed he held the little plane aloft that Pieter had made for him. It was a small-scale wooden model of a German Messerschmitt BF 109 painted to match the real ones. The full size plane served the Luftwaffe well as an air superiority fighter, a bomber escort, an interceptor, a ground attack aircraft and in reconnaissance. It would also score more aircraft kills in this war than any other aircraft.

As Max hung the plane above his bed with thread that Margrete had provided, he knew he really should be happy. The new plane joined two others that he had received for his birthday. This family treated him very well. Sighing, he lay down on the bed and watched the planes turn slowly, wondering when the war would end and fell asleep into the comfort of oblivion.

***

As 1943 came in, the year started badly. If there was news it was always bad and spread through the village like a cancer. Happy chatter that once bounced across the dinner table was absent one late February day as the whole family became subdued.

Melmans' son Reiner was shot down near Stalingrad. Officially classed as missing in action, the delayed news was just too much. He had been unaccounted for since November. Mr. Melman aged overnight caring little for anything, and Friedrich found that unless he did the chores the old man cared not that they were done. Frau Melman was afraid for him and hoped their other son Karl would return soon. Frieda spent days in bed weeping, inconsolable. She despaired that she would never be a bride.

Herr Melman had good cause to mourn. The bloodiest toll of the war was taking place now. In 1941 Hitler had reneged on his promises signed in the Nazi-Soviet Non-Aggression Pact two years before. He launched Operation Barbarossa, a massive Russian invasion. Josef Stalin, incredulous that Hitler could betray their pact at first denied it was actually happening and this delayed reaction resulted in hundreds of thousands of Russian casualties, as well as Nazi occupation of Russia.

However Hitler's failure to learn a history lesson from Napoleon's Russian campaign had devastating results. German forces were ill equipped for the frozen sub-zero temperatures of the Russian winter, coupled with insufficient supply lines. Stalingrad was the deadliest battlefront. In five months, the two sides suffered over two million casualties. As the Red Army pursued the fleeing Nazis, they inflicted massive devastation on everything in their wake. By 1944, on this Front alone, over thirty million people would die, almost half that being civilians. The festering wound that was Europe continued to emulate hell on earth as the carnage of unspeakable atrocities mounted.

As 1943 flew by Max and Friedrich settled in to routine with their surrogate families. They saw each other several times a week, but Friedrich had really taken to farm life and was often busy. Max being younger had little expectations put on him, but didn't mind when he was asked to pull garden weeds or dig up potatoes. He was grateful just to eat and live in a fairly peaceful village.

He also grew closer to Pieter who had never had a son and enjoyed having a boy around to do things with. It seemed that Pieter understood the boy, and some of Max's homesickness fell away from him.

The Brauers often sat around the table after supper and told tales and jokes, leaving the dishes till family time was over. Margrete listened if Max had something important to tell her, as his mom had, but it still did not keep him from missing Anna. Pieter now took Max into his shop and they made little projects together. Having more time on his hands as the storefront was less and less busy, Pieter began a project that really interested Max.

It was a cuckoo clock, so named because as it struck the hours it mimicked the cuckoo birds' cries in the forests. First Pieter took a hand drill and carefully made three holes in the bottom of a wooden box. These were for the chains and pendulum to hang through. Next, he took a piece of paper that he had drawn beautiful leaves and nuts on in a splayed pattern. Transferring the drawing by tracing on to a pine board, he then began to carve carefully with his tools. This would be the face of the clock, with a little trap door for the wooden bird to come out of.

Max was fascinated, and was given a little box to make one for himself. Being artistic, Max soon found carving was a pleasure. Pieter showed him how to hold the tools carefully and at the correct slant to achieve the depth of cut needed. He demonstrated how not to slice oneself, and how to shave away the curled wood with a steady hand. The two males found enjoyment in this shared activity and spent hours in the little clock shop whittling and discussing common interests. If there were lulls in the conversation, the soothing clocks would tick on together, and to Max it was a soothing rhythm that steadied his hand.

One August day Pieter announced a trip, for he had to yet pick up the inside mechanical workings for the cuckoo clocks. Excited for the day, the family's excursion would take them to the nearby city of Wurzburg. Maximilian was thrilled. He had not been in a city since leaving his home. Traveling in Pieter's Mercedes Benz automobile, they set out early with Gretchen and Frieda who wished to window shop. Margrete stayed at home with a headache.

Quite enjoying the adventure Max hoped to see normal sights, praying that Wurzburg wouldn't be a destroyed city of shelled out ruins. Pieter had promised to treat them all to lunch at an outdoor café he knew, and possibly a treat if there were any sweets to be had. The girls wanted yard goods to make dresses. Pieter's first stop would be for clock parts that should be waiting at the train station.

Setting out initially, the sun shone on a countryside that if one didn't look too closely, revealed little of the war. As they passed other villages, and a rippling creek, Max enjoyed the sights. He had almost convinced himself that he could forget the war today as the city of Wurzburg rose from the landscape. Pieter headed the car toward the large train depot and parked in the shade. The youths were eager to get out and walk around, and Pieter told the girls to stay near the car while he and Max would see to the packages waiting in the station.

Max followed Pieter along the boardwalk. It was growing warmer as it neared noon hour, and Max couldn't wait to get a drink of water. Pieter hunted through his pockets for identification papers as two gray-coated soldiers came toward them. Max thought they must be hot in those coats, and therefore so grumpy looking. While Pieter was having his papers checked, Max was suddenly aware of voices. He heard children crying and the muffled voices of many others. Confused as to where the voices may be coming from, he turned in a circle, and then back to the inevitable direction. Alongside the tracks beside the depot lengthy trains of boxcars were waiting on the sidelines.

The voices Max heard were coming from the cars to his left. He must be mistaken. People were crying and calling for water! Max stared at the small openings near the top of some of the cars. Incredulous, he saw the hands of people waving through the bars. Max could not understand. He once rode with his parents in a lovely dining car with large windows. These people seemed to be jammed together in the heat of the day in closed boxes with no air!

Having finished his business to the satisfaction of the guards, Pieter steered Max by the neck ahead of him. Max turned to look back. A child, who must have been on a man's shoulders looked vacantly out the top windows at Max. Max was not totally naïve. As realization dawned, he remembered boys at school talking about Jews being taken by train to concentration camps. Wolfgang in his class had whispered stories his father told him of death camps also. Max and those who wished not to believe had said they were scare stories that couldn't be true.

As guards posted at intervals along the tracks shouted to one another, clipboards in hand, the train whistle blew. Steam shot from beneath the wheels, as the first burst of power sent the cars banging into one another, and the melee inside them grew louder. The train chugged slowly out of the station as women wailed, unnerving Max further. He overheard guards confirming the destination of Auschwitz for this train, as Pieter hurriedly pushed Max into the shelter of the station, hoping the boy knew nothing about the extermination camp.

A lump of disgust and horror rose as bile in Max's throat. This terrible, 17th day of August would stay in his mind. Max felt sick. His happy day forgotten, he could not enjoy the fruit torten at lunch, imagining hundreds of hungry and thirsty people bound for a camp in Poland. Max wondered if it had not been for Kurt, could his family members have been among them. It was a quiet ride home.

Nearby, this day would also mark the first time that B17's would leave England to attack the ball-bearing factory at Schweinfurt. Fifty-two percent of all of Germany's ball bearings were produced there, making this a very important target. Over two hundred planes attacked, of which almost a third were destroyed by the Luftwaffe defending the factory. Heavy loss of life was the cost on both sides, and it was a devastating blow to the 8th Air force who did their best to cripple the Nazi war machine.

***

Next day Pieter brought a newspaper home with him. The headlines confirmed the massive tragedy that read, 'RAF Bombs Hamburg in July and August'. The article told of major strikes in which sixty to one hundred thousand people were killed in Hamburg alone. Fully one third of the houses there were destroyed. At this topic of conversation, Max asked to go outside. He couldn't comprehend a number that large lost. How would anyone survive this war?

Max went to see Friedrich. He needed to talk. He found Friedrich brushing down Matilda the big horse. Friedrich seemed surprised to see him, and asked Max to hand him the pitchfork. As he began lifting some soft hay from a bale into the stall, Max tried to form words that would describe how he felt. He couldn't. "Friedrich, are we evil?" he blurted out. Friedrich shot him a frown and pitched the next load of hay.

"No. No more than anyone. What makes you ask that?" Friedrich wondered where this was going.

"I mean, Papa used to read to us about Germany's victories. It all sounded so glorious. Our planes attack, and now, those who hate us fight back. Thousands of people are dying! Why doesn't Herr Hitler say he's sorry and just stop and surrender?" We could all go home! " Max complained.

"I don't know," Friedrich said between gritted teeth. He was just as sick of all this. Despite keeping busy on the farm, he had much time to think and worried about the very things Max did. He wouldn't admit he was afraid as well; afraid for his family at home, afraid life would never be the same again, afraid for the future.

"I saw one of those trains yesterday," Max said, waiting. When Friedrich didn't comment, he went on. "There were people on it, Friedrich! And it wasn't a dining car, it was a boxcar and they were crying out! It's true, don't you see? I mean, the rumors about…about the prison camps. The soldiers were talking about Auschwitz!" Max exclaimed, working himself up.

Friedrich stabbed the fork into the hay on the floor and turned to Max. "Don't!" he yelled at his brother, "Don't talk about it! Just be grateful it isn't us on the train! Be glad we are here and can wait out the fighting. Stop feeling sorry for yourself!" Friedrich shook Max by the shoulders. Max was afraid. Friedrich hadn't lost his temper with him in a very long time. Max began to sob. He was surprised himself that he couldn't stop the tears, but it had been held in so long, it now escaped with vengeance.

Sorry that he made Max cry, Friedrich threw his arms about Max's shoulders and held him tightly. "Sorry! I'm sorry Max!" he said, as tears burst unchecked from his own eyes. It was some minutes before Max could contain his sobbing, as his shoulders shook and he gulped back tears. Friedrich produced a handkerchief that Max used to wipe his face. "It-it's not you. I feel so bad for those people...for this whole war!"

They sat down in the straw. Friedrich told Max everything would be okay. "We just have to have faith, as Mama said, remember?" asked Friedrich, not fully sure himself what that meant. Max nodded. It was time to go. Walking back to Brauers' home, he felt spent. He thought again of the child who had stared at him from the train and unable to bear his thoughts, tried to forget.

Chapter Twenty-One

A Captive

***

Max and Dieter constructed a makeshift shelter on the edge of the forest by dragging boards and needed comforts out when they could. This was their secret headquarters, built on the side of a bluff and hidden from sight, yet it afforded a panoramic view of the skies toward the great cities. Despite hating the war, the boys were still curious, witnessing the aerial warfare as it unfolded above them. Soon the fort was quite comfortable with blankets, water, oil lantern, matches and a couple of old dishes. The dishes of course were for food, the best part of any day and the boys stalked up with some of Margrete's home canning from her pantry. Dieter contributed a map of the area to pin on a blanket wall and Max's book of planes was handy to identify enemy or friendly aircraft above.

So far only Gretchen knew about the fort, though not the location. She had seen Max leaving the house one day with an armload of things and her curiosity made Max let her in on the secret. Even though he had permission from Margrete to borrow the old items she assumed the children were playing on Dieter's yard, not realizing they were venturing almost half a mile from the village. Gretchen was sworn to secrecy for she would do anything for Max. Frieda and Gretchen enjoyed the amiable boy and spoiled him terribly, like a pet.

One autumn Saturday in 1943 Max set out after breakfast with promises to Margrete to be back by supper. It was chilly so Max ran back in for an extra blanket, and threw some of the lady's delicious rolls in his pack for the little journey. Dieter was to meet him there when chores were done and Max wanted to get there first to have some time alone to sketch. His pack held his artist materials and rolled up paper.

As he walked he again made sure no village children were following him. The fort wouldn't be secret if half the village found out. Besides, little kids could be nuisances and they could also be in danger there. Max daydreamed about many things, his parents often in his thoughts. Having made the trip many times his feet headed for the fort, his mind elsewhere. As he rounded a hill, he came upon a stag drinking from a small creek. The beautiful animal raised its head in alarm and looked at Max. Then leaping gracefully it bounded into the bushes. Max's heart was pounding with excitement. He wished he had not frightened the majestic thing away and sat down there and then to record what he saw with his sketching pencil.

The animal had a huge rack that reminded Max of the trophy horns on the wall at the hunting lodge in Oelde, a local inn near where his grandmother had lived. He hoped no hunter would find this deer as he sketched quickly, trying to get the correct proportions of the impressive antlers. Max finished up when the ground he sat on started to give him a chill and packed up his materials. Satisfied with his sketch, he carefully rolled it up so he could take it home for his wall. He started up the other side of the knoll when something colorful caught his eye in the valley below. Amid the trees an unmistakable red & white target circle from a plane wing peeked out from the foliage.

Max had seen other wrecks from afar but never one so close. He and Dieter would have to come back and explore this one. It was then that he spotted something else. About forty feet away a white ghost seemed to grow and shrink with the breeze beckoning him closer. It was a parachute caught in the trees ahead. Max suddenly felt vulnerable. Alone in the countryside, out of sight of the village, Max knew what this could mean. He looked around him spooked that an enemy could suddenly jump from the forest shadows and take him. He stopped, listening. But all he heard was the wind whistling softly through the aspens. He shivered. The clouds were building and a storm seemed to be blowing in.

Max forced himself to walk toward the chute. He could see that whoever had used it was now free of its bonds. The straps had been cut. Unnerved, he turned to flee when a moan like a wounded animal dying made an icy chill run up his spine. At first he sprinted away and then thinking better of it, admonished himself for being a fraidy-cat. Retracing his steps Max began searching around the chute and almost stepped on the body of a man. Max stared incredulously.

Here lay an enemy, wounded and helpless. The man seemed to be unconscious but moaned softly. An ugly red wound in his side, his lifeblood pooled beside him. Maximilian saw that the man was young, certainly younger than Kurt. Many things raced through his thoughts as he watched the wounded pilot gasp for breath. This very man could be the pilot who flew low over his home in the city, who strafed the streets with his machine guns, or dropped bombs on them, who even killed Rolf! Confused, Max was tempted to walk away. The man would die without help.

Max knew he could not do that. His tender heart and his upbringing would not allow it. He knew, enemy or not, that his mother would be already binding up the man's wounds. Once the decision was made, Max acted quickly. He bent down and covered the man with his blanket and tried to make him warm. His skin was cold elsewhere yet he seemed to have a fever. Max wondered how long he had been lying here. What else could he do? Max knew if he didn't find bandages the man would bleed to death. He must run to the plane below.

Where was Dieter? He had to pass by here sooner or later. Max couldn't wait; he'd have to do this alone. Leaving his things beside the patient, Max ran as fast as he could to the broken plane. Ten minutes later, panting, he came upon the wreck. Gingerly moving debris aside, Max squeezed inside the plane's broken shell searching for a first aid kit. There it lay, marked by the universal Red Cross sign. He glanced about for other supplies, perhaps a lantern, matches or anything useful. Max nearly cried out as his eyes took in the specter of death before him. In the bloody carnage lay a dead gunner. His arms were gone.

Max fled as soon as his feet would move and shaking, crouched low to retch outside the plane. Giving himself a talking to, he forced his weak legs to climb back up to the pilot. Crying silently, the boy tore open the kit and found rolls of gauze and pads. Remembering how the school nurse had done it once he compressed the wound with the pad and tried to wrap the gauze around the man, but he was too heavy.

Frustrated, Max checked for other wounds and fortunately found none. Seeing tape in the bottom of the kit, he decided to tape the pad to the man's skin. Removing the man's bloodstained shirt from the wound, Max spied a jagged hole below the ribs.

Max thought he heard someone approaching as footsteps grew near. Looking up in apprehension he was relieved to see only Dieter's astonished face. Dieter assessed the situation also and in quick agreement they decided to take the man to their shelter. But could they lift him? Dieter had a thermos of warm coffee and milk and held it to the man's lips. The aroma must have revived him somewhat because his eyes fluttered and then focused as he gazed at his two rescuers. Sipping the coffee gingerly, he sighed and mumbled a question they could not understand.

Fearing he may pass out again the boys gestured and signed that they wanted to move him. Moaning deeply he complied, allowing them to get under his arms and lift him. Struggling, the threesome limped their way to the shelter nearby. The man was shivering uncontrollably. Dieter helped him lie down on a tattered quilt and covered him with blankets. Max lit a fire in a rusty metal truck hubcap they had found by the side of the road days before.

Plying the patient with more hot coffee seemed to revive him further. It was beginning to warm up in the little place with a fire crackling before them. The trio stared at each other. Finally the man gestured with his thumb to himself, "Adam," he said. The boys understood and told him their names. The man gasped as he tried to reach into a pocket in his pant leg. Max gestured that he would do it and unbuttoned the pocket that Adam had tried to reach. From it he produced a picture, a handwritten note and a small flag patch, the kind one would sew onto a uniform. The flag was a Union Jack. "Canada," said Adam, pointing to his chest.

So, he was Canadian! The boys were excited and wished they could find out more about him. He seemed nice enough and that was the trouble with enemies. You just never knew when you were going to like them. Adam pointed to the picture as Dieter held up the lantern to see it better. It was obviously his young family and showed Adam, a pretty girl and small baby in her arms. Max watched the young officer's face in the circle of light as a moment of homesickness crossed his features. He kissed the photo lightly, and then pointed to the girl in the dog-eared photograph. "Lucy and Sam", Adam said and cleared his throat. He put the picture carefully back, pointing to his other leg pocket. This time Dieter did the honors and revealed a chocolate bar.

Max and Dieter stared, mouths agape as the man opened the wrapper and offered it to the boys. Chocolate! Max's mouth watered. Even the general store did not have chocolate anymore. Hard candies or licorice were all that was left. The boys nodded thanks and divided the chocolate into three parts, relishing the flavor they had missed for some time. It was culinary bliss.

Now it was time to make plans. Dieter suggested that they must get rid of the parachute immediately before it was spotted by Nazi troops that ranged throughout the countryside. Max agreed. First they would make Adam comfortable. Max started for the door and then remembered the biscuits in his pack. Offering them to the man, he pointed to the preserves he had taken from Margrete's pantry, inviting him to eat. Adam nodded and smiled weakly. They left him, promising to return. They hoped he understood.

Using their jackknives to cut the lines the boys had some trouble trying to untangle the huge parachute from the bushes. They worked quickly and silently, folding the billowing nylon into a bundle they could carry. When they got it back to the shelter the pilot was asleep. Adding a bit of fuel to the low fire in the hubcap, they made sure Adam was warm and set off.

The plan was simple. Bring lots of food and warm drink back for Adam. They would have to find some alcohol to clean the wound and clean warm clothing. He must get out of the uniform if he was to have a chance to escape. Both boys did not have a clue why they were helping Adam but it seemed like the right thing to do. Max found himself thinking of Fritz Faust and wondering what that cruel youth would have done.

Walking back the boys debated their decision to leave Adam. He might die from loss of blood from the bullet that was still in his body. If they told anyone Adam would surely be killed or taken prisoner. What to do? Both boys grew quiet with their own thoughts. Max remembered his discussion with Kurt. Sometimes one had to follow one's conscience. Kurt and Adam seemed to be two men caught up in a war that no one wanted, forced to defend their countries and the ideals they believed in. They just happened to be on opposing sides.

It seemed there was no choice. They couldn't let Adam die. He had a family. Dieter was to get the clothes. His brother Paul would be about the same size as Adam. Max would try and procure the other items though he wasn't sure he could do that without being caught. He would have to trust someone in the household and he knew just who to ask.

He was relieved to find the elder Brauers had gone out for supplies, but music told him that Gretchen was home practicing her violin in her room. Knocking at Gretchen's door, Max found the girl a sympathetic ear as he had hoped and told her the story. She was round eyed at hearing the tale but agreed to help him for she was a romantic at heart and couldn't bear to imagine the young wife and mother being left alone if Adam died.

A willing accomplice now, Gretchen found a large basket and got the supplies that Max needed. She had to hurry as Frieda and her parents were due home soon. However she was practical and wouldn't let Max leave without calling on the doctor, Herr Coleman. Max was afraid. What if the doctor reported the news to the authorities?

Together Gretchen and Max carried the basket beyond the rear gate and hid it under the vines. Then she steered the boy to the doctor's home hoping not to meet her parents along the way. It was now almost suppertime and time was running out. They hoped the doctor was home.

Dieter would be waiting for him beyond the village and wonder where he was. Max hoped they were doing the right thing in revealing Adam.

When they knocked the doctor himself opened the door. At first, Max just knew this had been a mistake. The physician appeared disgruntled and short tempered and Max almost fled from the porch steps. However Gretchen knew the man better and just how to handle him. Bothered daily by an old war wound, the doctor often appeared irascible but in truth had a soft heart. The cheery girl introduced Max and invited herself in, soothing the old man with her charming smile.

His housekeeper was off this day and so she offered to make him tea, which delighted him, but put Max into a sweat as he worried about the time flying and Dieter getting angry with him. The kettle soon boiled and Gretchen deftly managed a cup for the doctor, finding cookies in the pantry to sweeten the treat. The doctor accepted them and then turned to the girl.

"So my dear, I am sure you had better things to do than visit an old man. What brings you here today?" he asked, a little less gruffly as he sipped his tea.

"Herr Doktor," Gretchen began, "I have a very great favor to ask of you. But it must be a secret for it may bring trouble to all who learn of it." The doctor's eyebrow went up but he did not say anything. Encouraged, Gretchen blurted out, "Max here has found a pilot. He is wounded and lies out in the countryside. We need you to come and help him!" There, it was out.

Herr Doktor frowned and set down his cup. "One of ours?" Gretchen slowly shook her head. "How do you think I got this war wound?" he grumpily asked the surprised girl. "Am I supposed to run to the aid of an enemy?! What were you thinking?" With that, he rose from his chair and made as if to show them the door.

"Please Herr Doktor! He is only a young man with a little family! Please have mercy!" pled the dramatic young Gretchen. The doctor turned and studied the girl's earnest little face. She was a favorite of his and he remembered the day he delivered this child into the world. He took a deep breath and sighed, she was right, after all. War made strange allies and fools of us all, he mused. It wouldn't be the first time anyway.

Volker Coleman remembered back to a lonely trench in the first war when he had come across a young enemy soldier. He found the sole survivor among his dead friends. It would have been so easy to put a gun to the man and be done with it. But he could not, even then. War games seemed like murder when you had to look your victim in the eyes. Having compassion on him, Volker dressed his wounds.

The doctor snatched his coat from the hall hook and checked his black leather satchel to make sure he had all his supplies. The surprised Max and triumphant Gretchen followed him to the door. Then thinking better of it, he directed them to the rear door. They must not be seen. Nervously, for in a small place there were many inquisitive eyes, the trio got in the doctor's car and took the back road out of the town.

Gretchen was curious to see the pilot but realized it was better to stay behind and make excuses for Max. The doctor stopped the car at the end of her yard while Gretchen loaded the basket and returned to the house. She had to think of some reason why Max would not be at supper and did not look up or notice that a watcher saw the car drive off into the country.

Chapter Twenty-Two

Caught!

***

The sun was setting as Doctor Coleman drove the car a ways down the main road. Turning onto a little used path, the vehicle bounced through high grass as it disappeared into the trees. If he had set out across open fields sooner his fresh tire tracks would have surely attracted roving patrols to follow. Emerging onto open fields, the graying landscape could still be seen and so the doctor kept his headlamps off. Max alit from the car when they reached the rendezvous point where Dieter was to be waiting. No Dieter, or wait, yes, there he was. The boy stood up from his hiding place once he recognized his comrade.

"Where have you been?" complained the boy while climbing into the car. He had grown cold and frightened as the sun set. Then recognizing the doctor, knew they had help.

"Dieter, we had to trust someone," Max stated helplessly, "Or Adam would die." The boys directed the doctor to the grove of trees that covered the hill on the rear side of their hidden fort. There was no way to drive around the bluff, so parking where the car could not easily be spotted, the three got out. Carrying their burdens they trudged silently around the hill in the dark. A rising crescent moon and brilliant stars still were barely enough light to see by. Dieter and Max made sure they were there to steady the doctor on the uneven ground where the footing got tricky.

At the fort Dieter pulled aside a curtain and the doctor stooped to enter. The fire had gone out and so the boys hurried to light a lantern and get another going. Adam lay on his side, no visible sign of life evident. The elderly doctor gingerly got to his knees at some expense to his sore leg and puffing, bent to examine the man. His stethoscope told him that the pilot was indeed alive but breathing shallow. Enlisting the boys to help turn him over, Dr. Coleman checked the wound site. He could see that much blood was lost and the man was probably already a lost cause. However, the bullet missed the lungs and spine and if they were lucky, other vital organs. It had to be true however, for he should have been dead already. The doctor debated what to do.

Turning up the lantern to give the best light, the physician gently probed the wound. The wound didn't appear to be a bullet hole at all. Miraculously, the object could be felt not far under the skin. Could it have been a ricochet and not a direct hit? Only a deflected missile could have pierced so shallow. Perhaps the man had a chance after all. Directing Max to hold the lantern up and Dieter to hand him the alcohol, he sterilized the instruments and the wound and prepared to remove the offending metal from his patient. He was sweating despite the cold. Yet, he reminisced, he had surely operated in worse conditions on the battlefront. Max thought he might faint so looked away. Dieter who was fascinated by such things watched, as Dr. Coleman probed again only deeper, eliciting a cry of pain from Adam. They all hoped there was no one else around to hear. When the metal object hit the dish that the doctor had ready it was not a bullet as he suspected. In fact it appeared to be a small piece of twisted shrapnel, perhaps from the plane? Cleaning the wound and checking for other damage, the doctor was satisfied that muscle was the only thing badly torn. Now that he had removed the problem he stitched up the wound, binding it tightly when done.

Without an IV available, Max was instructed to try and get fluids into Adam. Lifting the pilot's head, some water was poured into his mouth. Choking at first, Adam came to enough to sip a bit and then lay back exhausted.

Dieter was sent out to bury the bloody cloths. He scooped out just enough soil to put them in and then hastily covered it all with rocks so as not to tempt wild animals. On top of this he poured a little petrol to cover the blood smell that would attract them. Dieter peered into the pitch-black darkness and suddenly felt spooked being out there alone, and hurried back to the shelter.

Volker sat back and wiped his brow. What trouble had these youngsters brought on him now? He watched the young pilot. He couldn't be much more than twenty with a life still ahead of him. Did he regret coming to save the young man? No. He did not. He would face whatever tomorrow brought tomorrow.

***

Back at the house Gretchen had some thinking to do. Did she invent a tale and perhaps have to eat her words later? She could say that Max was spending the evening at Dieter's home but what would her parents say when Dieter's father called on them? The truth would be all over the village in half an hour. And then there would be real trouble! She was just glad that Max had mentioned Dieter was in on the adventure. She had only one card to play.

***

Frau Hilda Metzger had watched silently from behind her sheer curtains in her upstairs window. The new boy next door in the Brauer home was always running off to the woods lately with that young Dieter fellow. Today however, they had returned seemingly in a hurry; nothing strange about that in itself. But it did seem suspicious to her that Gretchen had helped him hide a basket at the back gate. And so she watched and waited. Sure enough, within half an hour the good doctor's vehicle pulled up in the back lane, loaded the basket and left. Gretchen had returned to the house. What could this mean?

A widow since the First World War with no children to brighten her days, Frau Metzger had time on her hands. Her pinched countenance and sour attitude attested to her bitterness at life's cruelty. She also happened to be a card-carrying member of the Nazi Party and dedicated informant, should there be anything or anyone to inform on. Proudly displaying a picture in her living room of Herr Hitler her esteemed leader, she was not popular with most people of the town. Not that they would openly reject her, that would be foolish, but she seemed to cause other ladies of the town to scatter when she entered a store or business.

Certain of trouble that should be reported this time, she put on her shawl and ventured out. The general store had a telephone and she knew whom to call.

***

Sixteen-year-old Paul Neuman opened the door to a smiling Gretchen Brauer and almost dropped the pan he was carrying. The blonde beauty he dreamed of was actually standing before him. He had no idea what to say, so stood there dumbly.

"May I come in, Paul?" said the girl, glancing about the room for his father. She knew the effect she had on the young man. He snapped out of his trance then and invited her in. Hastily he returned the pan with supper back to the stove while self-consciously untying the apron he wore. "Is your father at home?" she inquired.

"Ah, no, no." He stuttered, not sure what to say. "He went to Ramsthal but will return tomorrow." Gretchen couldn't believe her luck. No explaining to the father was good. "May I sit?" she flashed a winning smile again and he hurried to offer her a chair. Paul had been besotted with Gretchen since third grade and had thought of many clever things to say to her if she ever gave him the time of day. Yet here she sat in his home and he couldn't remember one of them.

"I just came to tell you," she began, knowing that she was effectively stretching the truth to its breaking point, "that Dieter was asked to accompany Herr Doktor to another village with our boy, Max," she told Paul, hoping he'd believe it. "As you know, he is getting on in years and could use some help with supplies for the patients. They had to get going and I am sorry to say Dieter didn't have time to run home to tell you if he wanted to go along." At that she stopped, not believing it herself, and waited. In actuality she had told a similar version to her parents, omitting the part about another town, simply saying that Max and Dieter had joined Herr Doktor for the evening. It was the truth, and she thought, best to stay as close to it as possible.

Paul's thoughts were elsewhere and at the moment she could have told him the moon was made of Edam cheese and he would have believed her. Not that it mattered. He was glad to have a break from his mischievous brother for once. And having temporary respite from Dieter, he had an idea.

"I am just finished supper," he announced grinning shyly, "Would you like to take a walk?"

Gretchen thought it couldn't hurt to spend a little time with him, since he seemed to believe her story. She had always secretly thought he was handsome, but much too quiet. What do you say to a boy like that? As they took a stroll down the village street Gretchen shivered, and Paul saw his first opportunity to put his arm about her shoulders. She smiled at him gratefully as the young couple passed the general store, not realizing that Frau Metzger was on the public phone that very moment.

***

Frau Metzger wasn't sure if she should be glad or not. The bad news was that her regular contact was out, and she had important information for him. If he did not come out to Obbach tonight there might be no way to catch Herr Doktor at whatever game he was playing. The good news was that an important SS officer was even now in Schweinfurt and the report would be passed along to him promptly. She was sure that the neighbor boy and the doctor must be helping some Jews, somewhere. She hurried home to await the Sturmbannfuhrer's arrival and chuckled in anticipation.

***

Adam began to breathe regularly and Dr. Coleman checked him once more. His color was better. He left him rest, but hoped he would wake soon and take fluids. By now the families of the boys would be looking for them unless young Gretchen had a good explanation for their whereabouts. He would have to get them home. It was a hard decision to make, but he must leave his patient. The boys argued with this afraid to leave Adam alone to the elements, but the doctor explained that he would be fine. They had made him comfortable with a small fire in the hubcap and he had plenty of water within reach. They could come out tomorrow and check on him. It was nearing nine o'clock and he would have some explaining to do if they didn't return.

Grudgingly and with a backward glance, Max left the shelter last. Picking their way back in the moonlight the boys were secretly glad to finally get into the car. The car bounced slowly along uneven ground, heading roughly back the route they came with no benefit of headlights. Dr. Coleman looked up the road both ways and pulled onto it, seeing no other vehicles. Ten minutes after he dropped Max off in the back lane and headed to Dieter's house, the official car pulled up in front of the little house next door.

A knock at their own door ten minutes later brought a bewildered Pieter and Margrete, shocked that they should be staring into the faces of stern SS officers. Instructed to produce the boy and Gretchen and come to the neighbors' house, they summoned Max in his pajamas. Max complied, donning his coat. Gretchen had rehearsed what to say in her mind hours ago, and was ready.

As everyone crowded into Frau Metzger's parlor, the woman actually had a smug smile on her face. The good doctor was brought in along with the terrified Dieter who was still with him when the officers summoned them. Margrete thought she would faint, Pieter was racking his brain troubled by what this could mean, and Max thought he was caught. They were told that the Sturmbannfuhrer who had been traveling nearby had taken this detour tonight to question Max and the doctor. Max watched in trepidation as the tall uniformed officer who had been conversing with Frau Metzger turned around to face them. It was none other than Herr Kurt Schwartzkopf! Silently Max and Kurt locked eyes. Kurt gave nothing away and Max was too stunned to react. Fortunately Max did not reveal his familiarity or the result might have been vastly different.

The senior officer cleared his throat and said he would question this boy first. The other SS men watched the others as Kurt took Max from the room. When they were sure they were alone, Kurt hugged Max fiercely. In low tones he said, "Little brother, I am so glad you are safe here! Quickly, where were you tonight?" Max, incredulous that Kurt was here but glad to see his brother-in-law, whispered back explaining what happened. Kurt told him to tell no one else, ever. Max understood. It wasn't wise, his escapade tonight. Kurt also told Max not to show him any recognition. Their time was brief and too soon over.

Max left the room and Kurt took the Brauers next for their version of the evening. The elder Brauers knew nothing except what Gretchen had told them, that she had sent preserves along with the doctor to one of his patients. Lastly, Herr Coleman, who simply stated that he allowed the boys to help him on rounds. Amazingly, it was the closest to the truth and coincided with Brauers' version. Dieter simply nodded when Kurt recited the others' version of the evening, asking him if that is how it was. That would be the version in the report.

Coming back into the parlor, the smirk was effectively wiped off the widow's face when the Sturmbannfuhrer addressed her. "Madam, I am a very busy man. I am sure you have nothing better to do than spy on your neighbors, but I should be in Wurzburg in ten minutes and I am late. Be sure of your facts next time you have something to report and do not cause trouble for the good doctor who is simply fulfilling his function."

Her jaw would have dropped on the floor if it weren't attached. Trembling, she blurted out, "But, have you checked their story with any patients, Herr Sturmbannfuhrer? Why were they sneaking around with the basket?!" Her audacity to question the high-ranking SS officer surprised even her. She locked eyes with him, waiting. She feared she had gone too far.

The room was silent. Kurt stared coldly into Frau Metzger's eyes until she averted them. "How dare you question me, madam!" Clenching his fists, he raised the glove in his hand as if to strike her. The woman shook as if she might faint.

The other officers waited for Kurt's orders. Maybe they had an arrest to make tonight, yet. They watched Kurt lower his hand and take a deep breath. For over two years they had seen him handle the toughest situations with no emotion. Perhaps he just had a soft spot for foolish old women. They certainly weren't going to question the man they feared.

Doctor Coleman saw his moment and ventured a comment. "Forgive me, Sturmbannfuhrer, for intruding, sir, but my patients' business really is confidential."

"Enough!" shouted Kurt. "F-forgive me, Sturmbannfuhrer..." the woman mumbled. Kurt looked at his watch impatiently and signaled his men to leave. They turned on their heels and as they did so, Frau Metzger stuck out her chin and mustered a "Heil Hitler!" as her hand shot out in a salute. With that, Kurt tipped his hat, and the SS party left.

It was an awkward moment and no one in the room was quite sure what just happened. Uncomfortable, the Brauers left with Max and Dieter hurried out behind them, running for home.

As Doctor Coleman left, he put his hat on his head and watched the official car drive away. Having known the woman all his life he simply stated, "Hilda, we are too old for this. Let it go," and walked out into the night.

Later in his bed Max remembered that in the excitement he had not asked Kurt about his parents. For now, it would suffice that he had seen a family member from home and he would sleep well this night.

The next morning, Hilda Metzger took pen in hand. That high and mighty SS officer did not do his duty, she was sure of it. He was protecting someone. It had bothered her all night and now it was her duty to report him. She would have satisfaction. Revealing her suspicions, this letter would assure that Herr Schwartzkopf was at least reprimanded if not removed from his post. Hilda closed the envelope addressed to the Nazi High Command in Berlin. Since the post was closed she had only to wait for a patrol passing through to deliver it. She smiled.

Chapter Twenty-Three

More Derring-Do

***

Next morning, Max attended the Lutheran church with his adoptive family. Though the order of service was different than mass he found it interesting to be in this house of God each Sunday now. He bowed his head and prayed fervently when the congregation knelt, and asked God to take care of Adam. It was as if he, Max, had adopted the young father as family and now that he was committed, he felt responsible for him. It was difficult to be patient. He wanted to run out to the fort and see how the pilot survived the night. He could not show his eagerness however or the family would suspect something.

At lunch Margrete made a delicious meal of spätzle and Max ate his fill. Volunteering to help with the dishes, Max wanted to find what leftovers and scraps he could to slip into a towel for Adam. It seemed an eternity before Pieter announced his intention to have a nap and Margrete intended to catch up on her sewing. Max asked her if he could go play with Dieter. Gretchen shot Max a knowing look and went back to the book she was reading.

"Maximilian, haven't you seen enough of him this week?" Margrete asked, to which Max shook his head vigorously. "Alright then, but just for a couple of hours. And be home before dark this time!" she admonished, trying to look stern. The event last night had almost given her ulcers.

This time as Max left he knew he had to be careful. Since Frau Metzger had shown her hand as an informer, she was to be avoided. After meeting Dieter the two boys took their packs of hidden food and went the long way around the town. They must be extra vigilant now. The walk being much longer, the afternoon sun was far to the west and only an hour of daylight remained when they rounded the bluff near the shelter.

Opening the lean-to door, they were not prepared for what they saw. They hoped they would find Adam awake but he was gone. The hubcap was overturned, ashes strewn about with cold coals. The blankets still lay where he had been, but Max pointed to something that relieved them both. "Look! His uniform," Max said, hurrying to the corner to retrieve the bloodstained clothing. Adam must have put on Paul's old clothes that Dieter brought. Food was missing as well, giving Max hope that he got away safely.

Dieter still feared that he was taken, for it appeared that Adam left in a hurry. As the boys argued about this, they suddenly heard shouts and dogs barking in the distance. As one they bolted outside.

Quietly but as fast as they could move, they reached the overhanging oak panting in unison. Behind its broad trunk, they were hidden from the commotion below. Max counted eight soldiers swarming the downed plane. This meant for certain that they'd be looking for the missing pilot. Could Kurt have betrayed him? Max couldn't believe that. It probably was just a patrol. The two shepherd dogs were sniffing for a scent and Max was glad they had cut down the parachute, or soldiers would have seen it by now.

A whispered consultation and quickly they snuck back up to the fort. They must remove everything that pointed to Adam, or themselves. Hastily gathering up the uniform, parachute and things that would tie them to the place, Max also scuffed the dirt with his toe where the doctor had operated on Adam. He poured some petrol where Adam had lain only hours before. If dogs smelled blood, they'd have a scent. Max hoped Adam had a good head start. They took a last look around. It looked like a kids play fort again. Time to go. As Max turned he spied a small bit of color peeking out from under the makeshift door. He picked up the little embroidered patch. It was the Union Jack flag that Adam had shown them. Abandoning the blankets, they stuffed them behind some bushes down the hill as they left.

Sprinting from the fort, fear gave them wings as they ran for home. They would have to go back via the stream so the dogs would lose the scent if they were followed. Crossing over, they ran until they were winded. It was hard going with the heavy parachute between them. They rested a few minutes and were off again. Further down they crossed back over the stream and headed to the north of the village and Dieter's back yard.

Panting, Dieter pulled Max into the shed. "We have to burn the uniform and parachute! If they come here and find it, we'll be arrested." Dieter tried to convince Max.

"But if we burn it, won't the smoke and smell alert everyone?" Max cautioned. He was right of course. The only thing to do was bury it. No time now, Max knew he'd really be in trouble if he didn't get back soon. It was almost dark. Quickly they stuffed the items behind the ivy covered compost bin, hoping Dieter's family wouldn't have cause to visit it before they could move them.

Max arrived just as the family sat down to supper. He had made it! With a frown, Margrete told Max to wash up and join them. Throughout supper Max prayed hard that the soldiers he'd seen this afternoon would not find them. He didn't want a repeat of the night before. Margrete refused to let Max go out after the meal despite his pleading and heated the kettle for his hot bath. She saw the boy was filthy.

That evening a door-to-door patrol searched houses in Obbach, it being the closest town to the crash. Amazingly, Max and Dieter's luck held in that Frau Metzger had gone to visit her sister in another town that morning, so was unaware of the patrol visit. It would have been harder for the boys to explain the supply basket in new light of a missing pilot.

Max lay in bed listening to gruff voices of soldiers stomping through the Brauer house. Pretending he was asleep under the covers when two men came to his room, he hardly dared breathe. Turned to the wall, he kept his eyes closed as they pulled the eiderdown covers off his head. He didn't move. Seconds seemed like eternity as he waited. He then remembered the flag patch in his pants pocket that hung on the chair only inches from the soldiers. What if they went through his things?! Though terrified, he knew he must lay still or risk giving something away with his guilty expression.

As they discussed that this was just a boy, he began to sweat. He could hear one soldier handle his telescope as if looking to see what he found interesting through the lens. The other soldier acted impatient to leave; telling the first one that there was nowhere a fugitive could hide in this room. Finally closing his door, Max heard them descend the steps. When he was sure the front door had slammed, he breathed a sigh of relief. They must not have found the fort! Adam must still be at large, or they wouldn't yet be looking for him!

No one slept that night. War had followed them home. Next morning, Maximilian was up early despite not having slept. He ran to Dieter's house. Was Dieter even there, or had the soldiers discovered the stash out

174

behind the compost? Dieter indeed exited the house, looking subdued and as tired as most of the little village felt. They had been through a rough night.

"What happened at your house?" Maximilian whispered as they walked to school.

"The patrol came, but they didn't stay long." Dieter said sleepily. "Even though they checked our shed, they didn't turn around and look behind the compost. It wouldn't have mattered, after supper I threw the stuff down Gruber's old dry well." Too bad, Max thought, women were recycling parachute material for dresses when they could get it. For the next two weeks the boys had no desire to return to the fort.

The day after Max's twelfth birthday in October, aerial bombing again rained over Schweinfurt. It was the second major attack on the factories below, and planes battled fiercely to the death. The Brauer household watched the sky that night. This wasn't in the distance as recent previous attacks had been, but close enough to be a threat. Watching from darkened windows as night fell they witnessed in horror a plane's descent not a quarter mile away as it plummeted with a flaming tail into the fields below.

Next morning Pieter and some of the village men went out to see. Max, Friedrich and a few other boys followed. Markings on the wreck confirmed it had been an American USAF Boeing B-17 Flying Fortress. It was a large plane, a four-engine bomber. Max knew it from his encyclopedia. It carried a crew of ten.

Max watched, sickened, as men of the village brought broken and charred bodies out of the wreck in large sheets. The victims that were recognizable were all Negro servicemen! The boys witnessed silently as the grisly row of sheeted remains were being laid out, the putrid smell of burned flesh making them gag. The grim crew began to dig graves, each burdened with his own thoughts. These dead who had dreams of their own and may have laughed only yesterday, now lay silent forever as a testimony to the night's deeds. Max wondered if the dead men's families would hate Germans so much if they could see what he saw. That in giving them a proper burial, those who performed the task grieved for them also.

One other thing was destroyed, as Maximilian and Dieter discovered when they again dared venture out to their fort. As if a finger of warning had come down from the sky, a crater had remodeled the bluff where a play fort had once sheltered a lonely Canadian pilot, far from home.

Chapter Twenty-Four

Treason

***

In the city, Anna and Otto were overjoyed when Kurt gave them the news about Max. Once again, they were relieved and astounded that their son-in-law had been in the right place at the right time. Anna knew this had to be God's provision and was always amazed by that.

She had missed Max on his birthday, and wished she had been with him. She wondered if the host family had celebrated with him that day. Had Max thought of them? Anna vacillated daily between frustration and anger at the loss of her sons to strangers, and thankfulness that they were out of the city and comparatively safe. It was only a week later that she was feeling the latter as a horror unfolded one cool windy day.

Anna and Otto were never to forget that day. They had gone to pick up the usual government supplied rations as did others in the neighborhood. Holding their ration cards tightly, they hoped the provisions wouldn't run out again. They needed flour and the ground chicory that served as coffee in these times. Shivering, those in line waited patiently though the ration line was long and the day chilly.

Anna absently noted that Wilhelm Faust stood with his wife Maria further ahead in the line. He was the father of those troublesome boys who fought with her boys, but he seemed to be nice enough. Otto and

Anna were talking when suddenly the commotion ahead caused chatter in the waiting cue to cease as frightened citizens watched, disbelieving. Wilhelm was singled out of the line as Maria gasped in terror. Two Gestapo bullies were shouting at him as Wilhelm tried to defend himself. Thirty faces witnessed as his face crumbled in denial upon identifying his accuser. His own son Fritz stood to the side of the line with a scowl, obviously the informant.

To everyone's horror, Wilhelm was not even questioned or taken away. A swift decision and a single bullet to the head, and it was all over. Maria's screaming still echoed in Anna's mind. Fritz Faust just stared in confusion as his father lay on the street, the lifeblood draining from him. Fritz had not bargained for this. He only wanted his father to show proper respect for their leader! Now his misplaced loyalty had devastated his family as surely as if Hitler had done the deed himself.

When the murderers left, Otto, Anna and others rallied around the stricken, screaming woman. Nothing of course, could be done. The thing could not be taken back. Fritz had run off, it was too much for him to bear. Later, Maria lost her mind and her will to live. She did not enter the shelter when bombs fell again. Her daughter stayed with her. Both sons went to fight and they did not return. No one was sure if Fritz went because he still believed in his convictions that had betrayed his father, or if in hoping to die he would quiet the demons that now accused him.

Otto and Anna wept for a family destroyed. Talking about it was the only way to exorcise the event that replayed the tragedy in their minds for weeks. How could this have happened? What was this evil that was turning children against their parents! They had felt the Faust boys were mischievous and unruly sometimes, but this?! Never would Anna have thought she would witness such a thing, and hoped she never would again.

Wilhelm Faust had been a decent enough human being. He encouraged toughness in his sons as a necessity of life, but punished them for their bullying ways if he caught them. More than once Otto had seen him deal fairly with his boys when Friedrich and Max were involved. Wilhelm's greatest error however had been in supporting and encouraging his sons' involvement with the Nazi youth organization. At first, like most Germans he was proud of the new regime and the Führer that brought them prosperity and hope for a time. However, when the child transports began Wilhelm did not send his children away, preferring them to stay near him.

As time and the war progressed however, shortages and quality of life decreased and Wilhelm became disillusioned with Hitler and his promises. Seeing no end to war or honor in it and grieved by the loss of friends and neighbors, he began to mumble against Herr Hitler and his Nazi thugs. He let his disappointment be known to others and openly decried the regime before his family. Unfortunately, both Faust boys had been properly indoctrinated in all things Nazi and had vigorously pledged their lives to Hitler's cause. This dilemma surfaced like a wedge driving between them. Wilhelm had not realized how deeply. Now he was gone.

***

Chapter Twenty-Five

Death and a Miracle

***

Maximilian did not sleep well after the burial. He dreamed of charred bodies rising from the death plane and marching toward him, pointing fingers, accusing him. These phantoms changed into Nazi soldiers, marching, marching toward him. Max awoke in a cold sweat, panting. He had always been sensitive to others' feelings, and supposed he felt guilty for being German. He thought if his country had not gone to war, these men and countless others would be alive to see their descendents live. He remembered the man in the motorcar. What a different time that was! Full of hope, the people had been happy. Their leader and his troops in grandeur, paraded along the boulevard like conquering heroes.

Max sipped water from a glass beside his bed and shook himself fully awake. Everyone said Herr Hitler was responsible for this war. And Max, you fool, gave him flowers! But, he didn't know then, no one did. They had all fallen into a trap of their own making. He remembered that Mama used to quote the adage, 'pride goes before a fall'. What a fall! He didn't know he still had yet to experience other things that no child should have to know.

***

Every German was to be civic minded and contribute to the war effort, and so, as in other German towns, the children were enlisted to join in scrap retrieval. Local men took out groups on some Saturdays, Max joining others from his class. They were to fill a truck bed with bits of metal or rubber for recycling. The children were shown the types of scrap to look for and then would spread out through the lanes, alleys and ditches on their strange treasure hunt. Boys love to bring home odd objects and so this was actually quite interesting to Max and Dieter.

By midday, they had eaten their lunches and the scrap truck had progressed past the outskirts of Obbach. The two boys had absent-mindedly wandered farther than they realized while talking and the truck was soon a spot in the distance. The various paraphernalia they had acquired that day excited them. It included helmets, shell casings, various bits of war garbage, a bent bike wheel and other wonderful things.

Tramping through the knee-high grass behind a small hill, they suddenly were aware of harsh voices. They looked at each other in silence. A gruff authoritative voice was barking orders. The boys put down their collection and climbed up the knoll, crouching as they peeked over the top. What they saw made Max tremble. He glanced at Dieter who had gone pale. About a hundred feet away, three soldiers had lined up a sad looking bunch of ragged people. These included two children. Max estimated a dozen persons were standing on the edge of a long narrow hole. Piles of earth and shovels lay around the freshly dug hole, perhaps four or five feet deep. Some of the people had stars on their clothing. Some were almost naked.

As the horror unfolded before the two terrified witnesses, the rag-tag bunch of people began hugging each other and some were weeping softly. Then they were shot. The three soldiers did not stop emptying their rifles until all the captives had fallen into the hole. Some of them still moaned. Then there was silence. Pressing flat against the back of the knoll, Max stuffed his sleeve into his mouth to keep from crying aloud and alerting the death squad. Dieter pressed his eyes tight shut.

The boys lay still as their fear immobilized them. Finally, ever so slowly, Max peered through the grass to see what was happening. The soldiers seemed to be talking and laughing. As they finished their cigarettes, they threw them into the hole. Suddenly, a child began to cry. They were surprised one still lived! A soldier swiftly shot into the hole and the crying stopped. The leader of the soldiers instructed the others to help him cover up the vermin as they filled in the hole. The terrified boys lay quietly for what seemed an eternity, listening as shovels of earth fell on those who lay below. Eventually the deed was complete and the death squad climbed into a waiting truck and drove off.

Max wiped his eyes but the tears would not stop coming. He heard Dieter sob beside him. Max looked at his hands. He couldn't understand why he was shaking so violently, not realizing that he was in shock. Unable to run away, the boys lay on the hill and wept. They could not comprehend what they just witnessed. Those soldiers had laughed and called the people vermin!

Suddenly there was shouting in the distance, and this seemed to bring the boys back to the moment. Max identified his brother's voice. The two friends had been missing so long that others were searching for them. Now chilled by more than the early evening air, in shock they stumbled slowly back toward the calling voices. Trembling, their earlier adventure forgotten, the boys returned home as the children lying at the bottom of the unmarked grave would never do again.

Neither boy slept for many nights. These nights Margrete's motherly instincts comforted Max as she hurried to his room to find him crying in his sleep. She cursed the war. Soothing the boy until he calmed down yet again, she wondered about Maximilian's own mother. How she must feel and the heartache of not knowing how her son was! Well, Margrete thought as she whispered a prayer for the stranger Anna, I will guard him for you, don't worry, sleep well...

***

About a week later, a lonely figure slowly came up the road through the town. Some who were out on the sidewalks watched him, curious. Seemingly unarmed and clad in farmer's clothing and a skimpy coat, the vacant eyed man was apparently starving. No one stopped him as he limped by, no one knew him.

Frieda had been visiting with Helga and Werner Weber outside the general store as the man passed by. She stared and as she comprehended what she saw, screamed. This brought everyone within earshot running once the shock subsided. The ragged man stopped, trembling and just stared at her. Ever so slowly she stepped toward him raising and then lowering her hand. Did he not know her?

He blinked. Then, as if waking from a long sleep, a small smile crept into his face. Those who witnessed it could not believe it. The man who appeared to be in his forties was only twenty-two. It was Reiner Melman. The excitement in the village was contagious and they swept him up in their happiness, delivering him home. It was too much for him, he wept like a little child. Herr Melman left his chair and weeping also, enveloped his lost son in his arms.

Herr Melman recovered as a man from a bad dream. However, something was troubling Reiner. One evening soon after his return the family sat around the table. Reiner seemed finally ready to talk. Friedrich, being a member of the household now and treated like a son became witness to the awful story. And once it began, the tale poured out.

183

In late October of 1942 while flying a mission over Stalingrad, Reiner's plane was crippled and lost as reported near the Ukraine border. He was able to parachute from the plane, relieved that he came down in the Ukraine rather than the Russian side of the Volga River. Landing in a tree line, he was sure that Russian troops had seen him. Any moment he was expecting to be overtaken and shot. Quickly cutting himself from his chute restraints, he jumped into a nearby stream and half floated, half ran until he came to a deep eddy at a bend where the trees grew at the edge, overhanging the water. Hiding under these he could hear Russian troops calling out and running along the edge above him. He knew if he was caught it was certain death.

When he couldn't stand the icy water another minute, he climbed up the bank. As luck was with him the Russians had left. Shivering uncontrollably he saw a farm and headed for it. Crawling into a haystack he almost died that night of hypothermia. At dawn he pushed on keeping away from open spaces. Vacant gazes of the corpses he passed and burned out towns unnerved him, making him very nearly despair of hope.

Reiner spied a road heading west and followed it, keeping to the trees paralleling the road until it veered off to a village. Added to his hunger was the misery of the horrible cold he had caught from the icy stream. Stealing clothing from a deserted house to keep warm, he pressed on scavenging food if he came across any.

He was not alone. Other German soldiers were fleeing from the Soviet Army who now pursued them. Reiner was happy to meet a Landser, or German infantryman. Together he and Werner traveled together some days until they were able to steal a transport truck and drive cross-country. Crossing into Poland one night they were shot at. Not sure if they were German, Polish or Russians, Werner gunned the truck and didn't slow down until they were miles away. Even if it was their own forces they had no way of letting them know who they were. They were driving a Polish military vehicle. When the truck ran out of gas they walked.

Days on end were spent trying to stay alive and ahead of the Red Army that was advancing toward Germany. Glad for each others' company however, they spent evenings in hiding sharing their hopes, knowing tomorrow could be their last. Looking to join up with a German unit so they could eat, it seems the Nazi army was wherever they weren't. It had been six weeks since Reiner lost his plane and home was still so far away.

Starving, days and nights passed and the pair got careless while looking for food. A Polish farmer shot Werner. He stumbled but kept running, pulled along by Reiner until they got away. However it was too late. The wound would prove fatal. Losing consciousness, Werner clasped Reiner's hand leaving a crumpled and folded paper there. Reiner held him till he died. Then he ran until he was breathless. Diving under bushes to hide from roving patrols, he crawled into a nearby shed after dark. Unfolding the paper, he saw by the light of the moon that it was a letter addressed to Werner's wife. He would do his best to find her if he lived. Rolling into a tight ball for warmth, Reiner wept until he fell asleep, exhausted.

Again Reiner continued moving west and north for many days, hungry and cold, avoiding patrols and tanks. Once he had to cut the throat of a dog that barked; it would have betrayed his hiding place. He stole food if he found any when he passed by farms but more often didn't eat for days on end. Almost giving up, he considered taking his life when he found a pistol on a corpse. Then he realized the border was just ahead. Germany. Just maybe...he could make it home.

The worst night still tormented his dreams and brought him shame. That night he hid outside a small village in eastern Germany. It was near dusk when a Russian patrol bent on vengeance swooped down on the village, shooting what men were around and entering homes causing havoc and terror. They dragged three German women into the street. One of them was very pregnant. In horror, Reiner watched helplessly as the laughing soldiers brutally raped them with their rifles. Covering his ears tightly to block out their screaming, he couldn't bear it. Mercifully, they died quickly.

Weak from lack of food and unable to fight them anyway, it would have been suicidal to reveal himself, Reiner was vastly outnumbered. He knew he would be tortured if he dared venture forth. When the enemy moved on he emptied his gut of the bile that rose in his throat. Hunger drove him to raid the village houses that had been homes only an hour before. Averting his eyes from the bloodshed, his mind could not grasp the hatred and evil he beheld, the Russians had killed even the children. Chased by monsters borne of fear, his tortured mind kept him moving. Running house to house he sought sustenance but finding little food, he took what he could put in a pack and left the village of death.

Following the railway tracks like spidery legs from the station at nearby Stadtlengsfeld, he watched for trains going west. One night train passed. When a boxcar with an open door came past his opportunity had come. Running along side, he threw in his pack and jumped on. Before he could get his bearings something came at him from a dark recess of the car and knocked him out. He awoke sometime later in the frozen grass beside the railway tracks, his head pounding, dried blood in his eyes and mouth. A shadow blocked the rising sun. It had happened, he thought. He was caught. He didn't really care at this point, for he would be free of this misery.

While Reiner waited for death that was sure to come, the man that

LAMBS OF THE REICH

leaned gently over him lifted him onto the back of a wagon. Covering him with a tarp, Reiner could feel the wheels beneath him bump down the road. He passed out again. Waking days later in a bed with fresh linen was like being in heaven, he thought he must be dead. When his eyes focused a monk was shaking him gently. Offering him food the man tried to get him to sip some hot soup. He drank it greedily, spilling it everywhere, for he was starving.

After being cared for and fed he hid out as the weeks rolled by. Not sure if it was fear, comfort or roving patrols that kept him so long, he finally knew he must move on or risk betraying the monks' kindness if they were caught. When he was ready he thanked them and taking the food and water they provided, he snuck from a hidden exit below the monastery at night. That was three months ago.

Two nights later he was shot in crossfire between Russians and German troops. Left for dead, a German man and his wife came upon him while searching the pockets of corpses. Hearing him moan they dragged him into their flat and nursed him. Again incredibly, he was not to die. The bullet had gone clean through his side missing vital organs. Once able to leave he thanked them. They assured him it was their patriotic duty; they had two sons in the Army.

Reiner pressed on, his goal to reach home all encompassing. More bombed out cities and villages passed, corpses piled up on one another, stench and smoke and carnage paving his way home. He had almost given up again. Yet, as if led by a guiding hand, Reiner returned. The journey took almost eleven months.

Friedrich quietly left the table. He felt sick for Reiner, the world and himself. No one said anything. It was too much to bear. Heartsick for their son, the Melmans were only deeply grateful that Reiner was home.

It truly was a miracle that he was spared. Unfortunately, Reiner was not himself. The horrors he had witnessed were too much. Whether it was shell shock or soul sickness, Reiner was a changed man.

Chapter Twenty-Six

The Answer

***

One November day the weather was as chilly as Max's mood but he had to get out of the house. Aimlessly observing the village children play some tag game on the main street, he leaned up against the post office doorway. Max was asked to play but simply felt he had no energy. The horror of war had begun taking its toll on him. So he watched instead.

In the distance repeated bursts of machinegun fire were heard again. Another dogfight. The cacophony was an assault to the senses that now blurred in the background of their hours. What was a thrill to him once now meant death and it was no longer exciting. He smiled bitterly to see the little ones run around, carefree. Once that had been he.

Not sure what made him look up Max watched as a plane dropped rapidly toward them, smoking. The wings were gone! Max burst to life. Not a second to spare. He shouted to the children at the top of his lungs and running like a mother hen. Scooping up little Heinrich and Heidi, Max screamed at the others to run. Tossing the little ones inside a gate, he pushed the last strays into a doorway and ran in himself as the downed Messerschmitt bounced hard along the uneven cobblestone streets mere inches away, sparks flying.

Screeching along the road, pieces were tearing off the fuselage like a legless locust on its belly. Miraculously no airborne debris found targets as it flew in all directions. Coming to rest against the stone wall of the store, the remnants of the plane burst into flame. Though two older men rushed forward to try and save the pilot, it was too hot to get close.

The pilot however, was assumed dead already for holes riddling the side of the aircraft beside him told the tale. Next day the town buried the man, some German mother's son or husband. Herr Doppler carved a memorial for atop his grave, the first of several memorials that would be erected in the area to slain countrymen.

Max became the new town hero. The eleven children playing on the street just moments before the fiery missile hit were alive because of his quick actions. Mothers he barely knew embraced him when they saw him. Max didn't feel like a hero. He felt that he just happened to be in the right place at the right time.

A somber Christmas of 1943 slid into a cold January of 1944. Families of the village pulled together to provide what little comfort and food they could. Food was getting scarce, and even vegetables that had been in ample supply in summer were not available now. Margrete had canned everything she could then, but helping neighbors out was making the once stocked pantry shelves dwindle.

Pieter finally closed the store. No one was buying watches or clocks. There was no need. The war, like time, wore endlessly on. Pieter obtained a city newspaper whenever he could, eager to see if the balance of power was changing. He would read articles aloud sometimes, like the teacher did at school. Max thought he did that as if to say, see, things here aren't so bad. It helped if you put things in perspective, he told them. Aside from the ever-present war news other disasters befell the woeful planet.

A huge earthquake hit San Juan, Argentina in January killing ten thousand people. It was that country's worst natural disaster. Later in March the eruption of Mount Vesuvius was the big news from Italy. Max had studied about this volcano in school. Its famous eruption in 79 AD had destroyed the cities of Herculaneum and Pompeii. Yet, it was just an interesting fact.

Trouble far away paled when compared with personal trials. Humans were selfish, Max realized. Unless it is happening to you it doesn't seem real and therefore doesn't matter as much. Twelve-year-old Max was thinking too much. Instead of the carefree thoughts of boys his age in peacetime, Max worried about things much beyond his years. He was also mad at God. With the whole world fighting and making their own trouble did God have to allow natural disasters as well? The whole thing gave him a headache.

Retreating to his room with this tumult in his brain, he lay on his bed. He watched his planes rotating above him until exhausted, he dreamed. As if watching his life from a distance Max saw his parents. They were alive and well. He felt happy. Next he saw himself lying small beneath the covers, so sickly, and Liesl pleading with him to get well. The scene changed to Friedrich, his smile fading as he watched his friend die in front of him, shrapnel in his brain. Then Liesl with Kurt standing in front of them all, shooting any Nazi that tried to pass. Then he and his brother with arms outstretched as they drove down a dark tunnel, his mother's arms reaching out to them as she faded into the distance. Max awoke with a start.

Perturbed, he wondered at the strange dream. Quickly whispering a prayer of protection for his family was a constant habit, but suddenly he felt peace spread over him as if a matter had been settled. Like the answer delivered in a bolt of lightening it came to him. God would allow nothing to touch him or those he loved unless it was their time. For those who trusted God it was simple. " I must have faith!" he realized as it hit home. There were no coincidences.

He remembered stories of miraculous intervention and those who should have died but didn't. And he remembered other things. How Mama had told him that God sent Kurt to hide their Jewish ancestry. Friedrich had not perished in the Düsseldorf bombing. He and Dieter were not caught hiding Adam. Even being placed in Obbach was God's plan for him, he was sure of it! That was how they were saved from the flaming plane on the street! Even Reiner Melman had come home! Feeling at peace for the first time in months, Maximilian was revived.

Yes, people perished. The war continued. Freedom of choice allowed the evil deeds of men; but those were not God's fault. Despite even natural disaster God still held men in His hand. Max was relieved. He could not and would not believe that God didn't care. Max decided he didn't have to stay awake listening for disaster to strike. God did not sleep; He would take care of things. Whether he lived or died God was right there. This gave him a strange peace he couldn't explain. He knew he'd received the answer when he slept through the nights again. The best part was, the nightmares stopped.

***

In March a new arrival was taken in. Fortunately, it was Dr. Coleman who found her when returning from a trip to Dortmund. She had been wandering near the road, crying, hands outstretched, face raised to the sky, unseeing. Her story was related to Pieter who told his family at supper.

Heidi was a young bride in that city. One day she was away from home on an errand when the sirens began. She took cover returning home when the bombing stopped. Upon arriving, she found her home in ruins. She dug through the rubble only to find her mother and brother dead. A few days later a patrol shot her new husband for looting; he was searching for food.

Grieving, with nowhere to go she wandered through the city eating whatever she could find in the trash. Not being able to bear the sorrow, when she found a bottle of pills she decided to end her life and took them all. She passed out but awoke later totally blind. Amazingly, she wandered outside the town and then feeling her way along ditches came near the road where the doctor found her.

Again, Max was astounded by a miracle. That this young woman could walk blindly for miles and not encounter enemies or harm was unbelievable but true! It could only be that God sent angels to guide her. Now too it seemed the effects of the mystery pills were temporary and she was already regaining her sight, her strength returning. In the careful hands of God, Dr. Coleman and his housekeeper she would soon be well in body, if not in mind.

Chapter Twenty-Seven

The Blood Tide

***

Perpetual bombing on German cities in 1944 took their toll. Multiple attacks on specific targets such as transportation, the steel industry and electric power caused not only disruption but also disorganization and mass devastation.

The peoples' morale deteriorated after constant bombardment by aerial raids on the cities. Night raids were especially feared. Losing faith in any hope of victory after years of war, faith in their leaders and unrealized promises also wavered and died. Tired of the war, they wanted it to end.

Black radio listening was on the increase among German citizens. Rumor and fact circulated in opposition to the Regime. Active rebellion surfaced as well. In 1944 one German in a thousand was arrested for a political offense. Though Herr Hitler was victim to a second assassination attempt, it failed and two hundred suspected plotters were murdered for their trouble. It was a pity Pieter said, that Germans couldn't vote themselves out of the war, for who would deliver them?

If anyone was hoping their leader would tire of his mandate or give up the fight, they did not know the tenacity of the man. Hitler had always known the young people were his hope for the future. He had taken an interest in the nation's youth from the start; they were an integral part of his plan for a Germany that would rule the world for generations to come. In denying the end was near, he turned to his most loyal followers.

Correct in his estimation that adults grow weary and give up, Hitler saw youth as the only hope now for his vision of Germany. In desperation as troops were cut down, Hitler urged more and more trained youth from the ranks of the Hitler Jugend to take up arms. Drilled in total submission to the Reich and its Führer, who better to defend the cause? Boys who fervently believed and worshipped their Führer eagerly joined, unlike those who resisted the partisan indoctrination such as Friedrich and Max. Many HJ children were successfully influenced by the creed of German superiority, stripped of compassion and conscience, and so drilled in the Nazi belief system that victory or death was their mandate. The Thielmann brothers were fortunate indeed that they had been placed in a small village. They were likely forgotten.

As early as January 1943, exclusively Hitler Youth boys manned anti-aircraft batteries. War victory became their new calling, the boys serving first as postmen delivering draft notices and ration cards, or collecting scrap metal and other war materials. A recruitment drive started initially with 17 year-old volunteers, but younger boys joined willingly. Some being trained in Belgium, others at Defense Strengthening Camps, three weeks training was provided under the supervision of Wehrmacht officers. Principally trained in weapons handling, it included various pistols, machine-guns, hand grenades and Panzerfausts or bazookas. By this time unnecessary drills such as goose-step marching were eliminated.

In spring of 1944 the boy troops had been fully trained and named the Hitler Jugend Panzer Division. Immediately they were sent out to face the Allied invasion of Northern France. The young Division would battle a superior enemy but the Allies would see firsthand Hitler's loyal youth.

Beginning at dawn on June 6th, the Allies stormed the beaches of Normandy as if in answer to millions of prayers. British and Canadian soldiers were likely unprepared for the zealous fanaticism and death-defying bravery of the Hitler Youth they battled. Taking on tanks and fighting fiercely till the last survivor, males too young to shave were attacking Allied soldiers who had no choice but to kill them. The "fearless, cruel, domineering" youth Hitler had wanted became everything he hoped for in their bravery and contempt for danger. The result was that almost the entire division was wiped out.

When Caen fell to the British, this remnant of the HJ Division was moved from the Normandy Front. The once passionate young defenders of the Reich were now disheartened, exhausted and filthy. Mounting a counter-offensive in August the Germans were pushed back on three sides by the British, Canadians and Americans into the Falaise area, one narrow gap the only escape. Trapped, twenty-four German divisions waited while the HJ Division was sent to keep the northern edge of this twenty-mile gap open. While most were captured still twenty thousand Germans escaped including the last of the HJ Division. Over nine thousand of 12th SS-Panzer Division Hitler Jugend had been lost in Normandy and Falaise by September 1944.

As the first Allies crossed into Germany, HJ boys fought as guerillas against invading U.S. troops. In the Ruhr area boys hiding in the forests would wait as tanks passed and then attack the foot soldiers with grenades and guns inflicting heavy causalities. The Americans countered with air-attacks leveling villages in the area. Amazed that the boys did not surrender, the troops captured armed boys as young as eight, surprised that artillery units were operated solely by children, even some girls.

For the next few months country after country was taken back from

Hitler's clutches as the Allies poured in like a flood. Yet as they pushed forward countless souls were still dying as the Nazis stepped up the nasty business of annihilation. Endless trains still shuttled Europe's Jews by the thousands to the death camps in their relentless and gruesome task. Those who were not murdered were used as forced labor in the war industry to replace German labor shortages.

In last-ditch desperation German children were trained as spies and saboteurs in February 1945. They were to penetrate Allied lines with explosives and arsenic but most were promptly captured or killed. After failed attempts in two other skirmishes, the HJ Panzer Division would ultimately surrender to the Americans in May of 1945, numbering only four hundred and fifty-five left alive.

The Soviet Army advanced on Berlin, Nazi Germany's capital and Hitler's last stand. On April 23, HJ battalions were sent to protect the Pichelsdorf bridges by the Havel River. Five thousand boys hoping to oppose the Soviets guarded these Berlin bridges. They were clumsily clad in man-sized uniforms too large for them with oversized helmets. In five days of battle merely five hundred were left. Loyal to the end, many committed suicide instead of surrendering to the Red Army. All over Berlin able-bodied males were forcibly involved in the final desperate struggle. Those fleeing or deserting the fight were shot or hanged by roaming SS executioners.

A month before his fifty-sixth birthday Adolf Hitler publicly appeared in the chancellery garden to decorate twelve-year-old Hitler Youths with Iron Crosses. These were for their heroism in defending Berlin from attack. Awestruck, these children gazed at him as if in the presence of a god. This exceptional event was filmed as a final page in the collapse of Hitler's empire. Unbelievably when the presentation ended they were instructed to continue the hopeless fight. Ten days after his birthday on April 30th, it was reported that Hitler ended his reign by suicide as Russian troops neared his bunker. The Third Reich, designed to last a thousand years, crumbled in twelve.

Chapter Twenty-Eight

Freedom

***

As Hitler's dream fell apart reports of advancing allied troops came in from far and wide. It was at first rumored, then confirmed that Herr Hitler was indeed dead. Not sure how to behave in a world without their leader people of the village were unsure of the future. With no German government, what would happen now? Catholic leaders were among the first to give direction, and denounced any cooperation with the fallen regime. The new Catholic leader, Pope Pius XII seemed to confirm this in his radio address supporting Western leaders and their attempts to, "create a better Europe with human dignity...and above all, the holy principle of equality of rights of all people."

Pieter, a Lutheran, listened with disdain. "Humph," he grunted, "Now he changes his mind! He and his teacher, Pius XI, ordered Catholics to support Nazism! They actually helped Hitler rise to power. I well remember 1939!" Margrete clucked her tongue at him, not sure how young Max felt about the pope as his spiritual leader, being Catholic. The family sat in the parlor listening to history taking place as the radio confirmed the war was ended. She only knew that meant changes were here.

Max was outside when the first American troops entered Obbach.

They wore U.S. flag patches on their sleeves, as Adam must have before he removed his Canadian patch. Would they be nice, like Adam? Or would they hate and punish the German people for supporting their Führer and causing the deaths of many of the Allied forces? Many children ran out to see this spectacle as it happened. As the soldiers walked by Max was stunned to see pity on some of their faces. He did not realize how he looked to them. Most soldiers could not speak German but learned a few phrases to use and now called to the children who watched apprehensively from doorways.

Max could not believe his eyes as two of the soldiers handed out a few rations from the back of their supply truck, taking pity on the children. He couldn't know that they beheld thin, hungry looking waifs. The state of being un-full had been the norm for so long that it seemed normal. The adults were more cautious, were the Allies still enemies or liberators? Several parents even forbade their children to touch the food, fearing it was poisoned. What would happen now was anyone's guess.

The days that followed involved municipal and county leaders meeting with the new powers to determine what their needs were and procedures to follow. With sudden clarity Max realized what it meant to he and his brother. They were going home! Though it would take days or possibly weeks for arrangements to be made to transport children back to their homes, Max swung daily between eagerness and sadness. Fear, joy, sorrow, Max felt the gamut of emotions. He'd grown close to his adoptive parents and sisters. The girls had spoiled him and happy memories flooded his mind. He thought of the good times, playing chess together on Sunday afternoons and helping Pieter in the shop and how he showed Max the workings of clocks. Sometimes they sang together as Frieda played the piano. Margrete and he had some deep talks while weeding the garden. She truly was there for him during the toughest years of his life. He would also miss Dieter, his friend in difficult times and adventures.

Surprises were also revealed. Many times Max had passed the crumbling house on a back street of Obbach where glassless windows stared, dark and absent of life. Overgrown with ivy and wild oats the little homestead sat forgotten by generations. Wild things had overtaken the dilapidated house and the outhouse at the rear leaned precariously, the door torn off. A few steps behind this a small rise sloped gently upward forming a mound covered in overgrowth and foliage. Beneath the clinging vines the small door was virtually invisible. It led downward to an eight by eight foot room, a former root cellar. Someone had dug another exit for added ventilation through the hill. That was also cleverly hidden.

When it was learned that a Jewish family hid there for many months Max understood how they were missed the night the Nazi patrol searched the town. The family of four had somehow spent their existence with meager comforts in the candlelit room for months coming out only at night. They were alive but barely.

What was a bigger surprise was that both Dr. Coleman and his housekeeper knew of it, as well as Melmans and Webers. Within a day of American occupation the family cautiously emerged scarcely believing they were delivered. The families who risked death for them had fed them what little they had keeping them alive and warm until now. In winter they were sheltered in Dr. Coleman's attic to keep warm at great personal risk to the doctor. Max also learned that unknown to himself Pieter had recently sheltered other displaced persons for two days in the smokehouse at the end of the property. Amazed, Max perceived that many of the good people in the village were indeed anonymous heroes.

A week later the boys still waited for transport home. A small Red

Cross station was set up in the old post office to attend to the needs of ill people and relay messages from families trying to contact loved ones. There was one for the Thielmann boys! Eagerly they shared the letter like starving men sharing a single apple. Each line and thought was devoured with excitement. To their wonder, news from Liesl indicated a surprise or rather two of them when they returned. Anna and Otto sent their love and anticipation for their soon return. Overjoyed that everyone was well, they began counting the days till departure.

***

At least one person in the town was not overjoyed. Frau Metzger sat beside her radio in the parlor when the sad news was announced. She could not believe it. Her leader was dead! Every thing she believed to be true and hoped for was in ashes. The day the Americans marched into town like they owned everything she was filled with indignation. How dare they act like they were the mighty victors! In actuality only about 400,000 American soldiers lost their lives in the entire scope of WWII, probably due to their late entry into the war. Yet this number was but a fraction of the millions of Europeans and peoples of other nations that were killed in this war of wars.

Hilda was incensed. The Fuhrer's plans for Germany had made them a proud nation, soon to be free of the poison of the filthy Jews! Hilda Metzger was nothing if not loyal. She would show them! She would end this misery in her own way. She had lingered in her home for days now watching through the curtains, fuming at the Americans' audacity and wondering what to do. Daily she grew angrier. Now it was time to act. Rising from her chair made her legs ache. She hated being old and having arthritis. Slowly she made her way up to her bedroom.

The chest in the corner had not been touched since she buried her husband. Opening the brass clasp she determined to lift the heavy leather lid. The uniform that came to light was musty smelling but a faint aroma of his cologne lingered and she raised the cloth coat to her nose. Her eyes misted as a distant memory surfaced. She had not quite forgiven Wolfgang for leaving her alone all these years. Setting the coat to one side, she rummaged deep into the trunk for the treasure she sought. Pulling a faded lace curtain aside so she might see better, a sunbeam illuminated the contents. Finally, it was there! A solid object covered with soft cloth emerged.

Unwrapping the object carefully, a smooth pistol appeared smelling of metal and gun oil. It felt wonderful in her hand and she relished the sense of power it gave her. It was Wolfgang's Luger P 08, his army issue pistol from the first war. It was loaded. She always knew it was there, waiting. There had never been a need for it like the present.

Hilda Metzger put on an old oversized coat of her husband's though the June day was lovely. She hid the pistol in the roomy pocket. It concealed the gun perfectly. Walking purposefully toward the village center where the Americans unloaded a truck she tried to pick out the most senior officer. Slowly making her way up to the vehicle she watched the one who was the obvious leader. Clasping the hidden gun in her hand, finger on the trigger, she pretended she was just passing by...almost there now.

When she came abreast of the truck she stopped. The soldier who was unloading asked her a question she didn't understand. Realizing perhaps she was hungry, he turned back to his supplies to get her something. She had not answered him but kept her eyes on the other one, the apparent senior officer. The senior man was checking something off a list on a clipboard and his distraction was the break she was looking for. Deftly pulling the weapon from her pocket, she pointed the pistol directly in his face, breathless that she had pulled it off. Click. Nothing happened.

The Sergeant looked up at the sound of the hammer click. Their eyes locked. Holding her gaze, Hilda realized that he knew what she had tried to do. Hilda was prepared to die for her Führer. Nothing mattered now. She rose to her full height, chin jutting forward as if in challenge, waiting. She wasn't however, prepared for his reaction.

"Why thank you old mother," he said in perfect High German dialect, "how wonderful of you to present me with this fine relic of your conquered nation. It is a trophy I will keep always." With that he swiftly disarmed her before she had a chance to realize what happened. She had forgotten to take off the safety! Dumbfounded, she just stood there. It was Hilda's misfortune to have met one of the few Americans who knew fluent Deutsch. He'd already dealt with tougher foes than Hilda, well aware that Nazi sentiment still burned in the diehard loyalists.

The soldier who had missed it turned back from his business in the truck and handed the old woman a packet of rations. Effectively humiliated by the enemy, Hilda's cheeks burned with shame. The man she tried to kill had simply dismissed her, mocking her valiant attempt to murder him. He hadn't even given her the respect to admit she was a threat or even lock her up! She was a disgrace to her leader! Humbled and depressed, she walked home in a daze.

***

In some ways the morning of departure came too soon. Friedrich had said his goodbyes an hour before, packed and was ready to go before Max who was always disorganized. He had even gone to the barn to brush Matilda and say goodbye to the gentle horse. Stroking her soft upper lip, he gave her some wild oats he had scrounged and looked about the place.

He would never be here again, and wanted to imprint the place on his mind. Wiping a tear from his eye, he embraced Frau Melman and shook the old farmer's hand, promising vainly to write or visit sometime.

At the Brauer residence Margrete fussed with Max's clean and pressed clothing making sure he had packed everything. Max packed his remaining planes. He had given Dieter one of them the night before as a farewell gift. Margrete prepared a lunch of rations and included a few sweet strawberries that had ripened early. When the truck was ready the children were to line up. Friedrich hated long goodbyes and was waiting impatiently long before Max appeared. Max wondered why Friedrich was so grumpy, but perhaps he just missed the Melmans already.

Margrete began to cry as he carried his things to the truck. Gretchen and Frieda hugged him tightly and all the attention was making a lump in Max's throat. He would miss them too. Pieter held the boy's shoulder as if to make him stay a moment longer. "Maximilian, I have something for you," he said simply, "so you will remember us." With that, he produced a pewter pocket watch and placed it in the boy's palm. He could part with this. Pieter hadn't been selling watches for over a year, for there was no one who could afford to buy them.

Max didn't know what to say. It was a beautiful watch with a chain and he figured it must have cost a lot. Max opened the cover and looked at the crystal face with the prompt second hand gently ticking away the moments. Lovingly he closed it and traced the delicate etching on the cover. Shyly, he thanked Pieter and they shook hands. Max was crying now too. He felt like a baby, but these people had been his family for three years. Was he always going to have to face loss?

Max mounted the rear of the truck via piled up wooden apple boxes, hearing his name being called. It was Dieter and he was almost breathless from running. Although they had said their farewell the evening before Max was glad to see his friend had come. Dieter put something into Max's hand just as the truck gate was being closed. "For you Max. Don't forget us here," Dieter exclaimed putting on a brave face and looking for all the world like he lost his best friend.

When the truck pulled out of the village, Max waved until he could no longer see them. He tried to remember every nook and cranny of the place and the people who he'd come to love. He had even had a visit this week from his schoolteacher, Fraulein Kessler. Others had come to say farewell also; Doktor Coleman, the Melmans, and others who he'd befriended in the little village.

The truck bounced down the road as the driver shifted gears that complained noisily, and another chapter in their lives had ended. Max unwrapped the handkerchief bundle that Dieter had given him. Inside was a uniform patch that said simply, Capt. Adam Cross. Feeling in his pocket for its match, he produced the Union Jack flag. He hadn't known that Dieter had taken the name patch from the uniform before he threw it in Gruber's well. He stared at the patches, then pulled the smooth pocket watch from Pieter out of his pocket. His mind played over his adventures. He had come to Obbach a little boy and was returning a young man. "No, I won't forget you." Max whispered to himself as he wrapped the patches in the cloth together, "I won't forget."

Chapter Twenty-Nine

Home!

***

Obbach shrank in the distance as a fading memory while the children watched the countryside pass. At first excited and chatty, the miles fled by. As afternoon wore on with few stops for toilet breaks, meager lunches were devoured and some of the younger children slept upright on others' shoulders. Friedrich and Max squirmed like the younger children beside them, hoping this bumpy trip would soon end. Stops to pick up other children bound for the city made the trip unbearably long. Still Düsseldorf had not yet appeared on the horizon.

The nearer they got to the city, the less often towns were recognizable anymore. Many burned out or bombed ruins replaced once tidy rural homes. Sometimes the travelers averted their eyes as corpses still lay in fields or ditches. Survivors were yet reeling from the bloody recent months. Clean up and restoration would take time. First however they had to bury the dead.

Peering from the canvas-covered truck the children saw yet another of the little Bavarian villages approach. Skeletons of homes stood here as empty sentinels of forgotten dreams. The silent devastation reminded Max of tombstones in this country of graves. One such monument carried a poignant and fitting message. The words, "Aus der Traum" appeared in charcoal on a singular standing wall. Meaning, *"The dream is over"*, it mockingly spoke volumes about those who had dared to believe in it.

As suppertime neared the boys began to feel ravenous for their lunches were a now but a memory of hours before. Finally, Düsseldorf rose in the dusky sky before them. What familiar landmarks still stood made the boys excited. Other times they weren't sure of their surroundings, the cityscape remodeled as if crushed by a drunken giant. Friedrich barely recognized the soot blackened theatre where he and Rolf had gone the night Rolf died. Friedrich closed his eyes as the memory still brought pain. It seemed so long ago.

The truck finally pulled up on Hohe Strasse and the boys stretched stiff muscles before jumping down. They were home. Unbelievably, though the façade appeared worn and battered, home still stood. To Max who was looking for them now, it was another miracle.

Otto heard the truck and limping, came out the door. Enveloping the boys in his arms he held them until Anna who had been upstairs ran out. Crying with joy she pulled them into the kitchen exclaiming as she did so how tall they had grown. Friedrich and Max couldn't stop smiling as their mother pressed food on them. It was a wonderful homecoming. After eating, Anna saw the boys were weary and sent them up to bed deciding they could catch up on things at breakfast. The two tired brothers headed for their room. Upon opening the door it was like walking back in time; it was still exactly as they remembered it. Max almost instantly fell into a sound sleep but Friedrich lay for a long time taking it all in. He had changed and now his sin replayed in his thoughts, indeed it had returned to haunt him all day. He had a secret.

Back in March the Nazi regime had been flailing about in its final death throes. Some leaflets blown in the wind had fallen near the village. Likely dropped over nearby Schweinfurt and authored by the Allies, they warned of annihilation if the Nazis failed to surrender. Friedrich had read one and believed it. At age sixteen he was torn between gratitude that he had been sheltered from the fighting and confusion about where his alliances should lie. When the war truly was a lost cause he actually began to feel ashamed. Maybe the stories about Jewish persecution were blown out of proportion. Maybe the war was someone else's fault. He just knew he felt cowardly to be safe in the village when he was now old enough to make a difference.

That spring day Friedrich was out at the barn reading a sample of this Allied propaganda. Vowing under his breath that he would do something, he felt he should be loyal to Germany above all! The Nazi Youth training conflicted with his strict Catholic upbringing and his mother's admonitions to treat all people fairly. Never mind the rumor that he was half Jewish! These jumbled thoughts were interrupted when he heard shots in the distance. Normally he would have stayed where he was in comparative safety. This time his resolve to act coupled with curiosity got the better of him. He had to see for himself.

Hoping he wasn't seen as he opened the rear gate in the pasture he set off to find the skirmish. Friedrich ran crouched over until he had to stop and catch his breath. Glancing back he saw the farm buildings that now appeared as miniatures to him. Friedrich stood alone and unprotected. This fact was both scary and exhilarating but he was already committed. Creeping through the trees and keeping low, he saw the trouble.

Friedrich watched as two soldiers prodded a man and young boy of about six before them. The man was bleeding from a leg wound and stumbling but they shouted at him to keep walking. It was upon hearing their voices that Friedrich recoiled, disbelieving. These were the voices of youth, not grown men who pushed their captives roughly forward. Friedrich convinced himself that taking prisoners wasn't so bad, at least they were not being killed.

Suddenly the wounded man seemed to fall, distracting the captors while shouting for his son to run. As the boy broke free he ran toward Friedrich's hidden position. One young soldier aimed his rifle at the boy while the wounded man struggled with the other captor. Bullets whizzed by Friedrich not two feet from his position. Somehow the youth had missed as the child he hunted zigzagged away. In his haste to get off another shot, the boy soldier jammed the weapon. Frustrated that his target was gaining distance he dropped the heavy rifle and ran after the child, pulling a knife from his belt.

Friedrich instinctively grabbed a rock by his foot. Reacting without thinking, he jumped from his hiding place and let fly just as the boy soldier came within close range. The youth dropped like the stone that hit him squarely in the eye. Blood spurting from the wound, he screamed and held his hands to the eyeball that now hung down on his face. Horrified, Friedrich watched as the wounded youth flailed about on the hard ground holding his head. The screaming was unbearable. He could not let him suffer. Friedrich reacted then, holding the young soldier from thrashing around and took the rock, bringing it down hard on his temple. The uniformed youth lay still, his errand for the Reich now terminated in a premature death. Staggering back and sobbing Friedrich didn't know how suddenly things had gone so wrong.

Friedrich stared down at the young man whose life he had taken. Shock and revulsion registered slowly as Friedrich stared at the one soulless eye of a boy no older than himself. That he could be lying there instead was not lost on Friedrich and he fell to his knees as realization and abhorrence registered in his mind. Breathless, he turned to see that the adult prisoner had overcome his own young captor who now lay unmoving as well.

The child captive had gone to ground when the shots rang out. He now slowly rose from the grass a few yards away and looked fearfully at Friedrich. The boy was dirty and scantily clad but the tattered yellow star on his thin sweater told everything. The wind blew softly as a new silence stole over the terrible scene.

The child ran over to his father who eyed Friedrich for a moment. Wordlessly the man tied the tourniquet tighter around his wound. Aided by his son, the two figures then crept away from the road into the shelter of the forest. Friedrich stared after them. The freed captives had neither asked for his help nor thanked him for it.

Sitting in the grass afterward, Friedrich knew he'd have to move eventually. The surreal sight before him would not remain a secret for long. The Nazi army that once boasted thousands of troops had been devastated over the course of the war. There was no one left to fight now but the Nazi youth patrols that Friedrich realized had taken up the cause. It was obvious what story this scene would tell if Friedrich was found with the two dead German boys. He would be shot as a traitor.

Forcing his weak legs to move, he grabbed the youth's ankles and pulled him into the trees hiding the body in the brush. Friedrich found he was crying, shaking uncontrollably as he covered the deed. Running to the other body he rolled it into the deep ditch, where it wouldn't be found so easily. Friedrich bent and threw up until the contents of his stomach were gone. He stumbled back the way he had come. As fear conjured up phantom eyes watching his every move he ran as never before.

For many nights later he had not slept as the horror replayed over, accusing him in his mind. Scenes of the dead youth intermingled with memories of Rolf, laying in his own blood, his head smashed like a broken doll. Friedrich wept. He no longer wanted to fight. He only wanted his conscience to cease its condemnation.

Now safe in his bed at home far away, he knew he must forget or go mad. He was a murderer. That it was war was no matter. He had taken life and wondered if God saw the whole thing and hated him for it. Or, was he a hero for saving a child from certain death? He had not told Max and only a weak moment had made him reveal it to Herr Melman. Though reassured that he was not a monster, he could not forget the boy soldier's one-eyed death stare. Falling into a fitful sleep, Friedrich would never resolve the matter in his own mind. And so for now, he buried it.

Chapter Thirty

Heaviness and Healing

***

Next morning a refreshed Max and weary Friedrich joined the breakfast table. Otto looked tired as well but seemed to be in fair health to Max. Anna looked older and Max worried about the dark circles under her eyes. Of course, everyone was thinner. As they bent to pray for the meal each one was just grateful that they had made it through the darkest days to be reunited again. So many others hadn't.

Excited to present his mother and father with a memento of their time away, Max suddenly remembered his gift. Hurrying upstairs he returned after some moments to the kitchen with a cloth bag in hand. Max handed the square parcel to his mother. Anna was curious as she unwrapped the small package, soon revealing the cuckoo clock that Max had lovingly carved under the tutelage of Pieter Brauer. Gasps of awe and approval were uttered as Max grinned his widest. The little clock was indeed beautiful and his parents could scarcely believe that Max had made it himself. He was quick to assure them he had as they hung it in a prominent spot on the kitchen wall.

Anna's breakfast was simple fare but still tasty and the boys dug into the potato pancakes eagerly. The boys didn't realize that a few potatoes were almost all that was left in the cellar. Most of the current garden crop wasn't quite ready yet, being early summer.

Otto questioned the boys about their lives in Obbach. Anna listened intently while Otto quizzed them on the daily rituals of their homes there. Both seemed satisfied that they had been well cared for and glad their sons had gone. As the conversation continued, inevitable questions surfaced about acquaintances. The boys sobered as Otto related how some of their friends who had remained or left to fight in the last months were dead.

He told the boys of unbelievable sad but true events that had transpired in the last years of the war. He did this so they would understand why they were sent away, and be glad that they had not witnessed such acts of shame. One such act still brought tears of disbelief to Anna's eyes.

They told the boys about Wilhelm Faust and Fritz' betrayal. Friedrich and Max disliked the youth, but couldn't believe he had fallen for the Nazi lies that placed Hitler before his own father.

Another family on the block was caught hiding Jews and executed just last year. Yet down the street, the Adelman's secret guests had recently been revealed. Amazingly the storekeepers had successfully hidden a family of three for two years. Finally Otto stopped talking. He hadn't meant to say so much.

Friedrich and Max were quiet as they helped Anna dry the dishes. Each time the boys thought the worst had happened, more evil betrayed the imagination.

***

After breakfast Liesl arrived with her surprise. Two little girls toddled in the door into Anna's waiting arms, bringing sunshine into the gloom. Laughing, Anna introduced the two-year-old twins as Sofie and Steffi, while Liesl beamed with pride. Blonde and blue eyed with Kurt's smile, they only seemed shy of their uncles for the first hour. Soon both little girls were squealing with delight as Friedrich and Max bounced them on their knees or gave them rides on their backs. When the tiny girls had their nap the family talked on into the afternoon.

The boys had many questions about what happened in the city. They learned that the Americans had advanced almost to Neuss in February. By early March the Oberkassel Bridge was destroyed. German barricades and tank blockades were placed on certain Düsseldorf roads to impede the American advance. Iron girders, rubble and the ruined shells of vehicles and tramcars formed the blockades. On March 8th, the Rheinbahn's services stopped completely.

As American troops fired artillery from the left bank they ordered low flying air raids on the right hand side of the Rhine in Düsseldorf, where a tired and failing resistance held out. Gas, electricity and water were withheld making the possibility of epidemic very real for citizens who still remained in the city. Looting of public warehouses ensued. Finally, the Nazis surrendered three weeks later. At the end, over ten thousand Düsseldorf citizens had perished at the front or in air raids.

Almost afraid to ask about Kurt, Max broached the subject carefully. Liesl looked down and then sighed. When the Nazi government fell apart most of its principal players fled. A few diehard loyalists committed suicide like their leader, while others like Kurt waited for a reckoning to come. Kurt had come home and spent a few days waiting for his arrest, spending time with his little girls and cherishing the short days with his wife. When that day arrived Liesl wept bitterly. She had already shed many tears for the long separation that was inevitable. Kurt was not one of the brutal leaders that killed wantonly as others had. It wasn't fair that he had to go. She only hoped that the truth would come to light. He was to be imprisoned until a War Crimes Tribunal was scheduled, and that could take many months.

Max had often wondered why he and Friedrich weren't summoned as other Hitler Jugend boys who were pressed into action by the Wehrmacht in the last months of the war. When he thought about it, neither were Dieter and other boys of conscription age in Obbach. He and Friedrich now knew that Kurt was the reason behind the 'lost' orders for that village. In fact, once Kurt had learned accidentally about Max's whereabouts the night of the questioning, he'd made sure that he kept watch over the events near Obbach, ready to transport the boys out if danger came too close. Max was amazed by the provision of his brother-in-law, a man full of surprises.

Now the best news was that Liesl was to move in with Anna and Otto, which would be more affordable while Kurt was in prison. She had given up her flat and was moving in on the coming weekend. Max was ecstatic. After so long apart they would all be together again. Friedrich was happy, but subdued. Anna noticed the change in him and worried about him. She supposed it was just the effects of the war and hoped it would fade in his memory.

***

The next Saturday, Liesl moved in to the third bedroom upstairs. The boys gave the little twins their room, and moved up to the attic room. It was nothing new for Max and the window actually afforded a panoramic view of Düsseldorf. Sadly it was not the view it once was.

Max walked about the attic room touching familiar things and remembering another attic room far away. He wondered if the Brauers missed him yet. Would Dieter forget him? He couldn't think of them all without a lump forming in his throat. Confused, he felt guilty that he was betraying his own parents somehow as he pined for people that once had been strangers to him. Sometimes life's events made odd things happen to your mind, he mused.

He regretted that his little hedgehog had not survived his absence, but his old friend Heinz remained, still welcoming him with constant tail wagging. Older now with white whiskers intruding on his brows, his faithful friend looked up at him with a patient wisdom. He still slept beneath Max's bed, as if the passage of time had halted. Max closed his eyes and sank into a pleasant oblivion; it was almost as if the past three years were a bittersweet dream. Well, he'd have to live with that. He hoped Friedrich could too.

Chapter Thirty-One

Regrowth

***

As the year melted into the next, the family like all Germans struggled to survive in a different Germany. Occupied by foreign armies and overrun with millions of refugees from the east, Germans waited for the economy to improve and change to come. Its former enemies had divided Germany into four occupation zones under the U.S., Britain, France and Soviet Union.

The United States Congress approved the Foreign Assistance Act, arranging for aid that began to flow into impoverished economies in Western Europe. Destroyed cities, industries, and infrastructure were rapidly rebuilt as economies began to recover. Now repairs and rubble removal was a priority as the city struggled to return to normalcy like other cities in Europe. Importantly, the depots had to be re-built so operations could commence again. Burned out trams and building rubble blocked tram tracks and access roads. Crews were formed to do the work that could only be done by hand.

Initially the process was difficult and the laborers' malnutrition further hindered the process. About a fifth of these workers were former prisoners of war. To aid in the health of its employees, the Rheinbahn organized food for the stews made at the canteens and proved to be just what was needed.

Daily the boys busied themselves with helping Otto tend and watch over the little garden in the yard. It was raided several times by hungry drifters made bold by suffering malnutrition, and just keeping food on the table was an important priority. The piece of land Otto formerly purchased for their garden and chicken coop had been destroyed just a month before the surrender when an Allied bomb found it.

Fortunately Anna had some Styrian hen chicks she was keeping under a warm lamp in the house at the time the adult laying hens were destroyed. Realizing it may happen one day, she did not want all her eggs in one basket, so to speak, and decided to have a backup plan. It proved wise. Those three chickens grew and resided in a miniature coop in the back porch, their existence hidden from all but family members. Black market trading continued throughout the year and on into 1946.

Otto saw potential for his damaged garden plot. One day he visited the city municipal office to see a planning and building official to obtain a building permit. Friends told him it would be a wasted trip. Permits simply weren't handed out anymore, and few could afford to build privately in these tough times of reconstruction anyway. Otto smiled as he tucked a certain bundle in the car. He knew a little persuasion went a long way in these times of shortages. His gift was a success. The basket of eggs impressed the official who accepted the hard to obtain treat and was more than happy to provide what Otto needed. He returned home with the required permit. Soon Otto would be ready to build a house on the lot. It turned out to be a wise move.

***

Much awaited yet dreaded news arrived one day for Liesl. It was official notice that Kurt's trial was to take place at last. He had been in prison for almost a year and a half. Anna prayed and Liesl wept, and the family waited anxiously as Kurt's fate hung in the balance. Liesl hoped justice would be done now for Kurt did not deserve the same punishment for war crimes others had committed. Kurt was a good man! She held on to her belief that all would be righted.

Otto followed the trial as best he could, following daily transcripts in the newspaper. As damning evidence was presented they at first feared for Kurt. The prosecution brought in witnesses from Kurt's own subordinates, men who feared or hated him. For several days of the trial his future did not seem hopeful. Then, the tide turned as the defense uncovered not only testimonials, but also actual witnesses who had read about the trial and come forward. They had seemingly come out of the woodwork to testify on Kurt's behalf.

Otto and Anna were pleased but not too surprised to learn of examples of their son-in-law's humanitarian efforts to save not only Jewish prisoners, but also wrongly imprisoned captives. Ever mounting paperwork errors and overlooked transfers came to light as the once condemning tide turned in Kurt's favor. However, the ironic piece of evidence that would turn the jury and free Kurt was a letter presented on the tenth day of the trial.

Found in the files seized from SS offices within the Berlin based Nazi High Command, the document appeared to be written by a paid informer. Penned in 1943, the letter claimed that Herr Sturmbannfuhrer Kurt Schwartzkopf had been the investigator in the case of a doctor and some children that were certainly helping Jews to escape. She cited a poorly conducted interrogation and refusal to consider evidence or investigate her allegations. Signed by a Frau Hilda Metzger from the village of Obbach, the letter was undoubtedly meant to cause a very different outcome. In view of overwhelming evidence in his favor, the case against Kurt was at last, dismissed.

Freedom gained, Kurt returned to live with Liesl's family until he could find a new livelihood and other accommodations for his family. Being an officer of the Reich for so long and imprisoned since the fall of the empire, he was somewhat at a loss to know what to do with his new life.

The first year home, Kurt joined Otto in re-building projects helping out with restoration cleanup that was happening all around them. The family pulled together a new life out of the old, and time moved on. Yet the war left its mark on everyone, and certainly on Kurt as well. His time in prison had changed him, making him more withdrawn. Liesl sometimes worried about the new quiet, introspective soul that replaced the old Kurt.

Transformation happened daily, the new Germany emerging from its cocoon of destruction. The former war economy had made an oversupply of currency unmatched by its supply of goods. So in mid 1948 the deutsche mark was introduced to replace the Reich mark and controls were lifted by the Western powers over prices and basic supplies. This abruptly ended the black market but a new problem arose in Germany's Soviet-held zone.

The currency reform catching them by surprise, Soviet authorities hurriedly introduced their own currency for the Soviet zone and all of Berlin. It was too late. Deutsche marks were already distributed throughout their sectors of the city. Perceived as Western interference to undermine their agenda for a socialist society there, the response was sudden and dramatic, the Soviet blockade of Berlin. Sending troops to block roads and railways to West Berlin, they cut off electric power and halted river shipping and the delivery of fresh food.

The three Western powers reacted promptly, organizing massive airlifts supplying two and a half million people in Berlin's western sectors with necessities. This action kept the citizens alive for nearly a year. Failing to starve the Western Allies out of Berlin, the Soviet Union lifted the blockade in May of 1949, but the effects on that city were lasting. Unable to create a socialist Germany, the Soviet Union created its own municipal administration making Berlin a divided city.

Once more Otto knew they had witnessed history in the making. He sighed, contemplating the changes of the past decade. Never more grateful that his family was not in Berlin, he remembered he had once considered moving them from Düsseldorf before the war. He thought too about the fact that so many had lost at least part of their families. His own had come through the onslaught unscathed. Maybe Anna was right. It was quite possible that her God was watching out for them.

Chapter Thirty-Two

Movies, Girls & Dreams

***

The post war years slowly brought new optimism. No one wanted to dwell on the past, especially Germans who now looked forward to forgetting. If guilt for their indifference toward their Jewish brothers weighed on them, it didn't show. Those who had actively attacked or persecuted Jews had somehow slunk off into the shadows, defected to warmer climates or were dead. No one now wanted to claim responsibility for the horror. Three years into the restoration bombed out shells of businesses and churches were slowly disappearing, as were other visible reminders of war, and the country worked hard to return to prosperity. Those who wished so could pretend it wasn't so bad, but others remained affected for a lifetime, the hidden scars went too deep.

During this time that their sons had been home again, Anna was the happiest she had been in years. Her cup of joy was full. But Otto and Anna had missed the best years of the boys' lives and could never have that back again. Both parents now tried to make up for lost time and spoiled the boys as much as they could, as if to atone for their absence. Every day Anna saw time slipping away and she wished she could turn it back.

When either son asked to earn a little money for the show, or to buy something, more often than not they would be handed it. The boys were rarely asked to earn it, and no expectation of repayment was requested. Otto only wished he could give them more.

Hollywood movies were the rage with Max. From age fifteen he was found every Saturday at the local theatre house with one or two of his friends, or the latest in a string of girls who flirted with him. Max still held onto his plan to see America one day, and the movie pictures fueled his dreams further, as he imagined himself as any of the heroes portrayed on the screen. He didn't know how, but he was going to do it one day and soon. Errol Flynn, Tom Mix, Lawrence Olivier: all had a hand in selling Maximilian further on the idea.

Max especially watched the background scenery in these movies. He wanted to grasp what America was like and it excited him to think one day he would live there. He also loved the movies for how they portrayed such strong heroes. He decided the Americans' patriotism at least rivaled that of Germans. Only these heroes on the silver screen were filled with compassion, integrity and honesty. How different, he thought, from the promises their homegrown hero Herr Hitler had been. He thought bitterly sometimes, how his father and others like Kurt once had such high hopes for Germany and faithfully upheld their leader, until their hopes were cruelly dashed. Now Germans were hated and surely must be a laughingstock to the world once more.

By their mid-teens, Friedrich and Max had grown into handsome young men. Their thin frames were the only remaining evidence of food deprivation. Coy young women often flirted with the youths. However, Max seemed to get more than his share of the attention. This bothered Friedrich a lot. The result was a renewed sibling rivalry that often comes of jealousy. Friedrich had not dealt with his past.

Several things bothered Friedrich. He had always been the type to carry grudges, and had closely judged favoritism, real or perceived, that he held against his parents. He still remembered how they had fawned over his sick little brother and ignored him as a child. He couldn't forgive them for that, still. Or how he got more than his share of strappings if the boys got into trouble, because he was the oldest and should know better. He also fought with the damnable resurfacing memory of the Nazi youth he killed with a rock. All this made Friedrich a tortured and guilt-ridden young man.

When poison rots the soul at the roots, the fruit of it can only be tainted. Girls found Friedrich attractive enough, until he opened his mouth. He came across as vain and bitter, and his speech always carried the sharp edge of sarcasm. When compared with the gentle and easy-going manner of his brother Maximilian, the contrast was obvious, and Friedrich was left behind.

Anna noticed this disturbing change in Friedrich, even more than Otto who said it was a phase that would pass. She was helpless to stop it though, as Friedrich pushed her attempts to reach him aside. She could only pray that time would teach him things.

When Max finished school, Friedrich had already been apprenticing with Herr Mueller the goldsmith for over a year. Otto thought Max should try the same vocation. Max agreed, and was taken on as well. However, even though Max was creative and could design well, his mind and talents were elsewhere. After two months, Herr Mueller suggested that Max look for another career. Otto was upset at first, but then realized his sons were very different. While Friedrich was studious and task-oriented, Max was friendly and out-going by nature, and Otto realized, a born salesman. Who would have thought it? Otto mused, when the child was so shy as a toddler.

Maximilian tried different odd jobs during that first year until he found his niche. Always curious about machines, his tastes had turned from airplanes to motorcycles around his seventeenth year, since he couldn't afford to fly except along the road. Max wandered one day into a Bayrische Motoren Werke motorcycle shop that opened up a local dealership in the fall of 1949. A new postwar factory in Munich had begun producing the machines again for the adoring public. Often equipped with sidecars they were more affordable than automobiles, making them the transportation of choice for many households.

Max struck up a conversation with the proprietor. A kinship formed quickly as the man saw in Max a younger version of himself. Quick to learn and not afraid to get his hands dirty, Max was soon taken on as an apprentice bike mechanic. Max's enthusiasm and growing knowledge of the motorbikes' engines soon brought in other interested young men. Max was directly responsible for selling so many walk-in customers on the machines that soon his boss decided to pay Max for the favor. And so his sales career began. During the year with BMW, Max matured and finally learned to save. He knew he had to have money to carry out his plans. However, he was distracted by his desire to have a motorcycle himself, and decided this was something he wanted first.

By age nineteen, Max could afford his own bike. He grinned with satisfaction as he climbed on the sleek machine and started the engine, feeling the power vibrate beneath him. One dream fulfilled! He waved to his boss Heinrich and gunned the engine, pulling onto the street. Riding home, his elation was matched by the wind in his hair, the feeling of freedom for the first time in years, and pride in this accomplishment. Maximilian sped home to show Otto and Anna the new purchase.

"See Papa! " Max began, showing off the new toy, " It's a BMW 250-

cc single cylinder R24 model with a four-stroke engine and shaft-drive rather than chain-drive. The frame is of press-steel design giving it stability and making it lighter!"

Otto smiled and nodded his approval. It was good to see Maximilian excited about something again. Pride swelled up in his heart for his good boy. Max had not even asked to borrow a single mark to buy the cycle. As Otto watched his son talk, he thought that his sons had received the best from both sides of his and Anna's heritages. They were tall, both over six feet, like Anna's brothers. But the adventuresome nature and natural sales ability were from him. He only hoped his sons would be good men as well. He didn't worry about that however, Anna had been a good teacher and he also felt he taught them about the virtues of integrity and honesty, kindness and compassion. Now they were grown. Ah, it had happened too fast…

His mind elsewhere, Otto was suddenly brought back to the present by Max, who was excited about an upcoming race. "Papa, would you like to come?" Max was inquiring, grinning ear to ear.

"Sorry, son?" Otto was surprised that he was getting as soft-hearted as Anna, lately reminiscing a lot.

Max tried again. "Will you come with me to the side-car races? Klaus Enders will be racing the BMW RS Boxer. That model has side-shaft control and two overhead camshafts per cylinder. He's already won several World Championships in the last four years!

"Yes, of course son, if I can." Otto laughed. The father and son talked on as they basked in the afternoon sun, cherishing this casual conversation, the optimism of the moment, and the bonding that comes with shared pleasure. Anna came out to exclaim over the motorbike and Otto watched as Max took his mother for a spin up the block and back again. Then two girls strolling by found a reason to get that handsome Max to talk to them as they gushed over his new purchase. Of course they held tightly to him as well when at first one then the other were given rides on the new bike.

Friedrich watched from behind the sheered curtain in the window above. He did not rush out to congratulate Max, but let bitterness wash over him as he beheld the easy way Max talked to girls. Max seemed not to notice how the females worshipped him. Friedrich on the other hand, had girl troubles of his own, and hated Max's casual handling of the female sex that made them want him even more.

If Friedrich was not constantly comparing himself to Max, he could have seen he had a lot to offer, and was only making himself miserable. He hated that his 'little' brother had reached six feet four inches already, and Friedrich had stopped growing at six-one. Max was a better artist. Though it secretly delighted Friedrich when Herr Mueller had dismissed Max for lateness, daydreaming and lack of concentration, he had seen that Max could design more beautiful jewelry than he could. Constantly perceiving Max's talents as superior irked Friedrich immensely.

Two days later, Friedrich arrived home with his own purchase, a 500 cc version of Max's bike. Bigger and better, Friedrich swelled with pride as the family congratulated him as well. Unfortunately Friedrich was impetuous in every area of his rivalry, and in buying a bigger machine he didn't consider the need for caution or learning how to handle it properly. He challenged Max to a street race when he was out of his parents' earshot. Otto and Anna would not have approved.

Max knew that Friedrich's bike was faster and more powerful, but it was with desired camaraderie he accepted his brother's challenge. Thinking that Friedrich joined in his own passion for riding and a desire to spend time together, it never occurred to Max that the motive was much different.

Chapter Thirty-Three

Redemption

***

After supper the young men excused themselves, citing a rendezvous with friends. Otto and Anna smiled to see their sons go off on their bikes together. Reaching the top of the next street, the brothers had agreed to see who could get to the bottom intersection first. It was the least busy time of day since most people were either having supper or in for the evening, so traffic wouldn't be much of a problem. Friedrich had asked his friend Wolfgang to watch for cross-traffic at the bottom of the slight hill, and signal them when it was clear. Another pal, Mateas was to drop the flag to signal the start. These friends had spread the word to others and now a small crowd of young people had gathered, ready to cheer on their favorite brother.

It was a typical, lovely summer evening and Friedrich looked around. He saw the girl he had been trying to get to know, the lovely Ingrid. And Sylvana was here too! One or the other would be his when he won this race. He was sure of it. He glanced at Max who was talking to Hans. Friedrich almost felt sorry for Max. For once it would be he, not Max coming out on top of something.

Friedrich smiled. This was going to be great! With his superior ride he would easily beat Max and be the hero of the hour! The brothers turned their bikes around, lining them up at the crosswalk on the rise of the hill. Revving their engines loudly to the delight of the excited crowd, they waited for the signal.

The traffic at the bottom of the hill delayed the onset of the race, but it made time for a brief contest to see who could rev their engine the loudest and longest. At home half a block away, Otto and Anna could hear the loud engines through the open window and due to the decreased traffic noise. They looked at each other and came to the same conclusion together. Jumping up, Anna pulled on her sweater as Otto followed her out the door. Cutting through the baker's yard, they took a short-cut toward the raucous that could only mean one thing.

Upon Wolfgang's all-clear, Mateas lowered the flag and jumped aside. Max had more experience with his bike, so initially shot off the start first, leaving Friedrich behind. But Friedrich's powerful bike caught up in seconds and the two raced neck in neck. Almost in unison it was beautiful to watch, until mere moments later the unthinkable happened.

Pressing his advantage, Friedrich gunned the motor and changed gears. But the torque was too much for him, causing him to lurch ahead and lose his balance. Later, no one could agree if it was only this or the uneven cobblestones or inexperience that sent Friedrich flying into Max's path, causing the bikes to collide.

Otto and Anna were puffing as they ran. Emerging from the bakery's side path onto the street, they saw the accident as it happened. Fear now transformed it into slow motion. Anna almost fainted as she denied the horror she beheld. Friedrich flew up in the air off the bike that crashed loudly into a storefront. Landing headfirst on the street, his body lay still atop a manhole cover. Max also came off his bike, but rolled, scraping his limbs and his head. Horrified, Anna could see he took the brunt of the skidding on his face. Her scream joined the chorus of others who witnessed the accident.

Rushing to their sons, it was hard to know where to look first. Otto ran to his first-born, while Anna fell upon Max and cradled his head in her lap. The wild crowd of teens had come running, some entering stores to get them to call for help.

Otto feared Friedrich was dead. He knew Friedrich was badly hurt, but was relieved when he saw his chest rise and fall, ever so slightly. It seemed an eternity before the ambulances arrived. Anna would go to the hospital with her sons, but Otto, having a cool head in a crisis, would stay and meet with the police who arrived soon after. Some of the youth also stayed to retell their version of what they witnessed. Otto directed Friedrich's friends to get the bikes. Mateas Buhler nodded. He and Wolfgang would walk the bikes home. Friedrich's motorcycle was pretty wrecked, having gone into the storefront, but Max's bike appeared only a little scraped on one side. There would be damages to pay for, but for now Otto was only interested in getting to the hospital to his boys.

His heart was heavy as he drove to the hospital. And for the first time since he had stood in the trenches of the first war, Otto prayed fervently. Although he attended mass with his family, he had not felt close to God for many years. Not sure God would hear him for ignoring Him for so long, he wept out of a desperate heart. He basically pled with God for his sons' lives, trying to bargain with his own soul. Arriving, Otto rushed toward Anna and they waited for news together, praying as one for the first time in their married life.

Friedrich was alive, however just barely. The trauma to his head was the worst injury and he also sustained some broken bones. As the doctor sat with the upset parents he gently tried to cushion the news given the extent of the head injury. Friedrich was in a coma and they would do what they could, but it was a situation of 'wait and see' now.

The news about Max was better. Even though Anna had seen he was scraped up pretty badly and his right cheek looked like raw meat, the doctor assured them those were surface wounds. Max was being treated and would be released in the morning if there were no other complications.

When the doctor left, Otto and Anna went and spoke to Max first, comforting him as best they could. He apologized repeatedly, almost in tears with remorse. Gauze was wrapped around his head to hold the facial bandages and one eye was turning black. As the nurse finished up her duties with a tetanus shot to Max's arm, Anna tried to quiet him. Otto told him it wasn't his fault and not to worry. There was no need to scold. Otto felt the boys had received the worst possible punishment for their foolishness already.

Anna sobbed when she saw Friedrich however. His head was bandaged and both eyes had already turned black. Bloodstains from his ears and nose indicated the trauma the doctor had revealed to them. Tubes were everywhere and helping him breathe. An IV connected his arm to the drip bag. He was deathly pale. Otto wished he could trade places with Friedrich and save him from this. An arm and one leg were in casts, but these were the 'minor' injuries.

Despite surviving two wars and his own brush with death, Otto experienced helplessness and real fear only twice, both times when his sons were in danger.

***

Many days of vigil saw Anna and Otto watching worriedly over Friedrich. Max too took his turn at the bedside, his guilt in his participation of this outcome almost too much. Another daily reminder was his own painful skin that tingled as it healed and the drying scabs that drove him crazy.

The family watched as Friedrich's head became swollen and he no longer resembled himself. The weeks then became a month as they prayed for his recovery. Yet day after day there was no change.

One day Max was sitting with the sleeping patient when Anna and Otto went to get a quick meal. Max believed in God, but had never prayed so much in his life until the accident. Now, as he again asked God for his brother's healing, he was holding Friedrich's hand. He almost jumped as Friedrich's hand twitched. Raising his bowed head, he stared at his brother for any sign of life. Moments later Friedrich opened his eyes, at last. Max couldn't believe it!

Squeezing his hand, Max spoke his name, but Friedrich just stared at first, slowly awaking as from a long dream. Max ran to get a nurse and soon the doctor, nurse and residents were scurrying around the awakened patient. Anna and Otto came in soon after and couldn't believe their eyes. Over the next couple of days, Friedrich became more aware, and it was soon felt he was out of the woods and on the way to recovery. Elated, the family prepared to bring him home. But, there would be many more weeks before he would be able to walk or work again.

For Friedrich's part, he could not remember the race, and barely remembered the bike. Much later when he saw it at last, having limped out to the shed, he turned his back on the bent frame and broken spokes. He knew he would never ride again. The accident left him with permanent hearing damage in his left ear. The aching pain in his leg was nagging mockery to the pride he once carried. He felt humbled now and glad to be alive. Months of recovery had changed him.

Having finally won the attention he craved by being constantly waited on by every member of the family, he at last realized it was preferable to be whole and it was no treat being the sick one. He finally understood his parents' devotion when it was Max who was ill, so long ago. He wondered then how he could have been so stupid. His envious heart was redeemed. He guessed that some lessons were just learned the hard way.

Chapter Thirty-Four

A Revelation

***

The boom of 1950 had begun in West Germany. During this year Otto built a small house on the former garden lot and Kurt and Liesl moved into it with the twins who were just starting school. Friedrich was mending nicely and the markets were filled with ample food and consumer goods once again. The economy hadn't been this good since Hitler first came to power. Five years after the war things were looking up at last, and life was pretty wonderful for everyone, including a young man with ambition. Max almost gave up his childhood dream to go to America. Almost. But his dream called to him, as if fate would not be put off by procrastination. Over the next year, Max explored the options available for emigration to the United States. He wanted to save a bit more before he left.

By 1952 Max also had a steady girlfriend by the name of Petra Schlamp. A pretty girl with dark hair and high cheekbones, she reminded Max of Rita Hayworth, the Hollywood sex goddess. He did feel pretty lucky that Petra wanted him. She also was a fabulous cook and her mother fawned over him and knitted him sweaters. He felt that he probably could be happy marrying her, if he chose that path.

But Petra and her mother had not bargained for a man with a lifetime of dreams. Max had been researching entry into the United States and had visited the American Consulate twice. Frustrated, he was getting nowhere. It wasn't just all the forms to fill out and red tape to get through, but there were quotas to deal with and inoculations and restrictions.

Max kept all this from his family, and especially his mother. He felt that if it didn't happen, he would have worried her for nothing. And if, no— when, it did...well, he'd cross that bridge when he came to it. The latest bad news was that the United States had filled its allowable quotas of immigrants for this year. That meant that Max would have to wait almost a year to re-apply again.

As he returned home, he pulled his motorcycle up to the back lane and removed his helmet. Ever since the accident he had taken to wearing one. He had almost lost his brother from a head injury. He was thoughtful as he strolled into the house. What could he do? He didn't want to wait another year. At twenty, the whole world yawned before him and he was itching for adventure. The other problem was a beautiful girl who was hinting constantly at marriage. Although he was fond of her, he knew he wasn't in love, yet. He refused to be pushed into a domestic life that he wasn't ready for.

Maximilian Thielmann knew what he did want. He wanted new experiences. He wanted to go where the planes had come from. He wanted to see the ocean and the ships. He often pored over pictures of flat-topped mountains, and arid deserts that covered the southwestern states. He wanted to meet cowboys and Indians, even if they lived on reserves now. He bought travel books that showed him the Rocky Mountains and waterfalls with streams, and plants that were unknown to him. He wanted to see their quaint lighthouses on the eastern cliffs. All this and more was what Max wanted. It was even more than a desire. Some might call it fate, so strong was the pull on Max's mind and heart.

He entered the house. His mother turned from her stirring with a huge smile. "I made your favorite, wiener schnitzel and sauerkraut," she beamed. "There is rhubarb kuchen and cream for dessert." Max kissed her on the forehead, which was now below him, he'd grown so tall. He was going to miss her cooking. He often wondered if she sensed his restlessness and was using food to keep him near her.

Friedrich entered the room with a slight limp. He was much better than last year, and often joked now that he and Otto had matching limps. After the accident he thought his friends would think him a klutz for crashing his bike, but it had the opposite effect. The guys thought he was tough for surviving the accident, while girls clustered around to 'mother' him. He was quite happy, actually.

The nightmares had also disappeared for Friedrich. The weeks in a coma had cut off the repetitive thread of the dreams that tormented him. Gone was the face of the boy soldier he had killed. The deed seemed long ago now, and someone else's lifetime. Like the movies he watched, it belonged to another character.

Friedrich now eyed Max as he washed up for supper. Max kept his head down and seemed deep in thought. Friedrich knew something was up with him.

The family sat down to dinner when Otto came in. Friedrich couldn't wait to pick Max's mind. His younger brother always seemed preoccupied lately. "So," Friedrich began, handing Max the schnitzel, "Where were you today? Mateas and I waited for you at the cafe, you never showed up for lunch."

Max helped himself to the sausages and cut them up before answering. He did not want to let the cat out of the bag, so to speak, for Friedrich as always would run with the topic, distressing Anna. "Oh, I was busy at the library. Then I ran into Petra and we went shopping."

Anna asked Max what he was reading lately. Max had to think quickly. "Oh, the usual. Bike manuals mostly, some adventure." He did not want to say 'travel' but Friedrich was on top of it.

"You had some travel books too, I think," offered Friedrich. Max wondered how he knew that, but didn't have time to ask. "I ran into Petra too when you left, and she said you forgot one in her basket." Friedrich offered.

"Still interested in going abroad some day, Max?" his father asked between bites of sauerkraut. He drank his beer and burped with satisfaction.

Max nodded but kept eating. He didn't dare look at Anna. She had first learned of his desire to cross the ocean when he had shared with her shortly after their return from Obbach. In his youthful exuberance, he had not considered that his mother would not be overjoyed at the prospect of losing him again.

Anna had hoped Max's plans at age fourteen were different than what he wanted now. As she watched his face, her heart sank. He obviously was still very interested in pursuing this. "Max, if you want to travel some day, that would be wonderful," she ventured, "but have a wife and family first. You could travel with Petra, yes?" she asked hopefully.

"No. I'm not going anywhere with Petra, Mama." Max said while chewing faster, hoping to leave the table before arguments began. He hated having to persuade everyone that this was right for him.

"But, she is such a nice girl. Her parents are quite fond of you." Anna interjected.

"I'm not going to marry Petra. I want to go to America!" he blurted, wiping his mouth and rising from the table. Otto reached out and touched his arm, motioning to the chair.

"Please son, sit. Let's just think this through. If you go now, how will you live there? You don't speak the language, and I hear that English is very hard to learn. Why don't you take some courses first, and wait…" Otto started on his usual discourse. Max had heard this all a year ago, when he had foolishly mentioned this aloud before.

Max pretended to listen but tuned out Otto while he tried to figure out how to tell them he would not change his mind. "I'm not doing anything wrong! I only want to see America. I love you all, but this is something I have to do!" he gestured as he spoke with the conviction of one who is absolutely convinced. "Can't you let me alone? I am sure I will return if I don't like it."

Anna's face fell at that comment and she appeared as if she were going to cry. She got up and cut the rhubarb cake, putting a dollop of whipped cream on each piece. "Th-that means you won't return if you do?" she finally asked.

Max felt like a traitor. He got up and went to his mother. "Mama, I don't know. I hope to, I want to, but I don't know." No one knew what to say then. Friedrich ate his dessert with fervor as usual, Otto just sat with his hands folded, lost in thought. Max had lost his appetite and felt like a heel. He left and went to his room, his mother looking after him so sadly.

Max lay back on his bed and thought about his life. He had been through so much. They all had. He had tucked away the worst memories forever he hoped, the good ones he held onto. He had such a great supportive family. Was he an ungrateful son to leave his folks now? His mother was already sixty-two. He argued with himself in his thoughts. Oma Bauman was eighty-six and still going strong. Surely his mother would live as long as her own mother. And if he waited till then, he could be middle aged before his parents were gone!

His mind retraced the war years and then skipped to Obbach. He thought of his good friend Dieter and what they experienced together. He wondered how he was. Then he remembered Adam. He would have loved to be a bird and followed Adam that day. Did he escape? Was he even now at home in Canada with his family? He would love to visit him and see. Canada. The thought came as a revelation. He had not even considered this yet.

Max sat bolt upright. He could wait to join next year's U.S. immigration quota and keep arguing with his family, or he could check on Canada's immigration policies! Perhaps he could leave even now! This brought new possibilities to mind. With Canada as a new option, Max grew excited. He could always go to the States from Canada later!

The next morning he left early, there was a lot to check out. Taking the steps two at a time, he headed out the door. His optimism directly contrasted to Anna's apprehension as she heard the back door slam. Watching from her bedroom window she realized that for her, the apron strings were difficult to sever.

Chapter Thirty-Five

Deception

***

Petra waited for Maximilian by the fountain in the Hofgarten. She had worn her best dress for him, and eyed her reflection in a nearby shop window more than once. She liked what she saw and hoped Max would too. She checked her watch. He was fourteen minutes late. What could be holding him so long? Her frustration was at least pacified by appreciative glances from passing males, and she wondered why she gave Max so many chances. Other men would give their eyeteeth to be with her. Especially one other young man she knew.

Just as a troubled pout was forming on her pretty mouth, Max arrived. He was out of breath, but grinning with that perfect smile of straight white teeth, and her heart melted so that she couldn't scold him. Max told her they had a bit of a ride ahead and handed her a helmet. She climbed on the back of his motorcycle but said she hated to wear the sweaty headgear. It mussed up her hairdo. He refused to move until she put it on however, and he kissed her lightly on the lips for being a good girl when she did.

Soon they were off, breezing along the highway. Max hadn't told Petra where they were going, so she was delightfully surprised when they pulled into the nearby port city of Duisburg. First stop was the zoo and they bought peanuts for the elephants, a favorite attraction Petra loved. Strolling and laughing together on this spring day, observers would smile at the couple they assumed was in love. Max had asked Petra to spend this particular Saturday together for he had something to show her. The day continued well, with lunch at one of the outdoor cafés next to the waterfront.

Petra was getting increasingly excited. Max was so much fun and loved to laugh. Surely this might be the day she had been waiting for? But as lunch was ending, Max still hadn't asked her. When he suggested they rent a small boat at the harbor and take a small ride down the Rhine, she thought, how romantic! She just knew this had to be the opportunity he was waiting for. So distracted was she with her own desires, she had hardly heard a word Max was saying, nor did she realize what he was hinting at all day.

She stepped into the boat and Max manned the oars as they pulled out onto the sparkling afternoon water. Keeping near to the shore and out of the way of steamers and workboats, they headed toward the waterfront park upstream. Max was talking again, she thought absently, about travel. Petra had always known Max wanted to travel someday, but yawned and daydreamed when he went off on a discourse about his desires. She just knew she could change his mind once they were married, and he would soon give up that foolishness when he was a well-fed husband with his own children.

Max had been trying to prepare Petra all day. First he had talked about movies he'd seen last week when they were feeding the elephants. Then at lunch he spoke about the research he'd done on Canada, and what opportunities there were there. He even pulled a map out of his pocket and showed her the country of Canada, pointing out places of interest. She only thinly veiled her disinterest.

All day Petra repeatedly changed the subject, pointing out gowns in a wedding shop, or cooing over babies that mothers had tucked cutely into carriages. Once he asked her if she ever wanted to see other places and she looked at him blankly. "Why? Everything we need is here," she had answered.

Max thought a lot the night before about what he wanted. He liked Petra immensely, and if he let himself, he might just fall for her. But Max had been holding back. He knew if she wasn't interested in the same future as he, he'd never be happy and end up resenting her hold on him. Maybe his mother was right. He should see if Petra wanted to be with him badly enough. After all he could go to Canada with a bride. The idea actually appealed to him now.

He set down the oars and they floated aimlessly in the shade of huge trees. Where the sunlight streamed through the branches, dapples of light danced on the water. It was a lovely spot, and the water was calm here. It lapped gently against the boat. Petra sensed something was coming and gave Max a dreamy smile. He tried again.

"Petra, I have been trying to ask you something all day," he began, noting the anticipation on her face. "I have this for you." With that he pulled a small velvet box out of his pocket. Hidden inside was a delicate silver necklace with a teardrop pearl pendant. He hoped it would represent the memorable day and a promise of things to come, but if not, he hoped it would suffice as a parting gift, a symbol of what she meant to him. He wasn't prepared for her reaction.

Petra squealed with delight as Max put it in her hand. As she opened the velvet box however, her face fell. The sparkling diamond engagement ring she anticipated was missing. While the necklace was lovely, it was nothing more than what her father would have given her at Christmas.

Her bubble of elation broken, she just stared at it. Then, recovering stupidly from silence, she stammered her thanks. It was obvious she was disappointed somehow.

Max broke the awkward silence by racing ahead with his thoughts. "You see Petra, I wanted to let you know I'm very fond of you, you know that. I wanted to ask you if you could see yourself living in Canada. If so, we'll have a wonderful life there! I-I need to know if you will come with me. I have been successful in getting my name on the immigration list. I leave in six weeks, as soon as I've passed the physical exam and my inoculations are finished. My papers are in order already, all I need is your answer!"

Petra never was good at hiding her feelings. Not the type to mask disappointment either, she promptly slapped the necklace box back in his hand. "Maximilian Thielmann, what am I supposed to do in Canada, of all places?" she spouted angrily. "My parents, family and friends are here and I would never leave them. What is this obsession of yours!? Don't you realize you are leaving everything behind that is dear to you? Wake up! I love you. But you cannot have me unless you give up this hair-brained scheme of yours!" Petra yelled, working herself into a horrid mood.

Max, not used to being scolded and just as stubborn, quietly put the necklace back in his pocket and turned the boat around. Thankfully it was downstream now, and easier going on the return trip. A cool wind had come up to match Petra's foul mood as the clouds drifted across the sun. It was not a pleasant trip back to the pier as Petra could not let her disdain drop and verbally battered Max until they stepped out of the boat.

Max did not defend his plans, nor try to change her mind. In fact, he was very glad he had planned this day. It was an eye opening experience and had revealed what his future life would be like if he married the girl.

He could see himself hen-pecked and cornered and miserable. Silently, they returned to Düsseldorf. Max drove a little too fast, silencing the terrified Petra as she held on tightly. But that was okay by Max. When he dropped her off she stomped into the house and he left. There was nothing more to say.

A week later, Max had not called Petra and she began to worry. She felt she was too hasty in condemning his plans, and somewhat embarrassed by her outburst. Her mother even scolded her for her lack of control. "After all, you will lose Max!" her mother admonished, as if there were still a chance to keep him. Petra had assumed that her threat would make Max lovesick with worry and he'd come running to her door in contrition, pleading for her hand in marriage. She knew now she had better do some damage control.

Petra thought all day about how she could win in this situation. And then a plot formed in her mind, and the more she thought about it, the more she smiled. Yes, yes, that would be the only thing that would keep Max from leaving! And she would have to plan it carefully.

Luck was on her side, Petra thought, since her friend Elsa just happened to be having a birthday party this coming weekend. She was hosting a hayride and pig roast on her parents' farm and the timing was perfect for Petra's purposes. All the old friends from their school days were invited and that included Max and Friedrich. To make sure Max showed up, she enlisted the help of his friend Mateas, stating she had a surprise for Max and not to let on that he knew. Mateas promised he would make sure Max came, thinking that he was helping love along.

The evening of the party was lovely and warm. Several carloads of young adults came. Several were already married, others were dating couples and several were unattached. Max, Friedrich, Mateas, two new guys and some of the girls were of the last category. Petra feigned gaiety and indifference, trying to make Max jealous or at least take notice when she flirted with one of the newcomers. He didn't take the bait.

The girl knew she'd have to employ the other strategy. She sidled up to Max as they filled their plates and a little too loudly confessed her terrible temper, and that she regretted their minor spat of the past week. Standing close enough to touch his elbow as she leaned in to take a helping, she appeared to others as if she were indeed very familiar and comfortable with Max. Unsure of what she was doing, Max moved away a little but did not spurn her advances. In his naiveté, he thought perhaps she had reconsidered.

"Oh Maximilian, I've been such a bad girl, haven't I honey?" she, purred, looking every inch the contrite one. Max turned a little red at that comment, but allowed her to follow him over when he sat down. He couldn't very well push her away or embarrass her at her friend's home. And Max had always believed in giving people a chance to apologize. She made sure she was as pleasant and sweet as she'd ever been, and Max foolishly relaxed. He wondered though why he suddenly felt like a fly caught in a web and Petra was the spider.

After the meal the moon was out and Herr Mannheim had pulled up the horses and hayrack. The guests piled on amid chatter and laughter. Petra shadowed Max as he climbed up on the bales, cuddling up as close as she could while complaining she was cold. The ride was fun and the guests sang songs and teased each other and pushed others off the rack. It was a memorable evening. After at the farmhouse they picked straw out of each other's hair and headed in to see Elsa open her gifts. Next the floor was cleared of chairs for the dance, but Petra had other plans.

Max had just finished a dance with one of the single girls and was about to get her a drink when Mateas came up to him with a note. It was from Petra. All it said was to meet her at the barn. Max considered this. He finally sighed and apologized to the girl and decided to see what Petra wanted. He knew she wasn't right for him when she had revealed her other side in the boat. But he wanted to let her know that it was over, so she would stop pursuing him. Ever the gentleman, at least in the barn he could let her down without embarrassing her in front of others.

At the barn, which was set back behind bushes and a tool shed, he found only one light on over the door. He opened it and peeked inside. "Petra?" he called out. He walked in and thought it was deserted. Only the sound of a horse moving in the stall was heard, and small things scurrying in the straw. He was about to leave, thinking she had returned to the house when she called his name.

"Up here, Max," came the soft reply. Max did not stop to think about why Petra would be in the loft but climbed the ladder wondering what she was doing up there. He would rue this decision. As he rose through the opening above, he found her sitting in the straw, almost reclining. Her hair was spread out framing her face, which was quite seductive in the glow of a single lantern. Her dress was pulled ever so slightly above her knees and to Max she looked for all the world like one of the movie posters of a sexy star. "Come here Max," she beckoned with her finger.

Warning bells went off in Max's head. "I-I think I'll stay right here", he said, sitting on a low three-legged stool. "What do you want Petra?"

"You, you silly man. I've missed you! Max, can't we start again and forget that nasty business last week?" she smiled coyly, batting her eyelids just a bit.

"Petra, it won't work," Max stately flatly. "We're too different and want different things."

"Don't you want to be married and have children, Max?" she asked innocently as she rose from the straw and moved slowly closer.

"Of course. Someday. But not now." Max replied. He wondered as she moved ever closer why he wasn't jumping down the ladder. She was pouting slightly and looked so sexy with her tousled hair. She came to him and kissed him with those red lips, leaving lipstick on his collar when he turned away as she knew he would. She turned his face toward her and pleaded with him.

"Please Max! I love you! I'll be a good wife, you'll see. Don't go, don't go Max," she kept on as she unbuttoned his shirt. She had counted on this spooking him and as he tried to pry her fingers gently off, she held on, tearing two buttons off. Max knew he was in trouble.

"Petra please, stop! Don't do this. You can find someone else. You're a beautiful girl." Max said while trying to get up. Petra leaned in catching him off balance, pushing Max backward off the stool, pulling his jacket off as he rolled away toward the loft opening. He was breathing heavy.

"Max we're meant to be together! And you are not going anywhere!" Petra accused. Max reached for his jacket but Petra was too fast, pulling it behind her back.

"Petra stop it! I'm going to Canada!" Max attempted to get his jacket and she fought him, catching him off balance. They both fell back into the hay. Her plan was working perfectly. It was then she gave him a funny look as if to say, "Gotcha!" and then she began to scream.

Max couldn't believe he'd been suckered. As he struggled to get up, Petra held on and ripped his shirt, pulling it out of his pants. Max wrenched free and jumped down, falling down part of the ladder. Petra kept up her screaming and if Max could have seen the humor in it, she sounded a lot like an opera singer hitting the high notes. As she had counted on, everyone within earshot came running just as a frantic Max ran out of the barn.

***

Chapter Thirty-Six

Deliverance

***

The scandal, as it was referred to that spring, was the talk of the neighborhood. Or at least to those who'd known Max since childhood. People quickly fell into two camps, those who believed Max was innocent and those who just knew he was guilty. It is times like these that show a person who their real friends are, Max thought.

Not that Petra ever came right out and said she was raped. The appearance of it was enough to accuse him. She simply should have won the best actress prize of the year for her performance that night. Max felt she was good enough for Hollywood. He still cringed as he remembered eleven pairs of eyes staring at him accusingly as the crying and disheveled Petra dragged herself from the barn. She had acted too upset to talk, just pointing at Max and shaking while covering her breasts beneath the torn blouse. He didn't remember it being torn when he ran from her, as he thought about it later.

Max had lived through terror, loss and danger, but felt this night was the worst of his life. First he had to be interrogated by the police, then face his parents as the allegations were laid out. Of course Otto and Anna believed his innocence because it did not in any way resemble the Max they knew or sound like truth. Max was only sorry that they had to bear the shame of the allegations for his sake. Friedrich knew Max was innocent but wondered why Petra would pull a stunt like that. For once in his life, he became his brother's champion and came to his defense. He didn't realize how very much Max needed and appreciated it.

***

A few days later, Max and his parents were requested by post to attend at the Schlamp household. Curious about the purpose of it, Otto, Anna and Max discussed the possibilities. They were also surprised that criminal charges had not yet been laid. Max suspected a trap, but since Petra's parents were requesting the meeting, it was felt the three of them should go.

Arriving at the Schlamp household, Frau Schlamp came to the door at their knock. She stiffly beckoned them into the parlor, taking their coats. It was not meant to be a friendly meeting, for there was no tea or cakes laid out. As they sat down, they were introduced to Herr Krueger, the attorney. Petra sat to one side, her parents on the divan with the lawyer. She smiled innocently and hopefully at Max. Another wonderful performance, Max thought. Yet he could not hate her, he found to his surprise that he only felt sorry for her.

The attorney cleared his throat and in a nasal drone revealed the purpose of the meeting. Basically the terms he was to present them stemmed from the premise that Max had dishonored and deflowered the victim, Petra, and now the following offer was on the table. Petra, it seemed, still loved Maximilian and if the young man wished to do the honorable thing and marry her there would be no charges laid. If Max refused, charges would be laid and he would be sued for loss of reputation (Petra's), which could result in incarceration and/or retribution, and if pregnancy resulted, child support.

252

So that was it! Max thought Petra merely wanted to embarrass him as payback for rejecting her. Now the full truth of her deviousness suddenly dawned on him. Petra was still trying to control him! The Schlamps and their stuffy lawyer were proposing what basically boiled down to a shotgun wedding. Max saw his future evaporate in his mind, and could not believe Petra would ruin his life like this. He had never contemplated murder until now. Too bad, he thought, that it wasn't in his nature to carry it out.

As the Schlamps waited for his answer, Petra looked demurely down at her hands folded in her lap, like the innocent she wished to portray. However, she did not know Otto very well and wasn't prepared for a battle with him. She'd been counting on Max to crumble and cede after being caught in the damning charade, but now she had his father to contend with.

Otto frowned at the young woman who sat wrapped cozily with a blanket across her lap, as if she had been ill. She purposely hadn't worn any makeup for this meeting, giving her a very young appearance. Far cry from the vixen who had left lipstick on Max's collar, Otto thought.

Otto directed his words to everyone, but looked directly at Petra, locking eyes with her so she couldn't turn away. " I would like to inquire as to whether the victim," Otto paused, emphasizing the last word, "has any proof of her allegations. Has a doctor examined her and verified her claim? There should be evidence of it before we continue." Otto said, staring at Petra with reigned-in hostility.

"Ah, um,..." the lawyer babbled, " that will come out in the...ah...later." He had not been prepared for questions of this nature. Petra's parents just stared at Otto as if he was the devil.

"Also, I have a few other questions," Otto went on, "I would like to know why the young lady was in the hay loft. Why couldn't she request a meeting with Max near the house? What respectable young lady would ask a man to meet her in a secluded area?" Max saw Petra gulp. "We have the note written by her hand and given to Mateas. We will be presenting it to our lawyer." Otto stated.

Max was awed by the cleverness of his father. He had told Otto about the note, but didn't know if he still even had it. How astute of his father to mention it as evidence placing doubts on Petra's character, even if it was a bluff. Petra looked as if she was truly going to be sick.

"Maximilian has also let it be known to many that he has alternate plans which do not include marriage to Petra or anyone else. I would like to know, if he was going to attack Petra in a fit of passion, why he would be so foolish as to ruin those very plans?" Otto finished. Standing up, Otto told them the meeting was over and his own lawyer would be contacting them to bring suit against Petra for defamation of Max's character and entrapment.

The Schlamps did not understand how it happened so suddenly. They were now on the defensive and it was Petra's character that was laid bare for suspicion. Otto, Max and Anna collected their coats as the Schlamps tried to argue, Petra started to cry, whether for real or not was anyone's guess; and the lawyer tried to calm everyone down.

On the drive home, Max felt a million times better. Though he was not out of trouble yet, the scheming Petra would now have some explaining of her own to do. Unless she was pregnant by someone else Max did not have the paternity angle to worry about, but the damage was already done to his character by innuendo alone. He wondered what he had ever seen in that girl and vowed to himself to be more careful when choosing a girlfriend in future.

Anna vowed to herself not to try and make decisions for Max anymore. She had thought Petra was a decent girl. She now would have loved to spank her for being the spoiled child she was. Otto looked grim but determined, his son would not get the worst of this if he had anything to do about it. Max was never so grateful that his parents had been there. His hero of the day of course was Otto. Max had always respected his father, but that respect had even grown in the last hour.

Chapter Thirty-Seven

Preparations

***

As the days flew by, the Thielmann household waited for the next shoe to drop, so to speak. Daily they expected Max to be served with a summons to court for Petra's allegations and be formally charged. While this weighed on the family and frustrated Otto, the other matter foremost in Anna's mind was the probable imminent departure of Max. He certainly seemed bent on fulfilling his adventure in spite of recent developments, and had gone ahead and applied for passage on a ship bound for Canada.

Anna busied herself mending Max's socks, purchasing clothing that he might need for colder weather for the trip. They all moved through motions preparing for a future that could soon take him away from them.

Otto had secured a lawyer as promised, but until charges were laid, he had instructed him to wait. Confident the girl's family would wisely drop the whole thing, he was sure they would realize that their daughter would be sullied by her own accusations. He'd wait and let them make the first move.

Max kept to his purpose, preparing to leave on his appointed date. As yet, without any charges, he wouldn't be required to remain in the country. He wished away the days, hoping the whole thing would go away before he left. Two weeks before the trip, Max obtained his vaccinations and traveling Visa.

Friedrich watched everyone in his family go through the motions, but wondered when this awkward reality would end. If Max was really leaving, why weren't they talking about it? Did everyone think Max would change his mind? Or did they think Petra would ruin his plans after all and the only place he was going was jail? It certainly looked like he was really leaving them.

Friedrich talked to Max about this altered future one night shortly after. While the city moon played gently with the water on the Rhine far below their window, it drew shadows on the walls of their room. It was a warm night and the brothers lay restless in their beds, both awake with private thoughts. Neither could sleep. Friedrich glanced over at Max. He had to know. Now that the Canada trip was scheduled so soon, he couldn't believe Max would actually go through with it.

"Max," Friedrich began, to see if his brother slept yet, "It's hot isn't it?"

"Yes, I'm not sleeping." Max replied tiredly.

"You're really doing it, aren't you?" Friedrich queried. "I mean the trip."

"Sure. What did you think?" came back the reply.

"Max, are you sure this is wise? " Friedrich went on, "You will be alone, really alone. You don't speak any English, don't know anyone there, have no job or people to help you out."

Afraid he'd actually be convinced to stay or talked out of it, Max grunted irritably. "Friedrich, honestly, I don't know some of those answers. All I know is that it's what I've wanted since I was a small boy."

"Why didn't you ask me to come?" Friedrich suddenly offered, unsure why as soon as he said it.

"I-I don't know. I guess I didn't think you wanted to. Do you want to? I mean, you could I guess if you want to." Max didn't know how to feel. He'd shared everything with Friedrich his whole life, almost every adventure included his brother. This dream however, was his. Yet Max realized it wouldn't be as lonely having at least one member of his family along.

"I can't now Max, but later, maybe. I have to finish my apprenticeship with Herr Mueller first." There was silence in the shadowy moonlit room for a moment, then Friedrich spoke again. "You know you're breaking Mama's heart, Max."

"I know." Max replied. He did feel terribly guilty. But he had known this would be so. He just had to put on a brave face and go ahead with it, or it would never happen. His father had tried to interest him in other opportunities in the past year, almost bribing him to stay, and introducing him to other craftsmen that Max could apprentice under. Each time, Max politely said no thank you, and made his plans. He had finally convinced them all that he planned to stay only a year or two, and then return. It would take that long to learn English, get established, repay the voyage fare to the Canadian government and really see what living there was like.

He knew Anna had wept many tears and Max found her staring at him often, always on the brink of crying. It unnerved him. He made sure he talked with her often, to get her used to the idea. He also began doing sweet things for her, as he had as a child, reminding himself that while his life of adventure was just beginning, hers involved losing something she treasured. Max showed her his maps, where the ship would dock in Halifax, and where he was being sent to live. He had requested Alberta, reading about the cowboys and ranches there. He assured her he would write often, and keep her informed, so she would feel she was right there with him.

The thing Max pushed most often from his mind was her age. She had been older when he was born, and she had always considered him her baby. Now she clung to him in the only ways she knew how as the days to departure grew nearer. She baked his favorite foods daily, lavishing attention on him that made him almost pity her. She looked haggard lately. Otto told her to go to the doctor, but she refused, saying she was only heartsick. They all hoped that was all it was.

***

Petra wiped her mouth on a towel and looked shakily into the mirror. She had been feeling so ill lately. She lay down on her bed and looked at the ceiling. A lot had transpired in the last month. Perhaps she was just upset by it all. Petra glanced over at the basin where she had emptied the contents of her breakfast. It smelled awful. Well, her mother could empty it, she thought as she turned on her side. A selfish girl, she knew she was spoiled but quite willingly let her family cater to her.

The girl thought about the two young men she'd been seeing. She frowned. Rupert was a secret. Wild and proud, and as sneaky as she was, he had been her beau for five months and her lover for three. She shivered with the pleasure of remembered trysts, the thrill of their meetings when her parents thought she was with girlfriends. He had always been exciting since the day they met by accident on the bridge. He'd won her with his flirtatious words. Later, when they were alone, she loved the way he looked with his shirt off.

Max, on the other hand, had been convenient. She had started seeing him regularly when Rupert wasn't around and she was bored. Max was noble, handsome and unfortunately full of integrity, and this made him a bit dull. He would never take her before marriage or do anything dishonorable. She had honestly hoped he would in the hayloft. But she knew he was the better pick. That was why she tried to trap him after the party, until his father proved too clever. Now her father might not proceed with the lawsuit. He'd already stalled almost a month.

Again Rupert's face came to her mind. Rupert with his raven hair and flashing eyes could have any girl, but Petra knew he wasn't the faithful type. If only she'd been able to convince him she was enough for him. It bothered her that she couldn't wrap either of the two men around her finger. She so wanted Max to marry her, because although Rupert hadn't left her yet, she could see the writing on the wall.

Rupert was contacting her less and less, and she'd seen him with other girls, which hurt her terribly. He as much as said her days were numbered. The challenge was gone for him, and he resented her hold on him and her clinginess. A tear escaped her eye as she rolled on her stomach to ease the pain. Her tummy had been doing flip-flops all morning. This aggravation mixed with the jumbled thoughts playing over in her mind. Petra felt very sorry for herself.

Since she couldn't very well tell her parents about Rupert without revealing her dishonesty and rebellion, Max was supposed to be the one she could count on. And now, he was going too. It wasn't fair! Two of her friends were getting married in the late summer, and she would still be single! Petra felt abandoned and used. To top it off, she'd had this nauseating flu for over a week and couldn't shake it. Well, she would go to the doctor tomorrow.

***

Otto couldn't make up his mind. He looked over the options before him and frowned. The first was a sturdy leather set of two trunks. They would not only last the voyage but would serve Max well as he traveled and hopefully last through the voyage home also. The other luggage before him was a giant suitcase and a duffel bag to match. These were also well made, and Max could take the duffel more places because it was compact and he could keep it with him in the ship's sleeper compartment.

The shopkeeper smiled at him. "Going on a long voyage?" he inquired.

"No, no, ah, but my son is. This will be a present for him." Otto murmured. "He is leaving for Canada." Though he said it, it didn't ring true in Otto's heart. Now that departure was two days away, facing the truth was imminent. The shopkeeper's eyebrows raised at this bit of news, but he went on to point out the benefits of the more expensive set of luggage.

Otto finally left the shop with both trunks and the duffel bag. He felt Max needed it all for his things. Max may not be settled anywhere permanently for a time and may be gone for longer than they thought. As the shopkeeper loaded the items into Otto's vehicle trunk, he again smiled sympathetically at Otto.

"It's hard," he said knowingly, "my son has also gone to the States. It is a new era. They have opportunities now. I guess we can't hold them close forever." With that, the salesman shook Otto's hand and returned to his store.

Otto drove home heavy-hearted. He wished he could be happy for his son, but didn't fully understand this desire driving him to go abroad, possibly forever. Though he promised to try and return within two years, he would be missed dearly. Otto hoped he and Anna had properly prepared Max for such a journey. He was a good boy, always had been, but somewhat naive. Max accepted people at their word and made deals with a handshake. Anna had taught him such virtues and his nature was kind-hearted, but Otto tried always to warn him about people. Would

Canadians be as kind? Or would they see a hated Deutchlander, a Nazi? Otto read a lot and knew how other countries now viewed Germans. A strong anti-Nazi sentiment abounded in these post-war years, and as prejudice isn't selective, all Germans would be under suspicion, regardless of their beliefs.

Tonight Max would pack and the family relatives would join for one last get-together to say goodbye to him. Tomorrow the family would drive together to Bremen, the port city where the vast ship the Beaumont was docked. As Otto pulled up before his home, the realization hit him that after this night, Max would live there no more.

His sons were home and saw Otto pull up through the kitchen window. They both bounded out the door when they saw he lifted large items from the car trunk. Helping Otto bring in the luggage, Max could hardly contain his excitement. It was real! His parents were actually giving their blessing, he felt, in that they were helping him with this gift! Thanking them with hugs and laughter, Max admired the set and already imagined where these trunks would travel.

Anna helped Max pack, lovingly folding the clothing she had bought and making sure he had enough of everything to last awhile. Max kept telling her that he could do it all, but she brushed him aside, telling him that this was one of the last things she could do for him, and to let her do it. He looked at the time, kissed her and ran down the stairs. He had yet to get his final pay from the BMW shop and say goodbye to his employer. He'd already sold his bike to help pay his way.

When Max returned he showed his family the extra money Herr Finkel had insisted he take. It was for extras he might need, he had said. Max was feeling blessed and humbled. He had no idea he was so well liked. Acquaintances for days now were coming from everywhere to bid him goodbye. These well-wishers also assured him that they believed him and not that Petra girl who caused the scandal.

That evening was one of the best Max remembered in years. Relatives and friends joined with the family, including Liesl, Kurt and the twins in wishing Max a fond farewell. Many gave him gifts of cash to help out for the journey, others made him promise to write them about his adventures. The food and drink flowed until it was late. Finally, he'd been kissed for the hundredth time as tears and good wishes drifted out the door. Max was emotionally spent. Maybe he was making a mistake. How could he leave behind all these who loved him?

His reverie was interrupted by Otto, who reminded him they had to be up and gone by seven and it was already after midnight. Twenty-year-old Max the adventurer went to bed, falling into an exhausted sleep.

Chapter Thirty-Eight

Flight to Freedom

***

Petra Schlamp sat in the thin grayish gown and shivered. Why did doctors make you wear this skimpy rag and then make you wait half an hour on the examination table while they were busy elsewhere? She thought to herself. She sighed. She'd already peed in a cup, then the nurse had taken her height and weight and asked some questions, what more did they need and where was that doctor? She wished she had a cigarette.

Just then Doktor Wexler entered the small room. He smiled at her over his glasses and consulted her chart. After the usual blood pressure and temperature checks he asked about her last period, and other embarrassing questions then instructed her to lie down. He examined her, saying nothing. "So, you think you have influenza?" The kindly doctor finally asked. She nodded. The doctor then asked her to dress and come across the hall into his office.

Petra obliged. The girl had always thought herself smart and streetwise, but was totally unprepared for the doctor's diagnosis. He first asked her if she wished her parents to be present, and when she shook her head, he laid the truth out as gently as he could. Of course, he told her, it must be confirmed when the tests came back from the lab, but in his years of experience he had witnessed this many times. The doctor was quite certain that it was not the influenza that she had. The nausea was morning sickness. She was pregnant.

Petra wasn't quite sure how she made it home. She did not have any recollection of walking there or crossing the street, or which street she was even on. Her eighteen years had not prepared her for the news she just received. Lying in Rupert's arms had been the most thrilling, deliciously daring thing she had ever done, but she had not been prepared for consequences like this!

Her mind raced. That was it! She must tell him! If he ever loved her even a little, he would be glad to marry her and raise his own child. A few steps from her own gate, she turned on her heel and ran toward the tram that would take her to the other side of town.

***

The next morning, Max turned and looked back into the house. He might never see this old place again. He memorized the kitchen where his mother had made a thousand wonderful things to eat. The soft chair where his father read the paper each evening and the silver framed family pictures on the mantel above the electric hearth. He eyed the banister that he and Friedrich had slid down many times as little boys and the cuckoo clock he made with Pieter and presented to Anna seven short years ago. Max felt a lump almost too big rising in his throat. Then his father called. The trunks were packed and it was time to go. Heinz the dog had died a month before, as if he knew Max was going, so he'd better as well. That goodbye had been just as heart wrenching. Now Max turned and climbed into the car, but he looked back at the brownstone that he called home for most of his life until it was out of sight. Neighbors waved, as if they too knew they might not see him again.

Once the automobile was flying down the autobahn, it began to seem real to Max. He was actually going to do this! He tried to imprint every familiar sight he loved, to better remember when he was gone. At first a nervous chatter and lively conversation filled the car, but as the kilometers sped by, it died down, each occupant alone with their own thoughts. The vehicle took them northeast, stopping only at lunchtime so they could stretch and have a noon meal. Small talk was the norm then, as Max kept the conversation light and focused on other things.

One topic surfaced regarding the dramatic Fraulein Schlamp. They all wondered what had happened that Petra's charges had never been laid. It seemed Otto's threat had worked. The Thielmanns would have been surprised to know at that very moment Petra's father was requesting for the police to track Max down.

***

Petra was crying. Frau Schlamp was lambasting Herr Schlamp for his tardiness in dealing with the issue. It seemed that Petra had inherited her mother's tongue. While her husband phoned the police precinct as he was directed, the girl's mother ran her a warm bath and assured her the cad Max would pay for his crime.

Petra slid down into the luxury of the bath. Maybe all would be well after all. She wiped her eyes with the wet cloth and felt much better. Yesterday had been the worst of her life. Rupert not only spurned her, he rejected his own child telling her the bastard was someone else's. In that moment her heart broke. If she had owned a gun he would be dead.

But now Max would have to take the blame! They would have to catch him quickly, for she knew he had left for Bremen already. Though the lab tests were not back, Petra couldn't wait or Max would be gone, out of her reach forever. She knew the doctor's diagnosis was right anyhow. A woman feels these things, she thought. But Maximilian would not get off so easily. No matter that he had never touched her beyond a kiss. He couldn't prove the child was not his. Enough people at the party were witness to the barn incident. Max would be hers by this time tomorrow.

***

Arriving by early afternoon in the port city of Bremen, Max felt his chest would burst with anticipation. The ancient city was the oldest seaport in Germany and generations of ships had sailed down the Weser River to the sea, sixty-five kilometers away. Charming and beautiful, Max wished he had time to explore before leaving. His ship, the Beaumont was not sailing until morning. First they had to find the immigration office where his papers were to be checked. Certain formalities such as a physical examination had to be performed. No one in poor health would be permitted passage. Emigrants in the cue were to take a number and have their passports and vaccination papers ready.

The afternoon was spent dispensing with the requirements for passage. That evening they checked into a hotel Otto had secured for the night. No one could sleep, so tea was brought to the room and conversation kept them company until one by one they drifted off to sleep. Morning came quickly.

Maximilian was almost beside himself with eagerness, yet he had mixed feelings. He couldn't wait to get on the ship, yet he was already beginning to miss his family. He was to report to the docks like several hundred others and wait until called. He found some benches for them and was told he could wait with his family until summoned by a customs official. However as the clock struck nine, four pairs of eyes were not prepared for the sight of policemen as they came toward them. They had found the Thielmann family.

***

267

Herr Willie Schlamp was triumphant. He had succeeded in having the police track down the Thielmann boy. Everyone knew when young Max was leaving for Bremen. It had been easy enough then to have the Düsseldorf Polizei contact the Bremen Polizei and find him. Now he would have to be transported back to face his newly laid charges. Willie's little girl would have her day in court! Already he was anticipating the monetary gain that Petra would receive for damages and child support. That smug Otto would have some explaining to do now that his son was caught. Max couldn't get out of this one since Petra was found with child!

***

Mateas Buhler and Wolfgang Koch had been Max's closest friends since the post-war school years. Having gone through several grades together, they were as close as pals could be. These two young men were also witnesses the evening of the motorcycle accident that had almost claimed Friedrich's life. And as fate would have it, they were again to be there for their friend.

They not only believed Maximilian was innocent of rape charges, but they knew Max couldn't have done the deed for two reasons. Max was too polite and respectful of girls to ever consider rape. Mateas had given Max the note from Petra only because he thought he was helping out. He was sorry now that he got involved at all. Also the time frame didn't add up. Max was only in the loft for perhaps five minutes. He would have had to work awfully fast to rape Petra and get down out of the loft and barn in that time. If he did, Mateas admired his speed and prowess.

The second reason and a secret until now was the most damning evidence against Petra. The day before, Wolfgang happened to be at the bierhaus when a young woman confronted a man in an adjoining booth behind him. Hidden by a partition wall, Wolfgang overheard the upset girl accuse the man she called Rupert of getting her pregnant. He denied it and the two quarreled until she left in tears. The voice seemed so familiar, so Wolfgang watched when she stormed out, slamming the door. Sure enough, the voice belonged to Petra who had accused Max of rape! She must now have discovered she was pregnant and tracked down the real cad, the swaggering Rupert. So, Max indeed was innocent, it wasn't his baby!

Sharing this revelation with Mateas, the two were too late to tell Max, he'd gone yesterday. But news travels fast. Satisfied that Max was arrested by now and on his way back to face the music, Frau Schlamp went to the local grocery and smugly shared this tidbit with Frau Mangold. Frau Mangold who loved to gossip was eager to share news with her friend Cora. Cora happened to be Mateas' mother, and she mentioned it to Mateas the next morning. He listened, unbelieving. This would keep Max from his voyage and possibly ruin his chances to go this year or ever! Something had to be done and fast.

Mateas remembered that the ship was leaving by noon today. Not much time to lose. He thought quickly. The chances of finding this Rupert fellow in time were slim. Then, an idea occurred to him. The more he thought about it the better he liked it! And it would buy time for Max. They could always straighten the mess out later when Max got away and Petra challenged them. Mateas grinned to himself and thought if Petra liked fiction so much, she should be treated to some more! Jumping on his motorcycle he sped off to see Wolfgang.

***

Unknown to the Schlamps, Maximilian was not on his way back to Düsseldorf just yet. He was sitting in the Bremen Polizei precinct office while an officious clerk was prying information from Max for the arrest report. Otto was on a nearby phone to his lawyer and Anna was praying. Friedrich feared Max would not make the boat in time, if ever. The clock was now nearing eleven and nothing could be done until transportation could be arranged to return Max to the Düsseldorf police.

Max had been incredulous when he was arrested. That damn girl! How could she still ruin his opportunity when he was so close! His papers were in order and he had passed the physical. It was scarcely an hour to departure, and now this. He was so baffled by it all. What could have changed? He watched the clock hands march too quickly past eleven and saw his plans fall apart as he waited. By now the other passengers were loading and he would miss his chance. He wanted to scream.

His mother came over to him and put her hand on his shoulder. "Maximilian." She said, and he looked up at her in despair. "Don't worry son. If it is your fate, it will be well. God will keep your appointments if it's in His plan that you are to go." Max nodded mutely. He knew she would be happier if he stayed, but she was also selfless and wouldn't keep him here even if she could.

A moment later, the miracle that Max was looking for walked in the door. He was a friend of Otto's and a partner of the Düsseldorf lawyer Otto had hired previously. He smiled at Max and spoke quietly to Otto, then came over to Max. "Hello young man, Max is it?" he inquired, while holding out his hand to shake Max's own. "I have some happy news for you. All charges have been dropped. You are free to go, and I might add, you'd better hurry to catch your ship."

Max couldn't believe his good fortune. As they hurried out the door to the waiting car, Herr Mencken told them what happened. It seemed the Düsseldorf police were inundated with calls from several young men in the last half hour. All of them said they had a change of heart or a fit of conscience and had to confess that they had sex with a certain Petra Schlamp. Since they were all acquainted with the girl and most were at the party, the case did not look good for Petra. Outraged, the girl's father demanded if it were true. Petra denied it of course, but in her attempts to undo her sudden reputation as a tramp she confessed, pointing the finger to the only real offender, the elusive Rupert Sturn. "The police are picking him up today," Herr Mencken assured Max. "You won't have any further trouble with her."

Never had Max been so relieved or felt so sorry for the girl. He wondered where all these saviours of his reputation came from, but had a pretty good idea. Under his breath Max said a quick thanks for his friends.

***

The hardest ten minutes of his life to date had come to Max at last. Porters had loaded his trunks hours ago and now he had only to say goodbye to his family. Yet again. These long goodbyes were killing him. He hugged his father and brother as they dispensed some last minute cautions and wishes, hoping it would be enough. Friedrich told Max that he might visit him in a year or so. Even normally stoic Otto's eyes were wet now. Then Max turned to Anna.

She promised herself she would not do this, but even as she did, her soft mother's heart broke and she began to cry. Not quiet or sniffly, but full blown sobbing. Max was beside himself trying to comfort her. Holding her in a bearhug, he felt like a heel. It was some minutes before she could gain control, all the while being assured by Max that he would write every day and phone when he could. Anna fumbled in her pocket and pressed something into Max's hand.

Max glanced down at the rosary she put there. It was hers, the worn prayer beads linking her prayers for him to the silver crucifix. She made him promise to remember to pray daily, as she would for him. Just then, the large stack on the ship belched smoke and the warning whistle blew, loud and long. Time was up. Anna held Max's face in her worn hands and stared into his face, as if memorizing it for eternity. Max kissed her. "Don't worry Mama, I'll see you again soon!" Max said. He hoped it wasn't a lie. Then, he turned purposefully and walked away, each step he took weighing on him as if set in cement.

As Anna burst out crying again, Max knew that if he turned around to see her face once more, he would never leave. The most difficult thing he'd ever done was to keep on walking up the gangplank and into the ship.

Once more Anna witnessed a man she loved leave her behind. Her husband Hans of long ago now seemed to belong to anothers' lifetime. But this man was her blood. Anna watched her youngest leave her as he had years ago as a child, but this time she knew she would never see his face again.

Chapter Thirty-Nine

The Beaumont

***

Max simply couldn't handle turning to look or wave as they closed the doors behind him. He checked his ticket through tears that suddenly sprung of their own accord, making his vision swim. Looking up at the directions on the wall, he went to his allotted cabin. It was a dormitory room and made to hold probably a hundred persons. Several rooms like this one combined to carry the maximum of 780 emigrant passengers the Beaumont was designed for.

Max located his locker beside his bunk and threw in his duffel bag. He couldn't help glancing out the porthole window. They were still there and growing distant, his faithful family. Otto had his arm around Anna's shoulders and she was holding tightly onto Friedrich's hand, as if he too might vanish.

Fortunately the large room was almost deserted. Everyone else was topside waving goodbye or taking in the fresh air and sights of the harbour. Max lay on his bunk and thought for a long time. The anxieties of the last few hours had placed him on an emotional rollercoaster that wearied him. He fell asleep.

When he awoke the vessel was well on its way in the shipping lane gaining speed. He felt refreshed but for a moment wasn't sure where he was. When realization reminded him, he bolted from the bed and splashed his face with cool water from the small sink in the corner. He didn't want to miss a thing and hoped he could still see the coast of Germany before they set out into the ocean. He ran up the steps onto "B" deck and hurried to the rail. A stiff breeze accompanied the day and sent the stack smoke streaming out behind them.

Yes, there was his homeland, growing smaller now. Odd that he should feel detached, so excited was he for his new destination. If he could have foreseen how long it would be until he gazed on his birthplace again, Max would have looked back far longer as the shore disappeared into the horizon.

Max was surprised he had slept right through the voyage down the Weser River and past the port in Bremerhaven. Pulling out his camera to take a few pictures, he now strolled around the boat to take in more of things that interested him.

His father had given him a packet purchased in the dock terminal that included paper and envelopes to write to them of his sailing adventures, and impressions of Canada when he arrived. Max sat down on a deck chair and opened the packet. A few postcards of the ship fell out and a small booklet describing the history of the Beaumont.

This ship was originally called the *Hoher Turm* or *Hightower*. Built in 1940 by Hamburg ship builders, it was almost eight thousand tons with three decks. Since then it had seen service as a passenger ship and served as a U-boat depot ship during the war years. Purchased in the 1940's by a Canadian shipping firm in Halifax, it was refitted there to exceed nine thousand tons. Renamed the Beaumont, it now carried between six to seven hundred emigrants approximately once a month. Regular roundtrips carrying cargo eastbound to London and passengers westbound for Canada kept the ship busy. This ship also had a Canadian crew under Canadian registration. She was a beautiful ship to him, this refugee ship, and Max was glad he obtained passage on her.

Max set down the pamphlet he was reading and went to the deck rail. He breathed deeply of the ocean air, watching gulls diving and doing aerial manoevers much like the Messerschmidts he watched as a boy in Obbach. He couldn't yet believe he'd managed this! Three months before he'd found out about a program run by a Canadian Christian relief council that sponsored refugees from German frontiers. While not a refugee in any real sense, he applied anyway for the documentation and embarkation papers through the Bremen office. Once he passed health and security requirements he'd been accepted. The Canadian government offered passage fare in exchange for employment when emigrants reached Canada. Max couldn't wait to see where he was to be placed to work off his fare.

Maximilian Thielmann had great plans for the future. He knew that Canada was vast and he'd read that the crown held land for sale at a reasonable price. He was determined that one day he would own a piece of that great land. A feat he felt he couldn't have accomplished in Germany.

The supper bell rang echoing down the corridor as Max returned to his dormitory room. They were on open sea now and the waves rocked the ship up and down. Perhaps a storm was coming, but Max didn't worry. He seemed to have fine sealegs. He also was ravenous. Putting his jacket in his locker and grabbing a book, Max hurried to the cafeteria. He lined up as the large room was filling up rapidly. Getting his food on a tray, he looked around for anyone else who looked lonely. However, most people were grouped in families and kept to themselves. He sat down. The food wasn't gourmet by any stretch of the imagination, but ample enough he supposed. If not, his mother had packed a lot of food stuffs and packaged things for him to snack on throughout the journey.

As he ate, he thought he'd read his book. Max was well read and loved adventure books as much as the movies, but he was distracted by his thoughts. He truly was alone now. He tried to picture where his family would be at this moment, they must have already returned home. He also wished he could have seen the look on Petra's face when his friends pulled that prank, all claiming to have had her. He chuckled at the thought. Nasty boys. He sobered at the realization that he probably would never see them again, if it worked out the way he hoped in Canada or the States. Ah well, sacrifices had to be made. Max had always been an optimist, he was sure his sacrifices would be worth it.

Max returned to his room and read. The next morning he was cold and found he'd fallen asleep again on top of the covers while reading. He shivered. He stood up and peeked out the porthole to see a windy and rainy day. Bleak, like his mood today. Crawling under the covers, he tried to sleep again, but in a room full of men, it was too noisy as others were rising then. Max hoped he could get one of the spots in the showers, so leapt out of the cot and lined up.

As he showered Max noticed an ache in the middle of his back. Trying to reach back to see what it was, he couldn't quite touch it. Probably just a pimple he thought. He didn't remember having it before he left home, and hoped it wasn't a bite from bed bugs.

Days passed as his routine varied little. He would sleep, read, walk the deck and watch the endless ocean stretch out before them in every direction. Lovely days were a treat, one could take sun on one of the deck chairs. Max soon met and talked with other young men, but most were with their families and this made Max feel especially alone. He wished now he had convinced Friedrich or one of his friends to at least come for a year, to try it out. He was sure that once they saw North America, they would want to stay as well.

One day while sitting on the top deck, Max watched children playing with their toys, mothers chatting while walking by with their babies and men who sat dozing. A small table nearby hosted several others playing a card game of some kind. A young woman came up. Introducing herself as Heidi Lehmann, she asked him if the deck chair beside him was taken.

Max smiled at the lovely woman, motioning for her to have a seat. For some reason she looked awfully familiar. He just couldn't place her in any memory of his acquaintances. They made small talk about the weather, where they were from and their destination, yet Max found he was trying to solve a puzzle as she talked. She appeared to be in her mid or late twenties and wore no wedding ring. Could she be a friend of Liesl's? Even though he tried not to stare, Heidi caught Max doing so a few times. Finally she asked him why.

Max apologized. "It's just that, you look so familiar. I feel I should know you. Have you ever been in Düsseldorf?" Max inquired.

"No," Heidi said, for the first time noticing that Max too, seemed familiar. Until now they had not spoken about the war, probably the real reason each one carried emotional scars, the real reason a million others never spoke about it either. After a short awkward silence, it began to dawn on Max. Should he ask her, or would he offend her? He had to know. However, almost in unison they both spoke the word that had arrived in their thoughts. "Obbach."

Max knew at once who Heidi was. She had been the young bride who had lost all her family in such tragedy. She had tried to commit suicide by taking pills, and Doktor Coleman saved her in her wandering when the pills had rendered temporary blindness.

Heidi too now remembered the boy everyone called a hero for saving children from the burning plane that crashed in the town. Memories of Obbach were bittersweet. There dear Doktor Coleman had saved her life and she would always be grateful. In Obbach she began to really live again. But that was long ago. So much had happened since and Heidi was a new woman. The rail thin boy that Max once was had grown into this handsome young man. She spoke first.

"Oh Max! It is good to know you made it through. Those were terrible times, yes? " She paused, placing her hand on his, "But here we are! Facing new lives and a future unlike so many who never got another chance. We are so fortunate. Soon I'm meeting my future husband in Ontario and all is good once more."

Max put his other hand over hers briefly, and it did not seem too familiar at all. They were both survivors of an unfair war that picked its victims like Russian roulette. In having experienced such tragedy, all survivors shared a common bond, and he felt they were like kin. He grinned. "You are so right, Heidi," Max agreed, "I'm going to Alberta now for a new life too. It's what I've always wanted." Max explained he had hoped for the States, but that could be later. He was alone now, but maybe his brother or others would join him soon.

Heidi inquired if he knew anyone in Canada. When he said no, she thought him very brave. She gave him her fiance's address and phone number. Ontario was far from Alberta, but he could perhaps visit sometime or call when he wanted to talk. The two visited on through the afternoon. It was a great panacea for lonely Max, almost like seeing family.

Two mornings later, the ship steamed toward the slip of Canada that appeared on the horizon. Max was up early being too excited to sleep, and the recent malady on his back was bothering him. He had his duffel ready to go and got the hot shower first to wash away the cobwebs in his mind. He now stood on the bow point and saw the clouds part ahead as the sun behind him warmed the back of his ears. They would not land here at St. Johns, but would disembark at Halifax as their point of entry. As the ship turned south, Max took pictures of the lighthouses as they shone like white sentinels in the morning sun, the white surf breaking against the ebony rocks below in wild frothy sprays pounding the coast. Max remembered a similar picture in a book. It was more lovely than he'd imagined.

After breakfast while everyone was still present in the mess hall, the purser dispensed an identification tag to each person. The announcement was made for each emigrant to have it ready naming their destination. They were to form lines at the disembarkment point. Two trains with colonist and baggage cars were waiting at the port of entry. The first train would be routed to Montreal and Toronto. The second was bound for Winnipeg and points west, with almost every car destined to a different part of the country. In addition these trains pulled a dining car, one for recreation and a kitchen car to feed the refugees.

Dismissing them to assemble for docking, there was organized chaos. Eager families scattered to prepare. It wouldn't be much longer now. Heidi saw Maximilian through the melee and waved. Max smiled and waved back. This was it!

Exhiliaration grew in Max as they finally rounded the coast steaming into Halifax harbor, the flatter terrain here much different than the steep cliffs he'd seen in St. Johns. How lucky on this June day the harbor wasn't socked in with fog. Max breathed deeply of the salty air. Most of the passengers crowded the rails like Max, hungry to take in the sights and sounds of their new home.

Usually somewhat stoic like his father, Max found this moment suddenly quite poignant. Unsure how he should feel, the enormity of his choice had hit him at last. This was his new home. He had forsaken all for this dream, a dream now fulfilled. This had been all he had wished for since the horrors of the Reich had filled his young mind with fear, and he wondered how things might have been different.

Maximilian Thielmann was a sojourner in a new country, an adventurer, ready to discover all the bountiful riches his curiosity could hold. He'd known this was his destiny, had known it since a small child. Although he had made sacrifices to achieve it and many more might be in store, it would be worth it all.

Yet, for a moment he was also humbled that he should be the one to be so blessed. Max thought of Kaethe, and Rolf who died so young. He wondered about Reiner Melman, and Dieter, and Adam. He even thought of the Fausts, and how tragedy was the reward for their convictions. How many had been misled? They all had been. Some lived, some died, some were lost forever and would not be found, their whereabouts known only to God.

Max suddenly remembered his mother's words and said a prayer for his future and his family left behind. As the large vessel docked and much ado went on around him, it was for Max, a spiritual moment as the expectation of his new life loomed before him. He thanked God for safe passage, and the future God alone knew, for He had taken Max safely thus far.

Max would turn twenty-one in this new land. He wondered where he would be when that birthday came in October. With a grin and his heart bursting with anticipation, Max swung his duffel bag over his shoulder and followed others off the ship, stepping down onto his new home, Canada.

Epilogue

***

The character of Max was fictionalized after my father, Karl Maximilian. In reality, he never made it to the States to live, but found the fufillment he sought in making a life in Canada. As he travelled on the westbound train to Alberta, the problem in his back was discovered by the trains' physician to be a painful boil. Fortunately it hadn't appeared on the surface when he was examined for travel from Germany, or he would have never been allowed passage. He was taken off the train in Saskatchewan and the boil was removed.

When he recuperated the powers that be decided to place him with a farmer in that province to work off his fare. The mischievous man thought it great sport to confuse him, and liked to fool the young German. Once at a social gathering Karl gestured that he'd like to ask a girl for a dance, so the farmer carefully pronounced the English words for him. In repeating this request in the farmer's words he was soundly slapped for making an obscene comment about her breasts. Karl soon learned that jokes were always at his expense. Wiser now but ever optimistic, in spite of these experiences he eventually learned enough English to travel on when his debt was paid.

He wasn't alone too long. Dad's brother did join him later and stayed, eventually marrying and raising his own family in Canada as well. Dad's father visited Canada three times. Sadly, his mother died of cancer five years after he left Germany and as she had feared, never saw him again.

A year after arrival, my father landed a job at a packing warehouse in Saskatoon. On the only dates that they were both scheduled to work night shift, he met his future wife, my mother. It was love at first sight. A happy marriage and six children later, they moved from Saskatchewan to Alberta. Eventually able to purchase a quarter section of land in Saskatchewan, for my Dad it was the culmination of all he wanted, his dream came true. Ah, but that is a story for another time.

***

IN THE NAME OF CHURCH

By Edmund DuBois

In 1572, there is an uneasy peace in the bitter religious wars between Catholics and Protestants in France. Madeleine, daughter of a nobleman, and Colette, her bright but unlettered maid, find themselves fending off strange attempts by a Catholic bishop who is determined to take control of the maid because he professes to believe she is bewitched. A royal wedding in Paris provides the opportunity for Madeleine to seek excitement and shield Colette from the bishop. Madeleine and Colette have romantic affairs, but the Saint Bartholomew's Day massacre of Protestants turns the happy royal marriage into macabre tragedy and gives the bishop the chance to attempt his evil intentions- yet once again, Colette escapes. In a final confrontation, the bishop's true motive is unmasked, and believing himself possessed by the Devil, he goes insane. Madeleine, because of the terrible happenings "In the name of church," disavows affiliation with any church, and takes her worship directly to God.

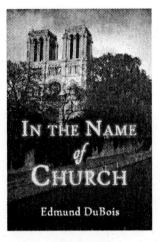

Paperback, 531 pages
6" x 9"
ISBN 1-4137-1763-2

About the author:

Edmund DuBois is a retired Army officer. He served in the Pacific during World War II and subsequently had assignments in the Pentagon and with NATO. He has co-authored one publication and is working on a sequel to the present novel. He resides in Sonoma, California.

010509c